POWER FORWARD

CHICAGO THUNDER HOCKEY

JODI OLIVER

Cover Design by Kari March Designs
Photography by Wander Aguiar
Editing by Sandra at One Love Editing
Proofread by Lori Parks and Jeanelle Ricketts

Content Warning: mc with depression, on page therapy, mention of past drug use, mention of past unalive attempt, injury related medical issues, on page anxiety.

Chapter One

Jackson

"At what point of the day do we get cake?" Elliot asks, fiddling with one of the elastic straps of his forest-green suspenders as he shifts from foot to foot. The guy is incapable of standing still. "I was promised there would be cake."

The ceremony doesn't start for another twenty minutes, but for someone like Elliot Olsen, twenty minutes is a long time. Something he likes to make sure we know whenever we're having a good offensive game because it means he spends a lot of time on his own in front of the pipes.

I personally don't see it as a bad thing, but goalies are known to be a little weird.

Okay, maybe not a little weird. *A lot* weird. But Elliot wears it well.

"When I got married to Katy, I suggested there should be cake at different stages of the day," Jonathan Peyton tells us, counting on his fingers as he lists them off. "Arrival cake, post-kiss cake, pre-speech cake, post-dinner cake, then the main-show cake."

"Dude, that's a lot of cake," Carter Lockwood laughs. "Imagine the sugar high."

"It would be magical," my teammate Zach Reid replies, flashing his boyfriend a big smile. "I definitely wouldn't say no to that."

"Same. I don't know why they didn't take my suggestion," Peyton says, perplexed.

Elliot falls into one of the chairs behind him and lets out a long, exasperated sigh. "Jacob told me about the cake he's made, and it's all I've been able to think about for *days*." He wraps his lips around the rim of his champagne glass and throws the liquid to the back of his throat like it's a shot, then bares his teeth in a grimace. "Champagne doesn't taste the same when it's not straight out the bottle or after winning the Cup."

"Drinking champagne in anything other than the Cup is plain wrong," Zach chuckles. The defenseman doesn't have a dainty champagne flute in his hand, having swapped his bubbly beverage for a coffee. Although, the coffee cup looks just as dainty, given his huge stature. His laughter trails off as he furrows his brows. "Wait. How have you been waiting days when he only told you about it last night?"

"Exactly. It has been days because in Australia, it's already tomorrow, so that means they have been waiting days, ergo, *days*." Elliot waves his hand out to the side and rolls his eyes, silently saying, *"Fucking duh."*

I frown in confusion, trying to understand his logic, but since I was traded to Chicago from Buffalo last February, I've learned not to question Elliot's thought process.

Like I say, *goalies*. Weird creatures.

The five of us are standing on the edge of the courtyard, where rows of rustic white wooden chairs are neatly placed in two sections. They're facing a colorful floral arch that looks out onto a sweeping view of the Santa Susana Mountains. It's very picturesque and romantic. The perfect setting for my teammate Blaine Olsen—Elliot's twin brother—to get married to his partner, Alex.

Sometimes I wonder what piece of advice I'd give myself in my rookie year. A tidbit to prepare myself for what was to come. I often think it would be this. That the second I signed my name on the dotted line of an NHL contract, I would also be waving goodbye to my off-seasons for the foreseeable future. Because the moment the hockey season ends, it officially becomes wedding season. There's a small window every summer between the end of the postseason and the start of training camp, and *boom*, it seems like everyone is getting hitched. It's a hectic dash trying to buy registry gifts and making sure the pants of my trusty wedding suit still fit over my thighs and ass, to booking flights to whatever scenic destination will be the backdrop to the vows being said that weekend.

Oh, and organizing childcare. Now that I'm a single father of two, it's not as easy to up and leave for weekends on end. Yeah, my parents help out a lot. Having their help with the kids was the main reason why I requested the trade, but I don't want to always rely on them because they do so much for me as it is. It wasn't so bad when I was younger and had no kids. I lived for the evening reception, where I could loosen my tie and just… let loose with my friends.

But those days are long gone.

Last year, I managed to avoid most of the weddings I was invited to, using the excuse of wanting to spend the summer exploring our new home with my kids. But I have a lot of respect for Blaine and Alex, and I'm honored to be a part of their special day.

As if on cue, my phone begins to vibrate. I slip it out of my pocket, and dread crawls up my throat. It's a video call from Ryan's iPad.

Worry prickles up my spine, and I excuse myself from where my teammates are standing and walk over to a quiet corner of the courtyard to answer. My children's faces fill the screen, and the first thing I notice is Isabela is visibly upset. Her cheeks are flushed a deep pink, and her eyes are glassy. My stomach churns, and my mind begins to race, thinking of all kinds of wild scenarios that could have happened to cause my daughter to be distressed, but I try not to let it show.

"Hey, what's going on?" I ask, pushing my sunglasses to the top of my head so they can see me. "Everything okay?"

"Hey, Dad. Isabela's upset that you're not here. I told her you're at the wedding, but she didn't believe me," my son, Ryan, tells me. He's got his arm wrapped around his sister's shoulders, and his iPad is propped up on his pillow where they're sitting on his bed.

"I miss you, Daddy," she whines, and then her chin wobbles.

Oh, shit. *Here we go.*

I suck in a sharp breath, waiting for the inevitable. My daughter might only be four years old, but it seems she knows how to play on my weak spots. Even though I'm expecting it—because she does this every time I'm on the road too—it doesn't stop the stab in my chest when she lets out a choked sob and tears begin to fall down her cheeks.

Fuck. I never should have left Chicago, wedding be damned.

"I know, peanut, I miss you too. I'll be home soon, okay? Do you remember why I came to California?"

She gives a shaky nod and hiccups. "B-b-blaine and Alex… getting married."

"Yeah, that's right." I smile softly, keeping my voice gentle and calm. "I'll take lots of photos so you can look through them when I'm home."

She blinks at me with her big blue eyes. I can see the fat tears clinging to her lashes through the camera. "And cake?"

Some of the tension leaves my shoulders as I laugh. "I don't think the cake will survive the flight home, but how about this? I promise I'll take you to the bakery, and you can choose a cake. Maybe I'll even ask Jacob if he can make you a special one."

And just like a switch has been flicked, the tears suddenly stop, and an excited expression takes over her face.

"Okay," she says gleefully, and I make a mental note to speak with Jacob about ordering a custom cake in the same flavors as the wedding cake when I'm home. Maybe it's a bad thing to promise sweet treats in order to cheer up my kids, but hey, a bit of cake won't hurt them.

I flick my gaze to Ryan. He's so grown up for an eight-year-old. A part of me worries he's had to grow up too quickly because of the shit he's had to go through recently.

"Where's Mom?" I ask.

"She's downstairs. She said she has some work to do on

her laptop," he answers. "I said to Izzy that we can do some coloring until Mom can take us to the park."

My head snaps to the side as music starts playing behind me. Peyton is waving his hand at me, motioning for me to follow. Shit, the ceremony is starting now.

I quickly return my attention back to my phone.

"That sounds like a good idea. You're a good brother, Ryan, and peanut, I'll be home tomorrow afternoon, okay? I've gotta go now because the wedding's going to start shortly, but I'll call you in the morning before my flight. Make sure you're good for your mom, and have fun at the park."

Ryan nods. "Okay, Dad. We will."

"I love you both," I say.

"I love yoooou, Daddyyy!" Isabela sings, and then Ryan ends the call with a quick "Love you, Dad. Bye!"

The call cuts off, and I drop my phone to my side, staring aimlessly out into the distance for a second.

It's hard being a single dad. I'm constantly worried about whether I'm doing the right thing or royally fucking things up. There's this huge part of me that believes I'm a bad father, especially now I'm leaving them for two nights to attend this wedding when I already spend so many nights away from them during the season. It follows me like a dark cloud, despite knowing they are perfectly fine with my parents or my ex-wife, Laura. She's a great mom, and they need this alone time with her. But it doesn't stop the ache deep in my chest that I'm failing them.

My kids and my career are the two most important things in my life. I'm one of the few single guys on the twenty-three-man roster for the Thunder, but I refuse to even contemplate dating again. Not until the kids are older, at least. Maybe I'll consider it when they go to college or something. I simply don't have time to fit another factor in my life when I'm already struggling to keep on top of everything.

"Yo! Wildsy!" Peyton calls out. "We've gotta go sit down."

I nod, holding up a finger to let him know I'll be right there, then bring up the text thread with my ex-wife. I fire off a quick message, hoping she won't take this the wrong way.

> Hey. Letting you know I've just had a call from Ryan. Isabela was upset about me being away. I know you've got some work to do, but could you take them to the park earlier than planned? Try to take her mind off me not being there?

Luckily, I don't have to wait long for the reply.

LAURA

> I'll finish this up and take them, but you know what she's like.

I bristle slightly. I can hear the unspoken accusation in her words.

Why are you surprised? You caused this.

It's not something I can deny because, yeah, I did cause this in a way. The move from Buffalo to Chicago was my doing, but it was necessary. Laura's and my relationship ended three years ago, shortly after Isabela's first birthday. We tried to make it work, but to put it bluntly, we fell out of love. We tried to put on a show that everything was fine for the sake of the kids, but when she got her dream job at a broadcasting network in Manhattan, we decided it was best to file for divorce to allow her to go into this new venture of her life without any legal tie to me. The new role would also involve her traveling a lot more, and I hated the thought of leaving the kids with nannies when they could have been with family while I was on the road.

So, I suggested putting in a trade request to move to Chicago and take sole custody of the kids. My parents live in the suburbs, and that way, the kids could stay with my parents while I'm on the road to provide some stability. Luckily, Laura agreed, and she visits whenever she can. But now, I can sense this underlying blame that I'm the reason Isabela struggles with separation anxiety and why it's always me she wants whenever she's with Laura. She doesn't seem to understand that I'm trying my best, and as long as the kids are happy, healthy and safe, surely that should be enough.

Sighing, I slip my phone back into my pants pocket and scrub my hands over my face.

"Dude, everything alright, eh?" Peyton appears at my side and claps my shoulder. "We've gotta take our seats 'cause it's about to start."

"Yeah, all good," I say because technically, it *is*.

Isabela is fine. Ryan is fine.

Everything is fine.

So why can't I make myself believe that?

I take my sunglasses from the top of my head and slip them back on over my eyes. I follow Peyton to our seats, taking a side step to grab one of the champagne flutes and swallowing it in one large gulp before returning it to the tray.

Hopefully, the fizz will ease some of the tension now lingering at the base of my skull.

Peyton sits down next to our defenseman Adam Kendrick and his wife, Maria, along with Zach and Carter. Elliot's moved to stand at the front with Alex's brother Jacob, and my newly retired teammate Ethan sits in the first row with a few of Alex's friends and colleagues.

The ceremony is only a small, close-knit group, and when almost everyone has taken their seats, I notice there's an empty chair next to me at the end of the row. At the same time, the hair on the back of my neck prickles with awareness.

No, no, *no*. This can't be happening.

Slowly, I turn to glance over my shoulder, and my body trembles when I see him. Dressed in a three-piece navy blue suit that fits his long, lean form like a dream, he oozes sex and sophistication. It's clear to see how he's made several best-dressed lists and received awards for the most handsome man. They used to call him the golden boy of the NHL. Not only because he had stellar stats to match his stellar appearance but because he had the type of personality that could win over even the toughest of critics.

He used to be known as the poster boy power forward.

I was fooled once before by the charm and the expensive suits and crystal-like blue eyes, but I won't be fooled again.

But despite my better judgment, I'm unable to tear my eyes away from him, watching him greet people as he passes. They fawn over him, so eager to say hello and shake his hand. I wouldn't be surprised if people dropped to their knees and kissed his fancy designer loafers. He has this air about him that causes people to gravitate to him whenever he's in a room.

I know about that all too well.

When Peyton jumps up and stretches over me to slap Hayden's back in a hug, my jaw clenches.

It seems the world wants to fuck me over a little bit more and flip me the double proverbial finger today.

He sits graciously in the empty seat next to me, crossing one leg over the other, and flashes one of his signature smiles my way.

"It's nice to see you again, Wilde."

My spine stiffens at the slight rasp of his voice, and my traitorous cock doesn't fail to notice. It clearly hasn't forgotten the times I forgot the world existed while he whispered sweet nothings into my ear.

Ignoring how my heart rate suddenly spikes, I tip my head to look at him. Dark sunglasses cover what I know are piercing, steel-gray eyes. I can still picture them so vividly from the number of times I'd lost myself in them. The early afternoon Californian sun highlights the sharp line of his clean-shaven jaw and chiseled cheekbones. His face has always looked like it's been cut from marble. I used to think he was too handsome for hockey. And like a fine wine, he's only getting better with age.

Fuck. I hate that my body still comes alive whenever he's around. A feeling that I've only ever experienced with him.

And I hate it even more so because he's the only person to ever break my heart.

My ex-teammate. My first love.

Hayden Cassidy.

Chapter Two

Hayden

If you had told me a few years ago that I would be sitting here today, watching Blaine Olsen getting all misty-eyed while reciting his vows on his wedding day, I would've gotten a cramp from laughing so hard.

No, seriously. He was the last person I expected to get married. As his agent, I've spent many years having to put out metaphorical fires. Whether it be keeping his place on the team and keeping his sponsors happy or on the internet after he thought with the brain in his pants instead of his head, but here he is. So fucking in love it's almost sickening.

Now, don't get me wrong, I *am* happy for him. His soon-to-be husband, Alex, has brought the best out in Blaine—and saved me from prematurely getting more gray hairs before I hit the big four-oh—and while today is filled with happiness and love, it's a stark reminder of everything I've failed at.

One of them being the man sitting next to me, and it's safe to say I failed him *big-time*.

The tension has been rolling off Jackson in waves from the moment I sat down next to him. His jaw remained clenched up until the happy couple started reciting their vows, and then he must have forgotten I was there because he finally relaxed. My attention should have been on Alex and Blaine, but I couldn't take my eyes off him as a million and one thoughts ran through my mind.

Was his blond hair as soft as it used to be? Was he still ticklish beneath his ribs? Did he still eat a peanut butter and jelly sandwich with the crusts cut off before every game? Was his mouth still his biggest erogenous zone?

I wanted to know everything about him, but my questions would remain unanswered. Because the moment he noticed I was watching *him* and not the ceremony, the tension returned to the broad line of his shoulders, and his jaw snapped shut so fast I heard his teeth audibly click.

It's kinda fucked-up to think his scowl is one of the most beautiful sights I've seen in a long time, but I don't blame him for feeling this way toward me.

I deserve it.

This is only the second time I've seen him in almost nine years, and I don't really know what I was expecting to happen when we saw each other again. I'm not delusional enough to think he was going to greet me with a '*hi, it's been so long, I've missed you*' hug. But regardless of the time that's passed between us, I would be lying if I didn't admit the guy still makes me weak in my already very weak knees.

Jackson Wilde has always been the one who got away. The one who was the reason why I could never completely hand my heart over to my ex-wife, Zara.

It was because he still owned it. Even now. Almost fourteen years later, he still has a tight hold on me.

And I have no idea what to do with that.

"Alex, do you take Blaine to be your lawfully wedded husband?" the officiant asks, finally pulling my attention away from the man next to me.

Alex flashes a wide smile and nods. "I do."

When she turns to Blaine, his chin wobbles. He presses his lips together like he's trying to keep a lid on his emotions. "Blaine, do you take Alex to be your lawfully wedded husband?"

Blaine's eagerly nodding his head before she's finished speaking, causing a ripple of laughter among the guests. "I do. I really fucking do."

Her mouth twitches at his slip of the tongue, but she manages to stop herself from laughing. She looks between them with a fond look on her face. "By the love that has brought you here today and by the vows you have pledged, it is my great honor from the state of California to now pronounce you husband and husband. You may now kiss one another."

Blaine grabs Alex's face with both hands and slams his mouth over his husband's. We all stand up, clapping and cheering in applause. Some of his teammates are hollering like hooligans.

Hockey players, you really can't take them anywhere.

Alex cradles Blaine's face, swiping his thumbs under his eyes to wipe away his husband's tears as they laugh into the kiss. The love they share is so palpable and pure. I could sense it the very first time I met Alex that they had a special kind of love, and it has only grown over time.

I had that once. That intense kind of love where you are everything to each other. The ability to communicate with a simple gaze. A deep-seated need to be together constantly. To have a level of intimacy that goes beyond just sex.

Twin flames, some might say.

Now, he can barely look at you, that small voice in my head reminds me.

I don't have many regrets in life. I like to think I've been pretty fortunate and made the most of the opportunities when they presented themselves, but there is one thing I regret. One thing that I've had to keep locked up and buried deep because our relationship during those three years was private. So private even our teammates didn't know.

My one regret was hurting him, and it's haunted me ever since.

I swallow down the thick knot that's crawled up into my throat and slip the mask back on, smiling as the happy couple heads down the aisle and into the villa. We follow, making our way inside to where the cocktail hour is being held while they convert the courtyard for the dinner and evening reception.

"Who woulda thought, eh?" Peyton says, draping his arm around my shoulder. "Blaine Olsen, *married*. Gag me. I'm thinking about setting up the divorced hockey players association. There's so many happy couples around me, and it makes me kinda nauseous. What do you think, eh? You in?"

I choke out a laugh. "Jon, you haven't been divorced for a year yet. You should be out there, reaping up the rewards of being the next potential captain of the Chicago Thunder."

"Dude! Shut your mouth! Don't jinx me like that!" he hisses, waving his hands between us like he can bat away the comment from the air.

I grin. Now I'm on the other side of it, it's fun to joke about hockey players and their superstitions. But I'm not kidding. He's in contention to be the next captain of the Chicago Thunder now Ethan Parkes hung up his skates at the end of the season.

He leans closer, his hulking frame casting a shadow over me. He wiggles his brows playfully and lowers his voice. "The ladies are gonna love me even more if I get the C, am I right?"

Jonathan Peyton is like an overgrown frat bro. He's in his early thirties and is a big puppy dog of a guy. He has the All-Canadian good looks down to a T. Blond hair, blue eyes, athletic build, and over six feet. He has a heart of gold, if you ignore the fact he cheated on his ex-wife every time he was on the road. They tried couples counseling, but ultimately, they decided it was best to call it quits. Sometimes people are not made to be monogamous.

But Peyton and I go way back. We played one season together in Boston after he was traded from New York, but then he went on to sign with the Thunder during the off-season. It was after Jackson was traded to Los Angeles, and Peyton became the unexpected friend I didn't know I needed. He helped me keep my mind busy while Jackson was tearing it up on the West Coast, being my wingman in bars and partying it up in whatever city we were in.

Not that I ever told him the real reason why I was drinking, dabbling in drugs, and fucking my way through North

America, but we've remained good friends despite our short playing time together.

Taking a step back, I run my gaze over him from his head to his feet, then let out an unenthusiastic noise. "Eh, maybe."

His jaw drops, brows lifting so high they almost touch his hairline. "Fuck you."

"Nah, you're not my type, but thanks." I clap him on the shoulder and steer him toward the bar. "Can you spot the hors d'oeuvres? I skipped out on breakfast this morning."

He follows me, ignoring my question.

"I can't believe you don't think I'm hot," he chides, sounding genuinely upset.

I have to swallow back my laughter. "Hey, I never said that. I said you're not my type. Plus, you're straight, if you've forgotten." I smirk.

He splutters, and I can't hold my laughter back any longer at the sight of his put-out expression. "Well, yeah, I am, but I also have feelings, and that kinda hurt, Cassie."

"Aw, I'm sure you'll get over it." I wink, pinching his cheek like my grandma used to do with me when I was twelve before heading in the direction of the waiter holding a tray full of food.

The rest of the afternoon and into the early evening passes by in a blur. The dinner was incredible. I've caught up with people I haven't seen in years. Now, the drinks are flowing, the vibe is vibing, and the fairy lights have been turned on, adding a soft glow to the sky as the sun sets behind the mountains.

Standing by the makeshift bar in the courtyard, I sip on a whiskey as I glance around. Throughout dinner, I had the perfect view of Jackson. Every time he laughed, my heart lurched in my chest. The need to talk to him has become borderline desperation. But I don't know what I would say. It isn't the right time to say I'm sorry for everything I put him through, but I need to speak to him. About anything or everything, regardless of the inevitable rejection that will come my way.

But I'll take anything he'll give me. Whether it be him telling me to fuck off or a tiny scrap of his time. *Anything.*

I spot him standing next to Blaine, Alex, and Peyton. His head tips back as he laughs at something Blaine says, and I realize this is the perfect opportunity. Jackson's too nice of a guy to tell me to fuck off in front of his teammates.

Right?

I place my empty glass down on the bar top, my body humming with anticipation and anxiety swirling in my stomach as I make my way over. Taking a steadying breath, I remind myself I'm confident and charming. I can do this.

Who am I kidding? I'm neither of those things. But I sure as hell can put on a convincing front because nobody knows what I've been dealing with in the almost nine years since I had the decision of my retirement taken away from me, except for two people. One of them being my ex-wife, Zara.

Jackson's laughter trails off as he sees me approaching, his face slipping into a frown.

Okay, maybe I was wrong. Maybe he *will* tell me to fuck off in front of his teammates.

"Hayden! Thank you for coming!" Alex beams. He wraps his arms around my shoulders in a welcoming hug.

The move earns me a scowl from Blaine, so I wink at him and give a cocky smirk over Alex's shoulder.

The first time I met Alex, he let it slip that he used to have a poster of me on his bedroom wall when he was growing up and how he had a crush on me. Something I like to tease Blaine about at every given opportunity because he's a possessive bastard.

Plus, if I'm teasing him, I'm not thinking about how old the comment made me feel.

"Thanks for inviting me. I can't believe I missed my chance," I sigh jokingly, placing a hand over my heart when Alex takes a step back. "We could've had such a fun love story."

Blaine wraps one protective arm around Alex's stomach and flips me off with his free hand. "Fuck off, Cassidy. You might be my agent, but I'm not afraid to punch you in the nuts."

I laugh. "I don't doubt that for a minute."

"You've met Jackson, right?" Alex asks, leaning back into his husband.

I risk a glance at Jackson. His blue eyes are hard with his glare. There's a deep crease between his brows, and the muscle twitches in his jaw when he gives a tight nod.

I clear my throat. "Yeah, I have."

"Wait!" Peyton blurts, his outburst causing me to flinch. "You go way back, eh? You played in Boston together before I was traded? I remember now! The power forward duo."

"That was a long time ago now." Jackson's voice has a cold edge to it, and a chill washes over me when he holds up his empty glass. "Excuse me, I need a refill."

I drop my gaze to the floor as Jackson walks away. Every

ounce of courage I managed to build up drains from me like liquid as silence falls upon the four of us.

"Huh," Blaine says, confusion lining his brows.

I lift my head, looking at him out of the corner of my eye. "What's up, Olsen?"

"Nothing." He shakes his head. "Nothing. I've just never seen Jackson be so…" He waves his free hand like he's trying to think of the right words.

"Standoffish," Alex supplies.

"He did get a phone call from the kids earlier. Not sure what happened, but maybe it's playing on his mind?" Peyton suggests with a shrug.

Or maybe it's me.

But I don't say that. That would mean explaining *why*, and that's not a box I want to open right now.

Plastering on what I hope is a convincing smile, I let them know I also need a drink, but instead of heading to the bar, I walk to the edge of the courtyard as numbness takes over my insides. A feeling that has been consistent since being forced to hang up my skates before I was ready.

When I stepped out onto the ice every night, I was loved. Adored. But the moment I retired, it was like I was forgotten. I became just another player to come and go from the sport. To have their career end earlier than expected. I went from spending a majority of my time with a group of guys to having multiple surgeries and nothing but my own mind for company while I recovered.

Nobody really understands how fucking lonely it is.

You're in the limelight, at the pinnacle of the sport that you've devoted your life to since you were a kid, then that's it. With a snap of the fingers, it's gone in a puff of smoke.

Now, you're someone who's only remembered on "hockey's worst on-ice injuries" clips online. Even the players' association didn't care once the doctors confirmed I wouldn't be returning to the ice.

I was brushed aside like a dirty alley cat, left to fend for myself with the constant reminder that I failed.

I failed Jackson.

I failed Zara.

I failed my career.

As I watch Jackson's retreating back disappear into the crowd, I can't help but wonder if he would look at me differently if he knew about the inner demon that's been living inside of me for so long. That I've allowed it to eat away at my life, stopping me from living. To just be… existing. Now, I'm living the life I loved so much through my clients instead.

Or would he see me as the weak man that I am underneath the façade I try so fucking hard to keep up?

Or would he be glad that he cut me out of his life when he did?

I guess I'll never get the chance to know.

Chapter Three

Jackson

"Whiskey, neat." I pull out a twenty-dollar bill from my pocket. "Actually, best make it a double."

"You got it." The bartender makes quick work of pouring definitely more than a double into a glass tumbler and slides it across the surface.

"Thanks," I say, stuffing the twenty in the glass jar. Turning on my heel, I head toward the edge of the patio so I'm out of the way. With it being an open bar and a bunch of hockey players in attendance, it's very busy and only getting more rowdy as the night goes on. The liquid burns my throat when I swallow it down, but I revel in it. It gives me something else to focus on other than my heart beating hard in my chest.

Whiskey isn't my typical drink of choice, but it was always Hayden's. For weeks after we broke up, it became my crutch. Loving how it tasted on my lips because it reminded me of him. But then the heartbreak turned into anger, and I haven't touched a drop since.

Until now.

It wasn't my intention to be rude and walk away from my teammates like a grumpy teenager, but fuck, I needed some air. Which is ironic, considering we're already outside, but being in close proximity to Hayden again is too much.

It's been fourteen years, damnit. *Fourteen.* Surely I should be immune to him by now. I shouldn't want to simultaneously punch him in the face and stick my tongue down his throat. I shouldn't want to bury my face in his neck, inhaling his scent until it's ingrained in my soul. I shouldn't care about him in any way whatsoever. He made his bed and lay in it when he threw what we had away without so much as a second thought. We both moved on, married our respective wives—albeit we both got divorced from those wives, but that's neither here nor there.

I'm struggling to understand why I'm still affected by him after all this time. It's like the Hayden Cassidy homing beacon that's been dormant inside me for over a decade has kick-started, and every single one of my senses has been programmed to focus on him.

It's stifling.

Throughout dinner, the only sound I could hear over the music and chatter was his deep, husky laughter. The smell of his spicy cologne has stayed with me all day, torturing me because he smells as good as I remember. And every time I looked in his direction, his eyes were zeroed in on me. Paying no attention to whoever he was talking to at the time, simply watching me with those intense gray eyes.

There was one thing I noticed, however, and that was whenever he laughed or smiled, it never quite reached his eyes.

What was he hiding behind that confident exterior? Was he using his charm like a shield, preventing anyone from seeing what was behind his three-piece suit of armor?

Then, I circle back to the same question that's been troubling me all night. Why do I care so much about Hayden fucking Cassidy?

Placing my empty glass down on the bar top, I take advantage of everyone being engaged in conversation or busy dancing, allowing me to slip out of sight unnoticed. I walk along the side of the villa until I get to a waist-high stone wall overlooking the vineyard. I rest my forearms against the wall and stare out into the distance.

My insides feel all cut up. Confusion mixed with age-old hurt. After we broke up, I managed to separate my feelings while he was still playing. It helped being on the other side of the country and only having to see him twice a season on the ice; then it was just a case of time. Because time is supposed to fix everything, right?

After he retired, we hadn't been in the same place for almost nine years until I saw him a few months ago in Zach's apartment, and it threw me off-kilter. All of the feelings I thought I had buried came rushing to the surface like metal to a magnet. Drawing me to him like no time had passed at all.

There was a time when I thought he was the one. That we would grow old and gray together. He would paint the picture of how our life would look after hockey while we were lying in his bed back in Boston. He wanted us to buy a cabin in upstate New York, or maybe even Vermont, where we could cook together before making love in front of the fire—his words, not mine. But looking back, all he did was feed me with empty promises he was never planning to fulfill. Because the moment I got the call telling me I was heading to Los Angeles, I saw something shutter in his eyes. But I ignored it. I was young and naïve enough to believe we would survive. That we'd smash the whole long-distance thing because I was convinced our love was real and strong and could withstand anything the world wanted to throw at us.

I couldn't have been more wrong. And fourteen years later, those words still cut through me like a knife.

I was never in love with you, Jackson.

The sound of shoes crunching on the loose stones pulls me out of the daze I was in, but I don't turn around. My body is so acutely aware of him I know who it is before he speaks.

"You didn't need to leave on my behalf."

Hayden's lips are tipped in a lopsided smile when I look over my shoulder. His hands are stuffed deep in the pockets of his pants, his suit jacket draped across his forearm. His body language is almost boyish, but there's nothing boyish about him. He juts his chin to the stone wall, a silent request to join me.

I nod once and turn back to look out at the vineyard. He places his jacket on the wall, then mirrors my position, forearms resting on the wall, and fixes his gaze on something in the distance. Every atom inside of me wants to turn to look at him. To take him in up close. To look at him now he doesn't have his sunglasses shielding his eyes or other people's attention on us.

I swallow hard as a heavy ball of emotion coats the back of my throat down to my stomach. It's a strange sensation to be standing next to someone who was once a constant. We went from being inseparable to becoming strangers, and sometimes you don't truly know the significance of that loss until they're standing right in front of you again. Like a mirage of someone you once knew.

Minutes pass by in silence, and I fight to keep my eyes off Hayden. I try to focus on how the sky is so clear, allowing the stars to shine brightly against the dark canvas. The music is still loud enough to hear but quiet enough to think. I manage to resist the pull up until he shifts and laces his fingers together. A flash of color catches my eye, and I snap like a weak piece of string. I take in the tattoos covering both of his arms. They travel from his wrist up past the fabric of his rolled-up sleeves. Not one inch of skin has been left untouched. One arm is black and gray; the other is vibrant color.

"They're new," I point out, then internally roll my eyes.

Seriously, Wilde? Of course they're fucking new. He didn't have one drop of ink on his skin when we were together. I would know, because I knew every inch of him intimately.

"Yeah. There's a lot of things that are new for us, Jax."

I frown at his tone, and I don't miss how my heart rate picks up at the sound of my old nickname. "What's that supposed to mean?"

"I mean—" He cuts himself off, sighing heavily. He raises his hand to pinch the bridge of his nose, then drops it again to look at me. "Fuck. I didn't want to do this here."

Those gray eyes lock on to mine, rooting me in place. They flash with an emotion I'm unable to decipher when he speaks again, "I understand why you hate me. In fact, I probably hate myself just as much as you do, if not more, but I'm not that person anymore, Jax. If I could go back and do things differently, I would do it in a heartbeat, but I can't. I have to live with the consequences of my actions."

Wait, *what*? He thinks I hate him?

Yeah, I'm mad at him. Infuriated, maybe. But hate is such a strong word. Even when he broke my heart and my hurt morphed into anger, I never hated him. I don't think I could ever hate him.

"I don't hate you, Hayden," I tell him, standing upright and turning my body to face him. "But you broke my heart. You threw away the years we spent together just like that." I snap my fingers. "Like we meant nothing. I'm sorry I'm not going to be happy to see you or be around you. Especially considering this is only the second time I've seen you that hasn't been during a game. But I don't hate you."

"You did mean something." He drops his gaze to the ground. His voice is quiet, almost pained.

"You could've fooled me," I laugh humorlessly. "I was sent to this brand-new city, all alone. I didn't know a fucking soul, and the one person who I thought had my back was nowhere to be seen."

My heart thunders in my chest, blood ringing in my ears as that wound I thought was healed reopens, exposing the hurt that I thought was dead and buried. But the words don't stop. They tumble out of me after years of being locked up.

"You dropped me so fast, Hayden. I didn't know what the fuck I did or whether our relationship was even real because next thing I know, you were posting you were engaged! You can't blame me for not greeting you with open arms. I spent so fucking long second-guessing whether our connection was genuine. Whether your feelings for me were genuine or whether you were just using me because it was convenient."

He squeezes his eyes shut, and his teeth dig into his rosy bottom lip so hard it turns white. "I wasn't using you, and it wasn't because it was convenient."

My body is trembling as I stare at him. I pump my shaking hands into fists, tensing and releasing to try and calm myself down.

I want to yell at him and shake him, make him know exactly what he put me through, but what use is it? It's in the past. I need to think of this as the closure I needed. To put a lid on the box that was us and never open it again.

We both remain silent, staring at each other for a few minutes. I can't help but take him in. His five-o'clock shadow is speckled with a silver tint, matching the silver strands appearing at his temples. His face is as handsome as I've always remembered, only now he has fine lines around his eyes, and he looks tired. The low lighting emphasizes the shadows beneath his eyes. Being back in Hayden's orbit is causing a lot of confusing emotions to war inside my chest because I shouldn't want to ask him if he's okay. I shouldn't *care*.

But there's the saying that you don't forget your first love. That they leave an imprint on your soul. And maybe it's true, but that also goes for emotional scars, and they can run just as deep.

A car pulls up and parks on the round driveway, the bright headlights causing me to squint. Hayden pushes himself off the wall and picks up his jacket.

He turns toward the idling car, and I find myself blurting out, "You're leaving?"

"Yeah, this is my ride." He glances longingly in the direction of the party going on behind before focusing his eyes back on me. "They're your crowd, Jackson. I'm sorry if me being here made things uncomfortable for you."

I open my mouth to tell him he didn't make things uncomfortable, not in the way he's thinking, anyway. Yeah, so it turns out I'm still fucking pissed at him, but that's my problem to deal with. The only thing I'm uncomfortable with is the whole heap of fucking mixed feelings going on inside of me.

"It was really good to see you again," he says after a beat because I still haven't spoken. This time when he smiles, it does reach his eyes, but it's full of sadness. "Take care of yourself."

I don't know why I want to ask him to stay. I want him to tell me why he's now covered in tattoos and the stories behind them. I want him to tell me what's going on in his mind and what happened to make his eyes become stormy. Like the flame that used to burn so bright has been snuffed out.

But I can't.

I can't do anything except watch as he gets into the back of the car and closes the door behind him. I stand there, a heaviness weighing on my chest, watching the taillights disappear into the distance.

I might not know what's going on inside of my head and heart right now, but there's one thought that's clear in my mind. When he walked away, he was limping, favoring his other leg that didn't end his career with a torn ACL.

His words come back to me like a quick-fire reel in my mind as I stare out at the now dark driveway.

There's a lot of things that are new between us, Jax.

I probably hate myself just as much as you do, if not more.

I'm not that person anymore, Jax.

Fuck. What does that mean? And why do I want to know who he is now?

Chapter Four

Hayden

A week has gone by since the wedding, and I've thrown myself in so deep with work I'm not quite sure what day it is anymore. I've needed to keep busy to stop my mind from replaying Jackson's words on an endless loop. They were filled with so much hurt. Hurt that I caused, and I don't know how to make it right.

I've been beating myself up. Thinking about all the things I could have done or said differently. But sadly, I don't have a DeLorean or any other type of time machine. I can't go back and change anything, which is the reason why I'm sitting on the comfortable, aqua-blue couch in Roberta's office, five weeks earlier than scheduled. She's been my therapist for over six years now, and she is now a crucial lifeline in my journey.

"So, how's everything going?" Roberta asks. She's kicked off her tennis shoes and tucked her feet beneath her on the armchair. She actively promotes that, inside these four walls, it's a safe space. I can cry or laugh and talk about anything and everything or nothing at all. Although, I know she doesn't like it when I don't say anything. She knows how chaotic my brain is, so there's always something to say. But the best part is she wants me to be as comfortable and relaxed as possible while I'm here, and if that includes taking off my shoes and kicking my feet up on the cushions, then it's encouraged.

Knowing she's not going to ask me outright what has caused me to move up my appointment, I avert my gaze to the jellyfish tank on the wooden unit lining the wall. Moon jellyfish swim in a mesmerizing movement under the blue light. Roberta's had them for a few years now, and I find them oddly relaxing. There's been a number of times where I've been envious of those tiny blobs because I learned they don't have brains, eliminating the possibility of their minds turning against them. Like mine has done with me.

After I received the news I would need a third surgery on my knee after a torn ACL ended my career, I found myself in a dark, downward spiral. I'd often stand in the ocean out the back of my house when the current was strong and wish for the water to take me away. To relieve me of the pain that only seemed to be getting worse inside of me, both physically and mentally. I didn't want to live like that anymore. Gone was the love and support I felt while I was playing professional hockey, and all I was left with was a fucked-up knee that didn't seem to be repairable and a mind that was telling me I wasn't good enough anymore. Even the waves didn't seem to think I was worthy because they never did pull me in.

It was during my fourth attempt that Zara found me and realized what I was trying to do. She found Roberta through a few of her medical friends, and if I'm being honest, if Zara didn't find her, I can wholeheartedly say I wouldn't be sitting here today.

They both saved me.

We went from meeting twice a week to bi-weekly and worked endlessly with my psychiatrist to find a medication that suited me, and then gradually, we've moved to meeting every three to four months. Or in instances when I need to seek additional support, like today. Her door is always open for me, and I appreciate it no end.

"I saw Jackson last week," I say, finally tearing myself away from the jellyfish tank.

When I look at Roberta, her expression remains calm and patient as she scribbles something in her notebook. If she's surprised, she doesn't show it. Her face never gives anything away. "How did it make you feel? Seeing him again?"

You broke my heart. You threw away the years we spent together just like that, like we meant nothing.

I squeeze my eyes closed as his words filter through my mind again, and the ache in my chest blooms. I may have broken his heart, but he has it all wrong about us meaning nothing. I *had* thrown it away because it meant *everything* to me.

"He could barely look at me, to begin with," I start, clearing my throat when my voice cracks slightly. "There was only one seat left when I got there, which, of course, happened to be next to him. He..." I let out a long exhale and focus back on the jellyfish when my heart rate picks up speed. The light in the tank has changed from blue to green, making them look like little green aliens floating around. "I think after seeing him at Zach's place back in March, I stupidly convinced myself that maybe we could… I don't know, talk again."

"I don't believe it's stupid to think that, Hayden. You were very important to each other at one stage in your lives. So, what's stopping you from talking again?" she asks.

Her question pulls my attention away from the tank and back to her again.

"We spoke before I left, and based on what he said and the anger in his voice, I don't think he'll wanna speak to me again."

The tiny thread of hope I was holding on to snapped that night.

A few minutes pass by where she doesn't say a word. I used to find it really unnerving. Long stretches of silence became torturous for me. It allowed the dark part of my brain to take over, to spread numbness throughout my body until I felt nothing but emptiness, but she's helped me through it over the years. Now, I find silence can be peaceful. Except at night. I might be approaching forty, but I can't sleep unless I have some kind of noise to drown out the chatter in my head.

"This was only the second time seeing him in quite a long time, right? Do you think there's a possibility he was surprised to see you, and his reaction was more out of shock than how he was genuinely feeling?"

I nod. "Yeah, before that time at Zach's, I hadn't seen him since I retired over eight years ago."

I think back to the puzzled expression on Jackson's face when my ride share pulled up and he realized I was leaving early. The internal war he was fighting was evident in his blue eyes, clear as day. A mix of disappointment, annoyance, and need. Disappointment I was leaving, maybe? A need to keep our conversation going? I don't know, but it wouldn't be the first time I've been delusional when it comes to Jackson Wilde.

She's right, though. There's a high possibility he was surprised to see me. Sure, he knows I'm Blaine's agent. I represent a few of his teammates too, but you can still be blindsided by your emotions when you're actually faced with something or, in this case, someone.

"And maybe he was surprised. I mean, probably?"

I tell her everything he said to me. About how I broke his heart, how he questioned everything we had and my feelings toward him, to the hurt he felt when I announced my proposal with Zara, and how he corrected me when I said he hated me.

He didn't hate me.

That's got to mean something, right?

By the time I've finished recalling our conversation, my throat is tight. I fight off the tears burning the back of my eyes, threatening to spill over, so I focus back on the jellyfish.

The light is now purple, and one of the blobs is spinning around like a whirlpool near the pump. Do they ever get dizzy? I guess not without a brain.

"I know I could've explained myself there and then, but the timing was all off. I didn't want to ruin his night more than I already had," I say, which earns me a disgruntled noise from Roberta.

I quickly cover my mouth with my hand as my lips tilt up in a smile when she doesn't call me out on my self-deprecating comment.

"Okay, so let's say he agrees to talking again. What are you hoping to achieve from that?" she asks after writing something else in her notebook.

Dropping my hand into my lap, I tug my bottom lip between my teeth and lower my gaze. This seems like a trick question. What *do* I want to achieve from being back in Jackson's life again? Ultimately, I want him back, but I know that's not going to happen. All the sad love songs say you don't know what you've lost until it's gone, and it's true. But my loss is so far gone, and I'm not sure it's redeemable after what I did to him.

Maybe I need to start small. That's what I had to do at the beginning of my therapy journey. That's what Roberta taught me. When something feels too big to take on, break it down into small, baby steps.

If we can start by talking first, then maybe it can progress to friendship. Once we're friends again, it's a step closer to making things right. I can explain why I was an asshole of the highest degree, and hopefully, we can both heal from there.

"I want to be friends again," I confess.

"How would it make you feel to be friends with him again?"

I automatically shrug, almost defensively.

Isn't it obvious? I want to say, but I don't.

"I don't know. Happiness, I guess? I was so happy when we were together. I want to make things right with him, but

I also want to open that door and see if there's another chance for us." I rub my jaw with my palm. My skin is beginning to feel too tight for my body under her watchful eye. "I'd start small, like you taught me. Ask if he wants to get coffee, then next time, maybe I can take him for lunch. Baby steps. I know he's wary of me, and I don't blame him for being guarded because I threw our relationship into a dumpster fire without so much as a second thought because I was scared."

She gives a small smile and nods softly. "But you want to try."

My breath comes out in a rush because that's just it. I want to try. I've been working on myself over the years to get to this point where I'm strong enough to try and get him back. Medication and therapy doesn't mean depression just disappears. I'm always going to be healing.

"Yeah, I do."

Her pen flies over her notebook as she says, "Okay, so if he says yes to coffee and you're back in each other's lives again, how would that make you feel?"

A smile lights my face at the thought of having Jackson in my life again. "Really happy."

"But what if it goes the other way? What if he doesn't want to be back in your life again?"

My smile drops, instantly replaced with a frown. I lift my hand, rubbing over my chest as pain ricochets through me. I'd be heartbroken. There's no other way to put it. I don't think I would be able to recover from losing him again.

"Then I'd want to give up," I admit, barely above a whisper.

As always, her expression doesn't give anything away. There's no sign of what she thinks I should do. I know she asks me these questions because she wants me to know nothing is guaranteed. She's leaving this for me to decide.

Without a word, she gets up and moves behind her desk. Her nails tap away on her keyboard, and then she comes back to her seat, curling her feet beneath her again. "I have some homework for you."

"Homework? Am I in school again?" I snicker, and she laughs.

"No, but I'd like for us to see each other again in two weeks. During that period, I want you to take some time to really think about both outcomes. Then I'd like you to write in your journal your feelings toward both sides. It's easy to have an instant reaction to things, but when we dig deeper, oftentimes our answers can be different."

I agree to her task, and we book an appointment for two weeks' time. Once I'm back in my car and heading toward my home in Hermosa Beach, I hit Call on Zara's name and wait for her to pick up. Even though we're divorced, we're still good friends, despite the lies I've said about her.

And that's a whole other heap of shit I need to make right.

"Hey, how did it go?" she asks as soon as she answers.

"Good. She's given me some homework."

Zara snorts. "Homework? What, are you in third grade again?"

I can't stop the bark of laughter that escapes. "You sound like me. She wants me to think about how I'd feel if I did get Jackson back and if I don't."

"And are you going to do it?"

I let her question linger in the air. I'm aware I'm putting a lot of pressure on this. Not just on Jackson but on myself. Placing the source of my life's happiness in one person's hands isn't healthy, I know that. And while I've come a long way since the first time I walked through the doors to Roberta's office, I'm still a work in progress. There might never be a completed version, but I've come a long way.

"Yeah, I am," I finally say after a beat.

"Good. You know I'm here for you if you need me. If you want to talk it out loud to me, or if you need me to create a diversion, I'm here."

A warmth spreads through my chest at the sincerity in her words.

When we decided it was best for us to separate, Zara didn't want the truth to come out about my struggles for fear of me spiraling further and destroying the progress I'd made. In order to avoid questions on why we were getting a divorce, she came up with the idea to say she had an affair. I personally thought it was a stupid idea, and if I was in a better mental space, I wouldn't have gone through with it. But she was adamant that she didn't give a fuck about people's opinions about her. She said the people who knew us would know the truth. She cared more about people's opinions of me, and fuck, did it make me feel like the biggest asshole who ever existed every time I had to spew those lies and play into the narrative she set.

But that's the kind of person Zara is. She puts other people before herself all the damn time, and I'm glad she's found happiness with Connor because he's a much better partner to her than I ever was.

Even if I do hold a tiny bit of resentment toward him

because he's ten years my junior and playing in the NHL. Lucky motherfucker.

"You're awesome, you know that?" I tell her.

I can hear the smile in her voice when she replies, "I know, which is why I'm gonna help you win your man back. No matter what it takes."

Chapter Five

Jackson
   3 months later - October

"Dad, have you seen my gloves?" Ryan asks, skidding across the wooden floor in his socks and stopping in the doorway. "They're not in my hockey bag."

I glance up from where I'm currently packing Isabela's bag on her bed. I leave for my first road trip of the season in less than two hours, and as usual, I've left everything to the last minute. I haven't had time to shower yet or have a coffee.

Being undercaffeinated and up against the clock is not a good mix.

"Where did you have them last?" I ask, folding a set of pajamas, but before I can quiz Ryan more on the whereabouts of his gloves, Isabela snatches the pajamas out of my hand and tosses them onto the floor.

"No, not them," she scolds and jumps off the bed.

I'm startled by her outburst, unable to do anything except stand there, wide-eyed, while she grabs another set out of her chest of drawers and hands them over with a sweet smile. Like she didn't turn into a wet gremlin a few seconds ago. "These, Daddy. Pink unicorns."

"Yeah, sure, okay," I say absentmindedly and stuff them into the bag. She's been throwing more temper tantrums recently. I don't know if she's having big feelings about being back at preschool and the hockey season starting again, but I've definitely been noticing more behavioral challenges than normal, and I'm not quite sure how to handle them.

When I look up again, she's taken her socks off and has started to pull various toys out of her toy box, scattering them across the floor.

My mom's going to flip when she sees the state of the house.

With a sigh, I squeeze my temples with my thumb and middle finger. I try to keep my voice as calm as possible. "Peanut, I need you to put your socks back on and put your toys away. Gigi is going to be here in less than twenty minutes, and you know Gigi doesn't like the house being in a mess."

The sound of rubber balls bouncing against the wall snaps my attention back to the hallway, and I'm unable to stop the loud groan escaping me. Ryan's dragged his pop-up goalie net into the hallway and is using his mini stick to hit rubber balls into it.

Why do my kids make things ten times harder than they need to be?

"Ryan, that needs to go back into your room. Now. We

don't have time for that. Where did you have your gloves last? They haven't grown legs and climbed out of your bag, so they have to be somewhere."

"Dunno." He shrugs, then continues to fire the balls at the net.

Tension crawls up the back of my neck, and I turn to face the window. I squeeze my eyes shut before taking a deep, steadying breath. It's always a stressful time whenever I need to go on the road, even more so today because I'm exhausted and in desperate need of a coffee.

It's not the kids' fault I'm an unorganized mess. There's no excuse for it. I've known about this road trip for a while. I've had plenty of time to get their bags packed and ready for my mom to pick them up, so I have no one else but myself to blame for falling asleep on the couch after opening a bottle of wine last night instead of packing my own bag.

Hello, failure as a parent, it's me.

It's only the first week of October, and I already feel like I'm burning the candle at both ends. But the fool that I am, I'm too proud—okay, maybe more like too stubborn—to ask for more help than I'm already getting.

The regular season is now underway, meaning my parents are pretty much taking care of the kids for me. Most mornings, I can take them to school and occasionally pick them up if it's not a game day, but usually, it comes down to my mom and dad. Isabela is now in preschool for longer hours, and Ryan has moved up into a mites hockey team and trains multiple times a week after school. It's been a case of finding the right balance.

Something I've failed to do so far.

I don't want to ask my parents for even more help.

They've already done the school run and hockey practice years with me and my sister. This is supposed to be their retirement. A time to relax and take it easy. Not picking up the pieces of my life after me.

I spend the next twenty minutes frantically packing both their bags, and by the time my mom walks through the door, I'm flustered and impatient as the coffee machine slowly whirls to life.

Her gaze bounces around the open-plan kitchen/family room, jaw gradually dropping open. There's stuff everywhere. Clothes, toys, colored markers, and pieces of paper. You name it, it's probably on the floor or the couch or the countertop. I'm grateful my housekeeper is coming while I'm gone, but it doesn't mean I don't feel like an ass for leaving it in this mess. I make a mental note to leave her some extra cash on the side.

"Wow, Jackson. I thought I'd taught you to be a lot cleaner than this." My mom picks up a plate with a half-eaten slice of toast.

Glowering, I take the plate from her and discard the food into the trash before putting it in the dishwasher and slamming the door closed.

"Now is not the time to be commenting on my house-keeping skills, Mom," I say between clenched teeth.

She holds both hands up in submission. "Hey, no need to be snappy. What do you need me to do?" She flicks her wrist to look at her watch, then eyes my disheveled state with furrowed brows. "Don't you need to leave soon?"

"Yes, I do, but I haven't showered, or had a coffee yet, or packed my own bag."

Sighing, she walks into the kitchen and pats my hip with

the back of her hand, motioning for me to move out of the way. "Go get in the shower and sort your bag out. I'll make you a large cup of coffee and deal with the kids."

And like they've been summoned, they come running down the stairs like a herd of elephants, shouting, "Gigi!" and launching themselves at my mom.

Not needing to be told twice, I disappear up the stairs without a word and into my en suite. I strip out of my plaid pajama pants and T-shirt and step under the warm spray.

As much as I love my kids and wouldn't change them for the world, I'm looking forward to this road trip. But the relieved feeling is soon replaced with guilt because what parent looks forward to a night or so away from their children?

I know Laura's and my divorce was for the best, but it's fucking tough being a single parent. I'm fortunate I don't have the financial pressures other parents do, allowing me to pay for a housekeeper and a chef to prepare meals for me so I only have to think about feeding the kids when my mom hasn't fed them already, but it's a constant juggling act. During the season, I'm working hard to keep my perfor-mance up, ensuring I eat well and rest enough. Being one of the older guys on the team means I have to work that bit harder than the younger guys. It's being on the road and missing important moments in the kids' lives. It's spending quality time with them, both together and alone, and making sure they know they're loved and supported while also providing structure and discipline.

And while I'm trying my best at doing all of that, it's remembering who I am too. Not as Jackson Wilde, forward for the Chicago Thunder and alternate captain, or Dad.

It's remembering I'm also Jackson Wilde, the guy who enjoys cooking and listening to Frank Sinatra and enjoys lazy Sundays in bed with a good thriller.

Because outside of every other hat I wear, I'm not sure *I* remember who I am anymore.

And it kinda sucks.

We arrive in Boston just before noon. Once my mom left with the kids, I headed to the practice facility for a light workout before our flight, and the moment the plane door closed, it was like the chaos of the morning caught up with me because I was out like a light and slept for most of the two-hour journey.

Now we're at the hotel, and we have some downtime ahead of tonight's game. Some of the guys head into their respective rooms, either to take a nap or FaceTime with their partners, but me? I always feel a sense of melancholy whenever I'm in Boston. The last thing I want is to hole up on my own, so I drop my bag, then head toward the elevators.

I haven't lived in this city for fourteen years, but it still holds a lot of memories for me. I started my career here. I was drafted at eighteen and spent a season on the development team in Providence before being called up to play my first game in the NHL game just shy of my nineteenth birthday.

And it's where I met Hayden.

I was already in awe of him before I was called up. He started his professional career as an undrafted free agent, and even early on, he was a polarizing figure, making waves from his first game. You could say I was captivated by him before he opened his mouth and introduced himself. It was easy to fall in love with him.

We had three blissful years together until I got traded to Los Angeles and it all fell apart.

"Hey, Jackson?"

I turn at the sound of my name, mentally snapping myself out of the cloud my head disappeared into. Elliot jogs down the hall, having changed into sweats and a hoodie that looks a few sizes too big for him.

"Are you going for a walk?" he asks, stepping into the elevator with me when the doors open.

"Yeah, I am." Normally, I go for a walk on my own, but something in Elliot's expression is telling me my goalie needs company. "Did you want to come with?"

"That would be cool, if you don't mind." He slumps against the back wall. He's staring at his Converse, blond hair falling around his face.

We're silent as we head out onto the street, and I lead us in the direction of Boston Common. It's only a short walk from the hotel, but it's always been one of my favorite places to visit. No matter the weather, I always make time to do a lap around the park. It's beautiful this time of year too. The greenery has started to turn a gorgeous, vibrant mix of deep yellow, red, and orange, making it a sight to behold.

"So, what's up? Is everything okay?" I ask.

"Yeah. I mean…" He sighs and shakes his head. "Yeah, it's fine. My brain's just a little loud at the moment."

I nod in understanding. "I get that. It makes it hard to nap when your brain's busy."

We fall into a comfortable silence again as we pass the bandstand and continue our way around the trail. It's a mild day, so we make sure to move out of the way of a few runners and dog walkers.

At least five minutes have gone by when Elliot's question catches me off guard. "Do you ever get lonely on the road?"

I tilt my head toward him. "What do you mean?"

"Like, everyone is pretty much coupled up now, apart from you and Peyton and a couple of the younger guys. But road trips used to be fun. We'd play Ping-Pong or gate-crash Zach's room to play video games, but now… Now, they don't wanna play Ping-Pong. They just wanna be in their rooms and speak to their partners." He shrugs. I can tell he's trying to appear unbothered, but I can see the underlying hurt. "It can be lonely, I guess. I'm not very good with change."

I think through my words carefully. I've come to learn that Elliot's a sensitive soul beneath the laughter and bubbly persona. He takes things to heart a lot more than others would, and I can imagine the change in the dynamic with his twin getting married has caused some of this.

"Sometimes," I admit, because it's the truth. I've only been in two relationships, but there are days where I miss having that someone in my corner, no matter how the game went. "But usually, I'm so focused on the game ahead and trying not to beat myself up for leaving my kids and feeling like a shit dad that I don't really have the time to think about anything else, you know?"

He stuffs his hands into the front pocket of his hoodie and nods. "Yeah, that makes sense."

"And when I'm not feeling guilty, I'm enjoying the fact I

can get a decent night's sleep without being woken up by getting kneed in the balls at 4:00 a.m.," I chuckle.

Elliot lets out a bark of laughter.

"Does this have anything to do with your brother getting married, by any chance?" I ask after a beat.

"Yeah, kinda. Don't get me wrong, I love Alex. I think he's so awesome, and I'm so happy he's my bro-in-law, but…" He worries his bottom lip, then makes a frustrated noise. "Ugh, I feel like such a dick for thinking this, but I feel like I've been replaced in Blaine's life. And I know that's not the case, but the irrational part of my brain doesn't want to get on board."

"I don't think you're an asshole for feeling like that. You two have a unique relationship, something only other twins can truly understand. Maybe it'll be easier once you meet someone yourself?"

A pensive look crosses his face. "Have you ever had that? Where you have the need to be with them all the time, even if it's over the phone?"

Hayden instantly comes to mind. Something that's happened a lot over the last three months. We were inseparable during our relationship. We spent every moment possible together, whether it be on the road, in the confines of our home, or even in the locker room. We would play together, train together, and eat together. At night, we would sneak into each other's hotel room on the road, and I pretty much lived at Hayden's apartment in Seaport until the day I was shipped off to LA.

A trickle of annoyance claws up my throat, making my skin heat. It's like he's planted his handsome ass back into my mind since the wedding, and I've been unable to think about anything else but him. Along with all the unanswered questions I have.

"Yeah, a long time ago. It didn't last, though," I say.

We finish our loop of the park, then head back to the hotel. The fresh air and Elliot's company have helped clear my mind, and hopefully, I've done the same for him. He's a good guy, and I hate knowing he's feeling dejected.

"Hey, Jackson?" Elliot calls out as I reach the door to my room. "I know it's easy for me to say, but you shouldn't feel guilty. You're an awesome dad, and you've got two awesome kids who love the hell out of you. You should give yourself some grace and stop holding yourself to this made-up standard." He smiles. "You're doing awesome, okay?"

"Thanks, El. I appreciate it." I smile back. "And I'm here if you need me, okay? You're not alone in this."

Once I'm back in my room, I set an alarm and strip down to my boxer briefs. My eyes are heavy by the time I slip under the covers, and like every time I'm in Boston, I fall asleep with the thought of Hayden on my mind.

Chapter Six

Hayden

One of the perks of being a retired hockey player turned sports agent is I can get free tickets to pretty much any game. NHL. NFL. MLB. NBA. You name a league, I'll have a contact. All I have to do is make a few calls, and within the hour, I've got a choice of seats to pick from.

Tonight, I'm watching the Chicago Thunder face Boston from the GM's suite. While I didn't have a smooth transition into retirement with minimal support from the organization, I didn't leave on bad terms. I held no shame when I dropped Boston's GM a call two weeks ago and asked if he would be able to spring a ticket my way for tonight's game. And I wasn't going to say no when he offered up his suite. There's always a fully stocked bar and unlimited food, and I make sure he repays for the tough years by drinking his expensive top-shelf whiskey.

I also have a perfect, uninterrupted view of the ice where the Thunder are currently up by one goal twelve minutes into the first period.

Did I need to be in Boston tonight? No. But this is all part of the master plan I've been working on over the last couple of months.

I knew they would be staying overnight before heading to Washington tomorrow, and what better place to invite Jackson for a morning coffee than in the city where we fell in love.

Corny? Perhaps. But I'm confident he won't be able to resist when I mention Rafe's Coffee House. It used to be our favorite place to go, and I remember how much he missed their hazelnut lattes when he got traded because he would tell me every day.

Until you ended it all.

I tell the voice in my head to fuck off because we're not going down that road. Not today. This is my chance to make things right, and I won't let that negative voice jeopardize my plan.

Sipping on a glass of whiskey, I watch Jackson skate smoothly across the ice. I loved playing on the same line as him. We were always so in tune with one another, silently communicating through our eyes, and we could connect passes without looking. I knew where he was on the ice at all times, and him with me. We were unstoppable, and nine times out of ten, if either one of us scored a goal, the other's name would be listed with the assist.

Our connection was magical, both on and off the ice. But ultimately, it was my own fear that severed that connection. It's kinda terrifying when you meet someone like that. Especially when it's someone you can't be with, like a teammate. The fear that rooted deep inside of me when he received the news of a trade took over and my mind began to spiral.

What if he found someone else? What if he realized how much I was head over fucking heels in love with him and decided I was too much? What if he realized he didn't really love me and decided to end it? What if the distance became too much?

I guess my anxieties started long before my injury because it was when Jackson had to leave that the voices started to take control in my mind. Those intrusive thoughts became suffocating, and the voices convinced me that I was the one who had to end things first because then I was in control. He couldn't break my heart if I broke his first.

I was twenty-six and immature. But even putting my actions down to immaturity doesn't make what I did right.

Boston fails to even the score by the end of the first period, and second goes scoreless for both teams. By the time the third period ticks down, the heat is on. Boston are all over the Thunder's forwards and trying to get under their skin. Blaine gets a penalty for tripping Mäkinen, one of Boston's defensemen, and argues his way to the box. He must say something out of frustration because the ref holds his hands up, forming a T.

Unsportsmanlike conduct.

"Fuck's sake, Blaine. Keep your head in the game," I murmur, resting my chin on my steepled fingers.

The next four minutes are like watching a disaster movie. Mäkinen capitalizes on a failed pass from Peyton, sending the puck over Elliot's glove and into the back of the net. Jackson's head drops back in defeat, and I can just imagine him rolling his eyes in annoyance. My lips tip in a small smile at the thought.

The final two minutes of Blaine's penalty is chaotic. Kendrick scores when Boston gets a hooking penalty, giving the Thunder a 2-1 lead, but then Mitch Henry takes a high stick to the chin that goes uncalled. Peyton drops his gloves at the first opportunity, grabbing the offending player by the front of his jersey, and lands an uppercut. The arena goes wild as the two fight it out while Mitch skates to the bench to get patched up. When the officials finally break them apart, Peyton makes his way to the penalty box, where Blaine gives him a fist bump and slaps his back. Boston evens the score once again, getting the puck past Elliot to make it two all.

My heart is in my throat as the camera pans onto Jackson, his face appearing on the jumbotron. His brows are pinched slightly as he tilts his head up to the screen. A light sheen of sweat coats his skin, and the scruff lining his jaw makes my fingers twitch with the need to touch it. To feel it between my thighs and the sensitive skin on my neck.

A shiver travels down my spine at the thought.

I'm on the edge of my seat as Jackson takes the face-off. He wins, passing it to Blaine, who's finally out of the penalty box, but Boston are quick to take back possession. I stop breathing when Jackson intercepts the puck, and then he's on a breakaway. Even at thirty-six, he's one of the fastest skaters on the team. The sheer power in his legs propels him up the ice, and within seconds, he's taking a shot on the net. It sails past the goaltender's shoulder, sinking into the top right corner. The lamp lights, and there's a collective groan throughout the arena while the Thunder fans celebrate.

I'm on my feet, clapping so hard my palms burn. My

smile threatens to crack my face in two. Pride is blooming in my chest when Jackson skates past the bench, tapping his gloves against his teammates'. I'm so fucking proud of him.

The final buzzer sounds, and Chicago wins 3-2.

My eyes stay locked on Jackson until he disappears down the tunnel. I manage to sneak out of the arena unnoticed, and on the drive back to the hotel, I type out a message to him. I end up deleting and retyping it three or four times. Because how can I say, "Please meet me for coffee," without sounding like I'm desperate?

I mean, I am desperate, but he doesn't need to know that.

By the time I make it back to my hotel suite, I'm tired, and my body aches from the chilled air inside the arena. I strip out of my suit, hang it in the closet so it doesn't get creased, then take a quick shower to warm up. Once I've dried myself off, I put on a pair of clean boxer briefs and slide into bed with my phone.

I managed to get Jackson's number from Peyton under the guise of "needing to send him something" after Blaine and Alex's wedding. Luckily, the Thunder's newly appointed captain isn't the kind of guy to ask questions, so he sent it over without me needing to think up some excuse. It's been burning a hole in my contacts list since the day after my visit with Roberta, but I've been waiting for the right time.

I type out another message, hoping it sounds light and breezy and not at all desperate. My thumb hovers over the Send button, and I quickly press it before I can spiral further into procrastination.

> Hey Jax, it's Hayden. Great game tonight! That goal in the third was a beauty. Can we meet for coffee before you head to Washington? Say 9AM at Rafe's? I won't take up much of your time.

My pulse quickens as three dots appear on the screen, letting me know he's typing.

Holy shit. It's kinda embarrassing how happy I am at the sight of three bouncing dots.

The phone trembles in my hand as minutes go by and that bubble keeps disappearing and reappearing again. Is he going to tell me to fuck off? That there's no way on this earth he wants to have coffee with me?

Before my mind can enter that dark spiral, my phone vibrates with a new message, and my breath whooshes out of me in a rush.

JACKSON

> Hey. Thanks, it felt pretty good too. Yeah, okay. See you at 9.

I stare at the screen for several minutes, waiting for the other shoe to drop. Is he going to ask me where I got his number? Or respond that he thought I was someone else and can no longer make it?

But then I realize I'm getting myself worked up over nothing. Because he said yes.

He said yes.

I roll over to put my phone on charge, and I fall asleep with Jackson on my mind and a smile on my face.

✕

Rafe's is a family-run coffee house that makes the best bagels in Boston. We used to come here all the time when I had a condo around the corner overlooking the harbor, and it became part of our morning routine. We would come down here, pick up coffees and a bagel. Sometimes we'd eat them in bed or in the car on the way to practice. Every time I've been in Boston for a work-related trip since I retired, I always come and order a hazelnut latte. Jackson used to drink it all the time, and I would tease him for it. But now *I* drink it all the time because it reminds me of how his mouth used to taste when I would steal kisses from him at every opportunity.

My knee bounces under the table, and nerves pool in my stomach. I knew it was a big risk when I sent that text last night. I've been working up to that moment for months. *Baby steps.* That's all I need to remember. This was step one, and in my mind, it was the biggest. Jackson could have said no to meeting up. He could have left me on read and ignored me completely. But he didn't.

He said yes. He said he was going to show up.

I take a sip of my coffee and glance at the time on my phone. 9:02 a.m. He should be here any minute now. I open up one of the apps I use when I need to distract my brain when the bell jingles above the door. My head snaps up so fast I get a twinge in my neck. Jackson's hulking figure is in the doorway, dressed in a charcoal wool coat and light gray toque, his eyes scanning the cafe before landing on me. The corner of his lips tip in a small smile, and it takes everything in me not to fist bump the air.

He came.

I'm unable to take my eyes off him as he weaves around

the tables. He places his coat on the other chair, then sits down.

"Hey," he says with a slight apprehension in his tone.

"Hey." I smile, hoping like hell it's relaxed, considering my entire body has gone tense with anticipation. I slide the coffee I got for him across the table. "I got you a hazelnut latte. I wasn't sure if you still drink it."

He accepts it, and his eyes widen a fraction in surprise. "Yeah, I do. Thanks."

"Great," I say with a relieved sigh.

Blue eyes assess me over the rim of the cup, and I pick up my own coffee for something to do. It's awkward, but not as awkward as the wedding. There's this level of nervousness between us, but it doesn't hold any animosity this time. It's weird. This feeling like you're in front of a stranger. There was a time we couldn't have been closer. Hell, I've had this guy inside of me, and I've been inside of him. Yet sitting here today, you never would have known we once explored every inch of each other's bodies with our mouths and wandering hands.

I trace my finger along the handle of the cup, trying to muster up something to say that isn't "please take me back," but Jackson beats me to it.

"So, what brings you to Boston?" he asks.

Well, shit. I can't exactly tell him *he* is the reason I'm here because then that automatically puts me in the desperation pool. That's something I'm trying to avoid.

"I had a few meetings, and I thought I might as well catch the game while I'm in town."

His head bobs a few times. "Was it weird? Being back there?"

"Kinda? I've learned to disassociate when I'm in agent mode," I say, then chuckle nervously. "If I allowed my own hurt and bitterness over my career ending earlier than I wanted it to, affect me whenever I went to games, then I wouldn't have many clients"

The muscles in my neck tense up at the sight of pity flashing through his eyes. I quickly change the subject because I don't want his pity. Rafe's is not the place where I cut myself open and expose my underbelly regarding the demise of my career.

"Thanks for agreeing to meet me this morning," I begin, taking another sip of my coffee to dampen my dry mouth. "I… I've had a lot of time to process what you told me at Blaine's wedding. It didn't come as a surprise to me that I hurt you, but I don't think I truly understood to what extent until that night, and I wanted to say I'm sorry. For everything."

His hand holding his cup pauses halfway to his mouth. The crease between his brow reappears, and his lips turn downward.

"Where is this coming from?" he asks warily.

I exhale heavily. "I don't want to go into things right now, but I just wanted you to know that I'm sorry for everything I put you through."

His frown only deepens. "Okay…"

I take another sip of coffee, then take a deep breath. I need to say it. Rip the Band-Aid off and get it out there. It's time for step two.

"I'd like it if we could be friends again. I know that sounds very juvenile for guys our age, but…" I take off my glasses and scrub my face with my palm. He's blurry, and somehow, it makes it easier to get my words out. "I've missed having you in my life, and I didn't know how much until I saw you at Zach's apartment that time with your daughter."

When I put my glasses back on, his expression is still full of confusion. The longer he's silent, the more my skin begins to feel tight and itchy.

Please say something, I inwardly beg, *Anything*.

His tongue darts out to lick over his bottom lip, and my eyes latch onto the movement.

"I don't know what to say," he finally answers.

"Say yes?" A small huff of nervous laughter escapes me. "You've got my number now. We can text, or if we're ever in the same city, maybe grab a bite to eat?" I shrug, trying to appear casual despite my knee bouncing an erratic rhythm beneath the table.

I sound like a fucking high schooler begging to be friends with the popular kid, but I don't care. This is a marathon, and I'm only at the very beginning.

Baby steps.

"Okay."

"Yeah?" I bring my coffee to my lips to disguise how my face wants to break out in a wide grin.

"Yeah. I mean, a lot has changed over the years, like you said at the wedding. We're not the same people we were last time we were here," he says, and I don't miss the slight defensive tone to his voice. "I guess it wouldn't hurt to be civil, considering we run in the same circles."

"Right." I nod in agreement.

He finishes his coffee, then pushes his chair back. "I've

gotta head off. The bus leaves for the airport soon, and I don't want to be late."

I stand up and try to hide my wince as pain shoots through my body. Luckily, Jackson is too busy slipping on his coat and doesn't see it.

"Good luck in Washington. Keep an eye on Young if he's in the net. He's been very pad-reliant recently—I think he's hiding an injury."

Jackson's face lights up when he laughs softly, and the sight steals my breath. "Thanks, I will."

We stand there awkwardly. Neither of us is quite sure how to say goodbye, but in the end, Jackson gives a firm nod.

"Take care, Hayden. It was good to see you."

"You too," I say, and I'm not ashamed to admit my eyes drop to his ass as he makes his way to the exit.

I guess there's one thing that hasn't changed.

Chapter Seven

Jackson

The sound of my bedroom door opening stirs me awake, followed by soft footsteps. I lift my head, blinking my sleepy eyes into focus to see Ryan heading toward me.

"Dad?" he whispers. "Can I get into your bed?"

"Yeah," I croak. "Course you can, bud."

I lift the duvet, allowing him to climb in and lie down next to me. Then, I crane my neck to look at the time on the alarm clock. 3:25 a.m.

We had a home game last night, and luckily, today is our day off. There's no practice or video sessions, and I don't need to think about anything hockey related until tomorrow morning. Though, I'll still do a workout in my home gym while the kids watch a movie. I set up a TV and couch in the gym purely so they could still be with me while I get in my cardio, but other than that, I plan on doing nothing except spending the day with my kids.

"You okay?" I quietly ask him after a beat.

"Yeah, just a bad dream," he whispers back.

"Wanna hug it out?"

I can feel his nod against the pillow more than I can see it, so I open my arms, and he curls into me.

It's not unusual for one or both of them to end up in my bed at some point during the night, but sometimes Ryan has nightmares. They are more frequent at the start of the school year, and again when the regular season starts. He hasn't elaborated on what happens in these dreams, but it's another arrow in my wing that I'm failing them. I can't fight them off for him, but I can give him a safe space to come to when they wake him up.

Pressing a kiss to the top of his head, I allow my eyes to fall closed again when he relaxes. "It was just a dream. I've got you."

"I know." A moment of silence passes before he says, "I love you, Dad."

My heart squeezes in my chest, and the back of my eyelids burn at those three words. There will soon come a day where I won't get to hear those words from him. He'll be too cool to tell his old man he loves him, so I cherish every single one.

"I love you too. Get some sleep. I'll be right here."

Between me falling back to sleep and waking up all bleary-eyed, Isabela has joined me and Ryan. Her little arm rests against my throat, and her hand cups my chin. A small smile creeps onto my face. At least she didn't knee me in the balls this time.

I carefully move her arm, tucking it under the duvet, and then I climb out of bed like a ninja so as not to wake them up. I throw on a T-shirt and head downstairs, making myself a coffee and opening the kitchen window to let in some air. After fifteen minutes, there's still no sign of the kids. I head back up with my coffee in hand and stop in the doorframe at the sight. Ryan's curled himself around my pillow, and Isabela has slipped one hand under his while clutching her stuffed elephant with the other. It's these moments that mean everything to me. There's no outside world getting in the way. It's just me and my kids and hours of uninterrupted time together.

I know I could have this all the time if I retired, but I'm not sure I'm ready to give up hockey yet. Sure, I get paid a pretty penny for my job, so much so I've got both their college tuitions stashed away in a bank account, along with money to buy them a car and a down payment for a house. And I've still got enough to see me through for the rest of my life.

Does it make me selfish for not wanting to give up hockey so I can be more present in my kids' lives? Maybe. But I'm trying to convince myself that it's not selfish because I'm setting them up to have everything they could ever need or want. And hopefully, they will be proud of me too.

Rounding the bed, I quietly place my mug on the night table. I slip back under the covers next to Isabela and place my hand on the top of Ryan's head, stroking the soft blond strands. He wanted to start growing his hair at the start of the year because Elliot decided to grow his. He thinks our goalie is one of the coolest guys ever, cooler than me by a long shot. It creates a warmth inside me that spreads throughout my body that my kids adore my teammates just as much as they adore my kids.

We had it good in Buffalo, but it wasn't until I came to Chicago that I truly felt part of a family. We're more than teammates. We're a band of brothers who love and care and always have each other's backs. They've taken us in and made us feel more welcome than any other team I've played for.

Except for maybe Boston, but it was more one person who made me feel like I was home rather than the whole team.

Deciding to make the most of this relaxed, peaceful morning, I pick up my book with my free hand, balancing it in my lap while I sip on my coffee. I manage to get through four chapters before they both stir awake. I close my book and put it aside.

"Finally!" I fake-cry, playing into the dramatics that ends up making them laugh. "I didn't think you'd ever wake up. I thought I was gonna have to spend the day on my own."

"You silly, Daddy," Isabela giggles around a yawn.

"I was close to calling a friend to help me out."

"Who's that?" Ryan asks innocently.

"The tickle monster!" I hold both hands up, splaying my fingers wide and tickling them both around the ribs. They burst into fits of giggles, and by the time I let up, my cheeks ache from my own wide grin.

"So what do you wanna do today?" I ask, settling back against the headboard.

"Let's make a cake!" Isabela shouts excitedly. "Lots of cupcakes. With sprinkles."

I laugh. "I mean, we can try. I don't know how well it'll turn out."

"It'll be fun!" Ryan chirps. "Can I do the eggs?"

"And me!" Isabela insists.

I don't think giving an egg to a four-year-old to break is

the best idea, but what's a bit of mess in the name of having fun?

"Sure. Okay. We'll need to go to the store first and get all the ingredients. But…" I trail off, grinning. "We do have ingredients to make blueberry pancakes. Who wants blueberry pancakes for breakfast?"

"Me!" they both shout in unison, then race each other down the stairs.

The kids help me with the pancake mix, and by helping, I mean throwing the blueberries and flour into the bowl with a flourish. Once we've eaten, washed, and dressed, we head to the store to pick up the cupcake ingredients with the help of a quick text from Jacob.

> JACOB
>
> Oh, wow! Good job for not going for a box mix, I'm proud of you ;)
>
> Okay so, you'll need unsalted butter, eggs, flour, sugar, baking powder, and vanilla extract. For the frosting, you'll need the same butter as the sponge mix, but also confectionary sugar. Call me if you get stuck and I can talk you through it. Good luck! Send me pics!

Ah, the perks of being friends with a bakery owner.

"Are you ready for this?" I ask them once we get home. I've just finished measuring everything out and placing them in individual bowls.

"They're gonna be so awesome, Dad." Ryan beams up at me.

I love how much confidence he has in me.

"Let's hope so, bud. So, first, we need to put in the butter and sugar."

I hand them a bowl each to pour into the main mixing bowl, and my phone vibrates on the counter with a new text message. I pick it up, and my chest does a weird spasm when I see Hayden's name on the screen.

"Who's that, Daddy?" Isabela asks, stretching where she's standing on the chair to look at my phone.

"One of my friends. Hayden. We played hockey together a long time ago."

The word tastes bitter on my tongue. I've never referred to Hayden as a friend. Even years ago, when we were hiding our relationship, I never once called him my "friend." It was always teammate or linemate because for some reason, those words didn't feel as devaluing to our relationship as *friend*.

I check the time and see it's 9:00 a.m. in LA, meaning it'll be one of his morning photos.

Every morning, he sends photos of his view of the ocean from his back porch and tells me to have a good day, along with a random fact about jellyfish. I don't know where this interest in jellyfish has come from because I can't recall him ever being interested in them while we were together.

He's also started to randomly send me a coffee and some variation of baked goods for the kids via DoorDash. Because they don't know him, they call him the cake fairy, and their sheer excitement every time there's a knock at the door tugs on my heart more than I'd like to admit.

I hold my breath as I click on the message and open the text thread.

HAYDEN

Good morning. Did you know the Turritopsis
dohrnii jellyfish is immortal? Spooky! Hope
you have a good day off with the kids.

"Wow! He lives on the beach?" Ryan asks, peering over my other side.

Sure enough, it's another photo from his back porch that steps out onto a stretch of golden sand. In the distance, surfers ride the waves, and the water glistens in the sun. A cup of coffee sits on a table next to a black leather book and a pen resting on top. It's in every shot he sends, and I'm curious to know what it is. Is it his notebook for work? Maybe a journal?

I can't help but snort at the thought.

Hayden wouldn't keep a journal. He didn't do deep thoughts and feelings except when he was in that post-orgasmic daze, high on the endorphins. But since we met up for coffee at Rafe's in Boston the other week, I haven't been able to get him off my mind. There was a vulnerability to him that he was trying hard to hide, but I knew his tells, even after all this time. I could sense there was something he wasn't telling me. The real reason why he wanted to be back in each other's lives now. I wanted to know so bad, but I didn't want to push.

It also means I've been on a wild roller coaster with my emotions, flicking between feeling touched that he's thinking of me and my kids to being angry that he thinks he can just waltz back into my life like nothing happened. That he didn't break my heart in such a devastating way.

I have whiplash from my own damn feelings, and I don't know what to do about it.

"Can we go to the beach?" Isabela asks.

"No," I say, locking my phone and placing it on the side. I'll respond to him later. "We're making a cake. Now, where were we at?"

We follow the recipe Jacob sent us step by step. Ryan carefully cracks the first egg, handling it with such care that no shell ends up in the mixture, but when it's Isabela's turn to crack the second one, she slams it onto the edge of the bowl. Pieces of eggshell go flying, sticking to the wall and the countertop, and the egg drips down the side of the bowl.

She holds her egg-yolk-covered hand up with a crinkle of her nose. "Eww, Daddy. Gross."

A rumble of laughter escapes me. Okay, maybe I shouldn't be giving eggs to a four-year-old. Lesson learned.

"You didn't need to hit it so hard," I say, wiping her hand with the dish towel. "Just a gentle tap."

I pick the broken pieces of eggshell out of the mixture and put in another egg, showing her how to break it. Not that she'll remember, but I try to involve them as much as possible when I'm in the kitchen.

When it's safe, obviously.

Once I've checked that everything is in the bowl, I slide it under the stand mixer and push down on the attachment. I switch it on, but I must hit the wrong speed because flour flies out of the bowl.

"Daddy!" Isabela shrieks.

I quickly switch it off, and when I glance down, all three of us are covered in flour, along with the wall and the counter.

"I think you went too fast," Ryan laughs, shaking his head like a dog and creating a flour cloud.

"You know, I think you're right." I rub my face, which only makes it worse and causes them to laugh harder.

Picking up my phone, I take a quick selfie of us and the destruction in my kitchen, then grab a cloth from the sink. I make quick work of cleaning up the kids, the counter and myself, then top up the bowl with more flour. I tense when I turn the mixer on at a slower speed this time, waiting for the floursplosion, and I sigh in relief when it doesn't come.

"Well done, Dad." Ryan pats my shoulder. "You did your best."

My mouth drops open. "Did you just pet me like a dog?"

He laughs, and Isabela lets out a loud "woof!" causing all three of us to burst into laughter.

These two fucking kill me.

I slide the cakes into the oven and set a timer for twenty minutes, then head into the living room to join the kids once I've finished cleaning the kitchen. I slump onto the couch next to them and kick my feet up on the cushion of the sectional. Their attention is fixed on the TV, where our favorite show, *Bluey*, is playing. I snap a photo, making sure neither of the kids' faces are visible, and upload it onto my Instagram stories with the caption, *Watching Bluey with these two is my favorite part of my morning.*

Then I open up the text thread with Hayden and send him the photo of the flourstrophe. I don't know if he would be interested in this, but he said he wanted to be friends and get to know each other again, and my kids are a big part of my life. I don't have to wait long, though, because his reply is instant.

HAYDEN

Wow… That's… I've gotta say, it's a good thing you're good at hockey. Not sure you've quite mastered the baking thing.

My kid praised me like I was a dog when I managed to put the mixer on the right speed.

HAYDEN

It doesn't come as a surprise to hear your kids sound incredible. Just like their dad.

Something goes weird in my chest at his words. What would happen if I opened the door and let him come into my life again? Would it be different? We're older now. Both of us are in different stages of our lives, experienced things that have matured us.

But what if it wouldn't be different? They say a leopard doesn't change its spots, after all.

I glance over to Ryan and Isabela. It's not something I can think about. They rely on me, now more than ever, and I can't risk losing myself again like I did once before, no matter how much my heart is being pulled in Hayden's direction.

Chapter Eight

Hayden

"From your latest imaging, your hip has progressed to stage 3, which will explain your increased pain and stiffness," Dr. Moore says.

There's an MRI of my hips on her computer screen, showing the narrowing space between my joints. It doesn't come as a surprise because I know my hips are fucked, along with my knees. It's not uncommon for hockey players to develop osteoarthritis. We use our hips, knees, and ankles a lot more compared to the average Joe, playing through injuries and trauma all in the name of the game, but mine seems more… severe. Or maybe it's just how my brain is reacting to my body consistently failing me.

I received my diagnosis during a follow-up of my third knee surgery. They wanted to do a full replacement, but the thought of having surgery for a fourth time while dealing with my depression wasn't a good mix. Instead, I have bi-yearly scans to monitor the speed of deterioration and cortisone injections to manage the pain and swelling. It's not a long-term fix, as Dr. Moore likes to remind me every time, that it can worsen the damage within the joint the more injections I have, but it gives me more time to come to terms with the fact I *will* need surgery in the near future. Maybe they can do it all in one go. Hips and knees. Double the surgery, only one recovery time.

"Am I going to need surgery?" I ask, giving voice to the thought.

"It depends on how it progresses, but yes, surgery is likely."

I open my mouth to speak, but she holds up her hand, a patient smile on her face.

"I know your reluctance around surgery given the history with your knee, which I fully understand. And while I can't force you to have the surgery, whether it be for your knees or your hip, I can advise it will improve your quality of life, Mr. Cassidy. It will significantly reduce the pain you're experiencing and give you back some of the freedom you've lost over the years."

Slipping off my glasses, I rub my eyes. I get what she's saying, but with the way my brain is wired, there's something that keeps asking, what's the point? Why go through the agony of recovery after surgery, for what? I'm still going to be a broken man.

"Are there any alternative methods he can try first?" Zara pipes up.

Some might find it bizarre that my ex-wife comes to my appointments, but she knows how these appointments can cause me to spiral, and having her here for support is monumental.

"I know it'll improve my quality of life, but I'm not ready for surgery just yet," I say before Dr. Moore can respond. "Can we stick with the injections for now?"

When I put my glasses back on, she's giving me a pointed look. I'd put money on it that she wants to shake me right now and demand I have the surgery so I can be out of pain and discomfort. I'm sure any other normal person would.

We don't use that term, Hayden, Roberta's voice filters through my mind.

I internally roll my eyes. She often has to remind me there's no such thing as "normal," but try convincing my brain of that.

"We can stick with the injections, yes, depending on your pain level. When I compared these images against your previous scan, it's only just moved into the moderate stage of arthritis, so I'm reluctant to give you the injection too early as it won't have the same impact as it will when the pain worsens."

I drop my head back and stare up at the ceiling. The sense of defeat settles over me like a weighted blanket. Do these doctors not know how exhausting it is to be so reliant on medication just to get through the day? I know I'm my own worst enemy, and my issues will probably lessen if I go through with the damn surgery, but still.

"Can you rate your pain in your hip on a scale from one to ten? One being minor, ten being completely unable to function in your day-to-day activities?" she asks, typing something into her computer.

"About a five right now," I murmur.

"Okay, that's not too bad. I would personally recommend you wait on the injections, but ultimately, it's your decision as you know your pain."

I turn my head to look at Zara. She gives me a sad smile before looking back to Dr. Moore when she continues.

"Continue with the anti-inflammatories as and when required, and we'll reassess in six months. However, if you need to see me earlier, you know you can call me."

That isn't any different from what I'm doing now, but I roll with it because I need to get out of this room. Out of this damn building. If I'm not in here, I'm not being made to think about surgery and how fucked-up I am. Not just mentally but physically.

"I can do that."

"Also, I know your occupation requires you to travel around the country and Canada, but as we move into the winter months, try and keep your visits to places with colder conditions to a minimum. Cold weather can sometimes exacerbate the pain."

My mind instantly goes to winters in Chicago. The snow, the frigid wind coming from the lake. If the best-case scenario in my plan does come to fruition and Jackson and I do get back together, how will I cope with my pain there? I don't want Jackson to end up caring for me when I'm in too much pain to get out of bed.

He might not even want you. You'll be a burden to him, and he'll end up resenting you. Do you really think he will want you around his kids?

Numbness begins to replace the feeling of defeat, seeping down my body limb by limb. My eyes fixate on a mark in the muted gray carpet while my brain tries to fight off the voice.

It's not real, I tell myself. *Think of the jellyfish.*

My vision blurs like I'm underwater, and I squeeze my eyes closed, forcing myself to picture the jellyfish in Roberta's office. I'm aware of someone speaking, but everything becomes muffled. There's an invisible heavy weight pressing against my chest, and my breathing spikes as my lungs struggle to inflate.

Baby steps.

One breath at a time.

When I begin to regain feeling back in my arms and legs and my breathing regulates, I open my eyes to see both of them watching me with cautious expressions. Pity flickers through Dr. Moore's eyes, and that's enough to get me moving.

"Okay, no problem. I can reschedule some meetings to video calls." I stand up, ignoring the pain in my joints from standing so fast, and button my suit jacket. "If that's all, I should be getting back."

Zara's frowning, but thankfully, she doesn't call me on my bullshit. We're silent as we exit the hospital and head to her car in the parking lot. She usually drives me to my appointments because I never know if I'll end up getting an injection, and there are strict instructions to rest for a few days after.

"What was that all about?" she asks once we're in the car.

"I don't know what you mean."

"Don't act dumb with me. Something happened in there. Like a mini panic attack or something." Her face softens. "Is it because she said you're probably going to need surgery?"

With a sigh, I tell her the thoughts I had about the surgery and the negative voice running through my mind about Jackson.

Her voice is quiet when she asks, "Does he know?"

I shake my head.

"*Hayden.*" She scowls. "You don't have to go through this alone, you know. I bet you haven't told him the reasons for your tattoos either?"

"No, I haven't told him anything."

She presses her lips together, clearly wanting to give me an earful of exactly how wrong she thinks I am, but she remains silent. For the entire drive back to my house, I stare out of the window and wonder what Jackson would think. Is this some kind of karma for how I treated him? For abandoning him when he needed me the most? Or have I just been dealt a shitty hand in life, and the only good thing is the multiple figures in my bank account?

We drive back in silence, and when Zara pulls up in front of my house, I'm feeling awkward.

"Thanks for driving me," I say, then place my hand on the handle to open the door, but she engages the lock, preventing me from getting out.

I turn to her with a frown.

"You're welcome. You know I'll always take you because I care for you, Hayden, but I'm pretty sure Jackson does too. I think you need to be more vulnerable with him in order for you to move forward. Open up. Share your thoughts and struggles with him. Give him something to see you're not the same guy who was scared of his own feelings." She smiles softly. "He's shown you a photo of his kids. That's a big fucking deal. He's letting you in despite being hesitant, so do the same for him. Give him a chance to see *you*."

Zara presses the button to unlock the doors, but I don't move. I chew on the inside of my cheek, digesting her words.

She's right. I've made the first move to try and make amends, but I'm still filled with fear. Still preparing myself for rejection and going against what I told myself I would do. I can't grow if I'm cutting myself off at the stem.

"Thanks, Zara." I reach over and give her hand a squeeze. "I appreciate you."

"I know." She winks. "Now, get out of my car because I need a big-ass coffee and an In-And-Out burger before Connor gets home from training."

I grin and push open the door. "Okay, okay. I'm going. Later."

We say our goodbyes, and I head inside with my phone burning a hole in my pocket. I place it on the arm of the couch and head into my bedroom to strip out of my suit, swapping my pants for sweats and my shirt for a soft ribbed Henley. In the kitchen, I make myself a coffee and whip up an omelet before taking a seat on the couch, angling myself to look out onto the patio leading to the beach. I bought this house two years before I retired, thinking it wouldn't be used until I was in my forties and ready to take up golf as a full-time hobby. It's all one story, with a garage built in underneath, and a patio that backs onto a beach. In hindsight, I wonder if past me subconsciously knew I would need a property like this, with no stairs inside to contend with, a lot earlier than I anticipated.

I finish eating my omelet and put my empty plate on the coffee table. Then, I prop a cushion beneath my knee to elevate it slightly and settle back against the couch cushions. Although I sent Jackson a text this morning with a photo of the sunrise peeking out over the horizon, I take another photo of my view from the couch and send it.

JACKSON

Damn, what a view. I would be out on that beach every day if I lived there.

It's nice. I love falling asleep to the sound of the water, it's so relaxing.

JACKSON

I think I'd be relaxed all the time having the beach outside my back door.

Sometimes it is, but sometimes it can cause discomfort. Walking over soft sand with bad knees isn't a fun experience.

JACKSON

You still struggle after your ACL repair?

You could say that.

JACKSON

Shit, I'm sorry. I had no idea.

I suck in a deep breath. Okay, here goes nothing.

It isn't something I advertise, and the league surely didn't want it to be known that their recommended specialist doctor did a number on me.

JACKSON

Wait, what?

Ah, this wasn't a conversation I wanted to
have over text. Can I call you?

JACKSON

Give me ten minutes, I'm just leaving the
rink. I'll call you when I'm home.

My stomach swoops like a damn fun slide, and my palms start to sweat. I can do this, right? I can open up and give him a glimpse into what these last few years have been like for me without trauma dumping on him. He doesn't need to know about the times I wanted to put an end to things once and for all. He doesn't need to know about Roberta. But he can know about my struggles with osteoarthritis and how it's a result of the game. Maybe it'll give him a mini wake-up call not to ignore the signs and to seek treatment at the first sign of discomfort so he doesn't end up like me.

Maybe it'll be an olive branch into something I want more than anything.

A chance.

Unable to sit still while my body trembles with nerves, I get up and put my plate in the dishwasher before making another coffee to keep myself busy.

Why does ten minutes feel like ten hours when you're waiting for a phone call?

Finally, my phone vibrates on the cushion as I sit back down. I take a deep breath and swipe my finger across the screen to accept, not wanting my excitement to show in my voice.

"Jackson, hey. How was practice?"

"Hey. Yeah, it was good. Coach has been trying a few new things to get ready for tonight, and I gotta say, it's looking good."

"That's great to hear. I'm sure you'll smoke Winnipeg into dust." I swallow hard. "So, uh… What I mentioned in the text, it's not common knowledge. As far as I'm aware, the guys I represent on the team don't know, and neither does Peyton."

So, in other words, *please don't tell anyone.*

There's a moment of silence, and I'm almost certain the call has disconnected until he speaks, and I can hear the sorrow in his tone.

"I saw you had it propped up in your photo earlier. It's not just your ACL now, is it?"

"No. I was diagnosed with osteoarthritis after my third surgery. I've just come back from the hospital, where they told me it's also in my hips."

"Fuck, Cas, I…" He trails off. "Fuck. I don't know what to say to any of that. The fact you've had three surgeries or that you've got arthritis. Like, you're thirty-nine. You're not old."

I chuckle under my breath, trying not to think too hard about the way he slipped and used his old pet name for me so easily. The times that three-letter word would spill from his lips when I made him come. It's a sound I've never forgotten.

"I appreciate the compliment because I sure feel like I'm seventy-nine most days, but I started playing hockey at a very young age. And you know I wasn't the best at listening to my body when it was telling me to rest or have a visit with the trainer."

He grunts. "You didn't get any better at that after I left, then, huh?"

"No." I grin. "If anything, I got worse."

There's another beat of silence, but this time, I don't feel concerned. I can practically hear his brain digesting everything.

"I'm sorry that you've had to go through all of this," he says, sounding genuinely sympathetic. "It can't be easy."

"It isn't, but you know, I've got the California sun to ease some of the aches, and the view isn't too bad either."

"That's true. That's a big perk." He huffs a laugh, and then his voice takes on an emotion I can't quite decipher. "Thank you for telling me. I can imagine it was hard, considering nobody really knows, so thank you. For trusting me with it."

A lump forms in my throat. I didn't know how cathartic it would feel to tell someone else. Apart from Zara, Roberta, and Dr. Moore, I've been battling it alone. And just having someone else know, who understands the struggles athletes face when it comes to either coming to terms with an injury or, in my case, an injury that results in hanging up my skates earlier than I was ready… It feels… revitalizing.

"Thanks for listening."

Another silence.

"I… I better go and nap ahead of our game tonight, but, uh… I'm here if you need someone to talk to. Or… you know, send more random facts about jellyfish." I can hear the smile in his voice.

A bark of laughter escapes me. "Hey, don't diss. Jellyfish are cool."

"As long as they stay the hell away from me and my kids,

sure. I'll think they're cool with a thick pane of glass between us."

My smile is so fucking wide my cheeks hurt.

"Thanks, Jax. I hope you have a good game tonight."

We hang up, and for the first time in years, there's a spark of happiness ignited inside of me.

Chapter Nine

Jackson

My days seem to blend together recently. It always does during the regular season. It's a repetitive cycle of training, home games, away games, and being a dad. However, tonight is the annual Chicago Thunder Halloween party at Peyton's house. Every year, the guys on the team compete for the most creative costumes, but this time, I think I've got the win in the bag.

"Daddy, you look funny," Isabela giggles when I walk down the stairs and into the living room in my costume.

I look down at myself, feigning innocence. "What do you mean? I think I look awesome."

Isabela falls back onto the couch and lets out a loud belly laugh that causes Ryan to look up from his Switch.

"Yeah, you do look funny, Dad," he laughs.

I place my hands on my hips. "Geez, thanks. You two sure know how to make your dad feel good."

They both burst into laughter, and I grin.

The thing is, would I have picked this costume if I was

shopping alone? No, but the kids happened to ask what I was doing the other day while I was searching for a costume. It went downhill from there, and that's how I've found myself in a blue Bandit onesie. *Bluey* is a big deal in the Wilde household, so it didn't come as a surprise when they begged me to buy the Bandit costume. I can't complain, though—it's very comfortable.

I also managed to order the matching Bluey and Bingo versions for them too, but I'll save those for Christmas.

I take a seat on the couch in between them, and they curl into me instantly. I wrap an arm around each of them and kiss the top of their heads. I might pull my hair out most of the time, but I do love them more than anything.

"Make sure you're good for Gigi, okay? No fighting her when she says it's bedtime."

"I'm always good," Isabela argues, and I give her a disbelieving look.

The tantrums have only increased recently, to the point her teachers pulled my mom aside the other day and expressed their concerns. She doesn't want to share or get involved with the other kids during playtime, preferring to play alone. I have a meeting scheduled with the school during the week to discuss what they mean by her maybe needing "additional support."

"Can we have ice cream after dinner?" Ryan asks, resting his head back against my shoulder.

"Sure, as long as you eat all of your dinner."

"Yeah, okay," he agrees easily and turns his attention back to playing his game.

"Daddy?" Isabela shifts until her feet are in my lap. "Can I come to the party?"

I twirl one of her pigtails around my finger. "You can't come, peanut, because it's a party for adults. There's going to be special adult juice there and loud music."

She sticks her bottom lip out in a pout, and my spine stiffens on high alert, preparing myself for the tears. Luckily, my mom chooses that moment to walk into the room and claps her hands to get their attention.

"Kids, dinner's ready. Say bye to your dad, and you'll see him in the morning."

"Have fun, Dad," Ryan says. He wraps his arms around my neck in a tight hug, then jumps off the couch and goes into the family room, but Isabela doesn't budge.

"Peanut, I'm only going out for a few hours. I'll be home later tonight," I reassure her, but she doesn't loosen her hold on me.

I shoot my mom a panicked look. I don't want to encourage this behavior, but I also hate the guilt that sits on my chest whenever I do things for me, such as spending a few hours at my teammate's house and having a few drinks for our night off. We've had a run of home games recently, and this is the first night I've taken the boys up on their offer of hanging out.

"Your mac and cheese is getting cold," my mom prompts, taking a step toward the couch.

Isabela huffs and glares at her out of the corner of her eye.

"Come on, don't be like this. I won't be long." I shift to the edge of the couch, and my sudden movement causes her to lose her grip on me. My mom quickly scoops her up and tickles her ribs. Isabela tries to resist, but eventually, she's giggling, and the bad mood disappears.

"Have fun." Mom winks at me over Isabela's head as she heads toward the family room. "Make sure you take photos of all the costumes, especially Ethan's." She lets out a contented sigh over her shoulder. "That man is beautiful. It's unfair, really."

For as long as I can remember, my mom's had a soft spot for Ethan. I don't blame her—he's a good-looking guy.

"I will. I'll see you later," I say and slip out of the house before the guilt can claw its way further up my throat.

Fifteen minutes later, I'm standing on the step outside of Peyton's house while he assesses me with quizzical eyes. "Who the fuck are you supposed to be?"

"Bandit. You know, the dad from *Bluey*."

He blinks, a clueless expression on his face. He's dressed as a spartan warrior, and the lack of fabric shows off his impressively strong body. The opposite to mine because I might as well be wearing pajamas.

"The TV show?" I add, then roll my eyes and shove the six-pack of beer into his chest. The movement causes him to stumble backward. "The kids picked it out, okay? Just roll with it. Bandit is cool."

"O-okay. If you say so, dude," he says in jest, closing the door behind me.

As always, Peyton's gone all out with the decorations. There are banners and streamers covering the walls. Fake spiders hang from the ceiling, with carved pumpkin lanterns scattered around, and there are so many balloons I'm pretty sure he must have emptied out the store. Dance music pumps from the built-in speakers installed in every room, and the battery-operated candles create the perfect spooky party ambiance. Aside from me, he's the only bachelor on the team with a house and usually ends up being the host for any parties.

When I walk into the kitchen, the countertops are covered in copious amounts of food, and I cough out a laugh when my eyes land on a tapped beer keg.

"Are we back in college or something?" I ask, pointing to the stacks of red Solo cups. "Who's setting up the beer pong?"

"It's Peyton, what do you expect?" Kendrick snorts, taking a swig of his beer. His wife, Maria, is tucked against his side. "I'm pretty sure he'd still live in a frat if he could."

"That's true," I agree, then point to their costumes. They're dressed up as Fred and Wilma Flintstone. "Original. I like it."

I pour myself a beer and lean back against the counter to take everything in. There's a lot of people here. All the players and their significant others are here, along with some of the front office staff. Some of the furniture has been pushed to the sides of the room to create a makeshift dance floor, and I almost choke on my beer when I spot Zach's boyfriend, Carter, dancing with Elliot. Carter's dressed in a tight white dress that leaves nothing to the imagination, a pair of white Air Jordans, and a Princess Leia wig. Zach stands to the side in a Han Solo costume, watching his boyfriend dance to a remix of ABBA's "Gimme Gimme Gimme" with a loved-up smile on his face.

"Dude! You came as Bandit!" Elliot hoots after he's finished dancing, tapping his cup against mine. "I fucking love *Bluey*."

"Thank you!" I say, casting a glare at Peyton. "I'm glad someone appreciates my effort."

"Dude. You're accepting praise from the guy who came dressed up as his crush," Peyton quips, pointing to Elliot, who responds by flipping him the bird.

I take in Elliot's navy tactical pants and matching navy T-shirt, then notice the Chicago Fire Department Engine 3 emblem on his chest and grin. "Got yourself a T-shirt, huh? How long did it take you to ask for that?"

Elliot's crush on the lieutenant started last year during the annual Chicago Thunder family fun day when the local fire department was invited to bring along an engine and ladder. It was more for the kids, but Elliot, being the lovable guy he is, got really excited over the fire trucks. But his anxiety can often prevent him from putting himself out there, and while we tease him like we would a little brother, I always make sure he knows our teasing is playful because sometimes he struggles to differentiate.

"Fuck you both very much," Elliot huffs. He throws back the remnants of his beer before mumbling, "I got it the other day."

Peyton and I struggle to hold back our laughter as Elliot walks off in Blaine and Alex's direction.

"I fucking love that guy," Peyton proclaims, and I whole-heartedly agree.

Time passes by as I chat with some of the Thunder's front office staff, talking about how the kids are doing at school and how they're enjoying Chicago. I play a game of beer pong with some of the guys and manage to beat Blaine twice, then retreat to a corner of the kitchen to catch up with Jacob and Ethan.

"Who knew retirement for a hockey player would be like normal people's retirement?" Jacob jokes, smoothing a hand up Ethan's chest. My old teammate is due to have surgery on his knee in a few weeks. "I had to look up whether I needed to install a handrail in the bathroom."

Ethan grabs Jacob's hand and presses a kiss to his palm. "You make it sound like I'm having a double hip replacement or something."

My mind instantly goes to Hayden and what he told me the other day. It wouldn't come as a surprise if he ends up needing a knee or hip replacement, given his diagnosis. I ended up going down a rabbit hole when I got home from my game that day, reading up about the symptoms and restrictions it causes as it progresses into later stages. It made me feel something I didn't think I'd ever feel for him again. A need to protect him. Then, I ended up getting pissed off with myself for feeling that way.

It's fucking exhausting being confused.

"Jesus fuck. Don't put that into the universe. Please." I snort.

"Ha! Dude! Did you and Jackson plan to come in a couple's costume or something?"

I turn at the sound of Peyton's voice, and my breath hitches.

Speak of the devil, and he shall appear.

Hayden stands in the archway to the kitchen, a bottle of champagne in one hand and what I assume is a bottle of whiskey in the other.

And wouldn't you know, he's wearing a Chilli costume.

Chilli, who's Bluey's mom. Bandit's wife. They are a *couple*.

Peyton's head snaps my way, amusement dancing in his blue eyes. "This is hilarious. Did you plan this?"

I shake my head, stunned speechless.

Hayden watches me cautiously. There's a tense line in his broad shoulders. His eyes focus on mine behind his black frames, a silent question flashing through them: *Are you going to freak out?*

And that's the thing. Maybe I *should* freak out because why is he here, wearing that? Does he know the significance of this? Of what it means to me? Or is this some kind of weird coincidence?

I took a photo of me and the kids earlier before I left, but I haven't shared it anywhere, so it's not like he could have orchestrated this intentionally.

"Hey," he rasps when he finally pulls himself away from Peyton and Blaine and every other one of my teammates who monopolizes his time.

Jealous?

Ugh, fuck off, conscience.

"Hey," I echo, suddenly feeling raw and exposed.

He retrieves a cup from the side and pours himself a drink before leaning back against the counter and watching me over the rim of his cup. He crosses one ankle over the other, and the movement causes my eyes to drop. I take in his long legs and trim hips. The costume is slightly big on him, but I can still make out the smooth lines of his body.

My mind begins to wander. I want to know if I pulled on the zipper of his costume, would he be wearing anything underneath? Would it expose inches of smooth, golden skin? And how far do his tattoos go? Is it only his arms that are inked, or is more of his body covered?

The fucked-up thing is, even after everything, I want him. Badly.

When my gaze meets his again, the glint in those slate-gray eyes tells me he's witnessed me checking him out, and a smirk kicks the corner of his mouth.

I lick over my dry lips. I can almost taste him and the whiskey on his tongue.

This is bad. So very, very bad.

I've gone fourteen years without this primal need to taste him. To capture his lips with mine and steal his breath like I used to do all that time ago. Then he comes in here, wearing a fucking Chilli costume, and I'm folding like a bad poker hand.

He places his empty glass on the counter behind him and turns to look at me. With his eyes locked on mine, he runs his thumb over the corner of his mouth, and then he's moving.

But he doesn't come my way.

He walks right past me and heads toward the stairs, quickly glancing at me over his shoulder before making his way up.

I clench my fists at my side. Frustration replaces the heat coursing inside me. Frustration that his reappearance in my life is making me question everything.

Before I can think better of it, I make sure the coast is clear and take the stairs two at a time. I rest my hands on the doorframe to the bathroom, and when I hear the sound of the tap switch off, I'm ready. The click of the lock disengages, and the moment the door opens, a flash of surprise flicks over his face. Like he can't believe I actually followed him.

"Jackson? What are you—"

He doesn't get to finish his sentence because I grab a

fistful of his costume and push him back inside. I flick the lock on the door behind me and crowd him against the vanity.

I don't know why I'm getting so worked up over this. So he came in the matching costume to me? It doesn't mean anything.

It *can't* mean anything.

"Why?" I ask, my voice barely above a whisper.

"Why what?"

"Why this costume? Did you know I was coming in this?"

His mouth opens and closes several times, and then he shakes his head. "No, I had no idea."

"So, *why*, Hayden?" I demand.

I know I'm being irrational right now. I'm not thinking clearly. My body is trembling with frustration and need, and being in close proximity to his fucking scent again is making my cock thicken.

His gaze drops between us, and he takes a deep breath. "When I saw you that day at Zach's apartment, I noticed your daughter had a backpack with these characters on it. Then you posted the other week on your Instagram about how watching this show with your kids is your favorite part of your morning."

I blink at him.

Okay. I wasn't expecting any of that. I should be pissed that he's been keeping tabs on me, but the blood filling my dick tells a different story.

I open my mouth to respond, but he cuts me off.

"I... I guess I wanted to be part of your favorite

morning somehow." He chews the corner of his mouth with his teeth. "All I know is I can't stop thinking about you."

I can't stop thinking about you either.

I can't tell him that. I can't let him know that since he has come back into my life, I'm suddenly off-kilter. I can't go down this road again. I can't let him in like I did before. I have my kids to think about now. They are my biggest priority. But I also can't ignore the undeniable connection between us that's still there. It's tethered and frayed, but it's still there, hanging on tight.

All I know is tonight, I might be making the biggest mistake, but I can't bring myself to care.

So, I throw caution to the wind and worry about the consequences later and slam my lips against his.

Chapter Ten

Hayden

I must have imagined what this moment would be like more than a thousand times over the years. What it would be like to kiss Jackson again. I'd often think about the softness of his lips, his low, breathy moans, and the addictive taste of him as my tongue dove into his warm mouth. I've thought about it in so many ways, but none of them were like this.

The possessive way he grips my head in both hands, fingers burying into my hair, holding on to me like he's afraid I'm going to disappear. His greedy pulls on my tongue and the low growl from deep in his chest make my toes curl.

I cautiously place my hands on his hips. With the desperation that's thrumming through my veins, I don't want to be overzealous by grabbing him and hauling him closer like I want to do, but I need to touch him in some way.

I need to know that this is real and not some figment of my imagination.

He responds by pressing a thick, muscular thigh between mine. He rolls his hips, and I gasp into his mouth when his hard length rubs against the underside of my dick.

Fuck. He's going to make me lose my mind.

He deepens the kiss, and there's no way on earth I can stop the moan that escapes me. The edge of the vanity digs into my ass cheeks from the weight of his body pressing up against me, but I'm not going to complain. I don't want to break this moment. Not when I've finally got Jackson in front of me.

Not when I've finally got his lips on mine again. His body pressed against me, enveloping me in his heady scent.

His tongue sweeps into my mouth in hungry strokes. He tastes like beer and frustration and a whole heap of want. He bumps my glasses with his nose, shifting them to sit awkwardly on my face, but I don't dare move to right them. He can knock them onto the damn floor for all I care. Anything, as long as he doesn't take his mouth off me.

Giving in to temptation, my hands slide up the hard planes on his body. He feels so much bigger than he did before. Like the last fourteen years have been kind to him. The thin material of his costume does nothing to disguise the ridges and grooves of his solid obliques, and his muscles shiver as my hands travel higher. When I reach his chest, I smooth my fingers over his pecs, then pinch his nipples between two fingers.

"Fuck," he hisses, tugging my bottom lip between his teeth.

My lips tip into a wicked grin at his reaction. He's just as sensitive as I remembered.

He rests his forehead against mine, and minutes go by as

we stand there, eyes closed while trying to catch our breath. My heart is beating a mile a minute, and I'm starting to feel a little light-headed from the blood that's rushing down to my cock.

But that euphoric feeling doesn't last long. He takes a step back, and it's like I've been doused in ice-cold water when he whispers, "I'm sorry."

I rear back and right my glasses so I can see him clearly.

"What?" I sputter. "What for?"

He takes another step back, increasing the distance between us, and runs an agitated hand through his hair. "I shouldn't have done that. I'm sorry. That was a mistake."

Well, fucking *ouch*.

My fight-or-flight instincts kick in, chest tightening, pulse quickening. That kiss didn't feel like a mistake to me. It felt like it was fueled by hunger and desire with a hint of frustration wrapped up in one Jackson-flavored package. I won't let him take this moment from me. Not when it's the first time I've felt alive in years.

Straightening my spine, I say with all the confidence I can muster, "Well, I'm not sorry."

His gaze snaps up to meet mine. "You're not?"

"No, I'm not. If it isn't obvious already, I'm kind of a mess for you, Jackson. I always have been."

"I… don't understand. But you used to be married?" he asks, brows pinching.

"Yeah, I was, and I'll love Zara until the day I die because she's an incredible woman, but I married her for the wrong reasons."

He watches me for a beat. There's a mix of emotion swirling in those brilliant blue eyes. Obvious desire, but also fear. I want to know what he's afraid of so I can show him he doesn't need to be. I want to show him I've changed, that I'm not the same guy I was.

I might be broken, but I'm not stupid enough to throw away his heart for a second time. If I'm so lucky enough to catch it again.

He runs a hand down his face and drops down to sit on the closed toilet seat. "I'm so fucking confused."

"About what?"

"You. Me. This." He waves a hand between us. "I don't want to want you again. I can't risk falling into your hands only to get hurt, Hayden, because I barely survived the last time. I have my kids to think about now."

"I don't want to hurt you," I admit quietly.

Quite the opposite, actually.

"I know I asked this in Boston, but why now? If you've been a mess for me all this time, why now?"

I lean back against the vanity, taking some of my weight off my knees. I wet my lips with my tongue, then rub my fingers against the cool marble top, tracing the shapes and lines. It's hard for me to open up and be vulnerable about my past struggles. Most of the time, when people hear you have depression, they don't know how to act around you. Or worse, tell you that you have nothing to be sad about or other people have it worse, or you'll get over it, or that everyone gets sad sometimes.

Zara's words from the other day about being more open with him come filtering back through my mind. Jackson was always my safe place before I fucked everything up, and the level of care shining in his eyes right now tells me he can sense my reluctance. He's always been more emotionally mature. I know he won't spew the other shit, but I also know I can't dump all my trauma at his feet.

I can do this. I trust Jackson, and if I want this to happen—for *us* to happen—I need to tell him.

Give him the option to escape.

No, I can't think like that.

Baby steps.

"It took me a long time to realize that I had married Zara for the wrong reasons. Years, in fact. It was during one of my therapy sessions that I realized it had always been you, but I screwed up big-time. I needed to make sure that I wasn't that same guy who broke your heart. I needed to work on myself to make sure I was worthy of you before I tried to reach out. The way I ended things with us wasn't okay. I was scared and immature. I believed the negative voices in my head telling me you would be better off without me, but that's no excuse for the way I treated you."

He stares at me, brows still slightly furrowed, but there's a new emotion in his eyes. Empathy. His voice is soft when he asks, "And how long has that been? That you've been working on yourself before reaching out?"

"Six years," I manage, dropping my gaze to the floor. I can't look at him when I tell him this. I can't bear to see the pitying look on his face when he finally knows the truth. *I can do this.* "It was after Zara found me trying to end my life."

The bathroom is silent, apart from the music coming from downstairs and the blood rushing in my ears. When he doesn't speak, I lift my head, and the expression on his face knocks the breath out of my lungs.

His eyes shine with unshed tears, cheek tinged pink as he swallows hard, trying to keep his emotions in check.

"*Cas*," he whispers, voice cracking.

I dip my head again. Shame coats me like a shroud, like it always does every time I have to say those words out loud.

I'm aware of Jackson standing up, but I'm not prepared for when he steps in front of me. His fingers grip my chin, and he angles my head up to face him. My eyes lock with his.

"I'm glad you're here," he whispers with a shaky voice. "Really fucking glad."

My face goes hot. "Yeah?"

"Yeah, I am." His tongue darts out to swipe over his bottom lip, and then he takes a deep inhale. "I need time. I'm not saying no, but I can't say yes right now either. It's not just my life anymore, Cas. It's Ryan and Isabela too. I've put them through so much fucking shit with the divorce and moving to Chicago that I can't risk bringing any more chaos into their lives. Not that you would be chaos, but any new relationship would be a change for them. And I need to figure things out in here—" He taps his head, then his heart. "—and here first."

Swallowing down the puck-sized lump that's formed in my throat, I nod as best as I can with his hand still holding my chin. "I understand."

This has to mean something, right? I wasn't expecting him to jump in my arms and tell me we're getting back together. I knew it was going to be a progressive thing. A marathon, not a sprint.

Baby steps.

I'll give him the time he needs. I'll wait until the end of time for him if he asks me to.

"I think it's best if I go," he whispers, tracing over my bottom lip with his thumb before letting go of my chin.

I open my mouth to argue that these are his friends, his teammates. If anyone should be leaving, it should be me, but he holds up a hand to stop me before I get the chance to speak.

"You should stay. Enjoy yourself. I just… I need to clear my head."

Jackson takes a step to the door and clicks the lock open. I grab hold of his wrist before he can open the door. He looks over his shoulder, patience radiating in his eyes as he waits for me to speak.

"Can I still speak to you?"

A soft smile crosses his lips. "Yeah, you can. I'd be disappointed if you didn't enlighten me further on random facts about jellyfish every morning."

I huff a laugh, suddenly feeling sheepish.

"I hope you'll tell me the story about them one day."

"Yeah. I will," I say quietly, then let go of his wrist.

He opens the door and gives a gentle nod of his head to say goodbye. I watch him leave, my chest heavy with emotion.

Okay, so that went better than I expected. Opening up wasn't as scary as I made it out to be in my head. If anything, it's done what Zara predicted. It's created an olive branch between us, opened up the door for whatever might happen in the future.

Turning around, I splash my face with water and use a towel to dry off. When I head back downstairs, Jackson's nowhere to be seen, but the disappointment I would've felt before doesn't come.

Can we talk about progress? High five to me.

I gaze around the open-plan kitchen living room area, and it seems everyone has been preoccupied and too busy to notice I disappeared upstairs until my eyes catch a set of brown eyes staring at me from behind black-framed glasses.

Ethan Parkes is watching me. His face is stoic, expression giving nothing away. Except when he arches one brow, silently letting me know he noticed, and clearly, he saw Jackson leave only moments ago.

Steeling my shoulders back, I take a steadying breath and head toward where he's standing with Jacob, Alex, Blaine, Zach, and Carter.

"Hey!" Blaine greets me with a wide smile, then looks at my empty hands. "You need a beer?"

"Whiskey, if there's any left."

I risk a glance in Ethan's direction, and his dark eyes still bore into me as he takes a sip of what looks like my whiskey.

"Here you go," Blaine says, handing over a glass. "So what did you come as? I can't tell if you're supposed to be some kind of cat."

"I'm Chilli, from *Bluey*."

"Huh, didn't Jackson come as something from that?"

"He did," Ethan answers, his grumble barely audible over the music playing. Nobody picks up on his pointed tone, though, because Ethan's always been on the quiet and grumpy side. Add in the fact he's dressed up as the Beast while Jacob has come as Belle, and he's only adding to the part.

Needing to change the subject, I wiggle my finger

between Zach and Carter. "This is iconic. I never would've guessed you'd come in *Star Wars* theme."

"It was my idea." Carter grins, ignoring my sarcasm. "I can't wait for him to be punching into my hyperspace later." He wiggles his brows suggestively and thrusts his hips while Zach groans and drops his face into his palm.

I choke on my drink, and the others burst into laughter.

"Thanks for that visual," I deadpan.

"You're welcome." Carter beams.

"You should have heard some of the things he was saying earlier about us," Alex pipes up. He's in a Pikachu onesie, similar to my costume, and Blaine has come as Ash from *Pokémon*.

"It's not my fault you come in such innuendo-worthy costumes," Carter retorts.

"You literally asked us if I smack my balls against Alex's face and pretend to catch him," Blaine points out.

"And? I don't see the problem with that."

My gaze bounces between them in amusement, and then a guy I recognize from the wedding appears at my side, holding out his hand.

"I don't think we've met. Hi, I'm Nate," he says, laying the charm on thick.

"*Nate*," Alex warns.

"What? I'm introducing myself."

"I thought you'd be all over our goalie," Zach says.

Nate chuckles. "A guy can dream, but in all honesty, we're not suited. Could you imagine the chaos we'd cause together?"

"Yes," Alex chimes in quickly. "Plus, I warned you to stay away from him."

"Eh." Nate waves his hand dismissively. "That only encouraged me. Don't get me wrong, I think he's hot as sin, but our personalities would clash too much, and he's not the kind of guy you have a one-night stand with."

Blaine visibly shudders. "Please don't talk about fucking my twin in front of me."

"Who wants to play drunk Twister?" Peyton shouts, holding up a plastic mat with colorful dots on it.

"Aaaand that's my cue to leave." Twister and bad joints are a recipe for disaster. I down the remnants of my drink and place the glass in the sink. "Thanks for the fun night."

"What? You're leaving already?" Nate coos, placing his hand on my chest.

I look down at his hand, then back up at him. He's bold, I'll give him that.

"Nate!" Alex scowls. "I swear I am never bringing you again."

Nate flashes a flirty smile and saunters off while Alex gives me an apologetic look. I give him a wink, letting him know it's okay, then make my rounds to say goodbye. When I head outside, my ride share is waiting. I slide into the back seat and rest my head against the headrest, watching the bright lights of downtown Chicago pass by. I'm feeling oddly… content. I wasn't sure how tonight was going to go, especially turning up in this costume, but I'm glad I did.

My phone vibrates ten minutes later as the door to my hotel suite closes behind me. I slip it from my pocket, and my heart lurches at the sight of Jackson's name on the screen.

JACKSON

I meant what I said earlier. I'm glad you're here, Cas. You've always been important to me. No matter what happens, I want you to remember that.

I raise my hand, shielding the smile that threatens to split my face in two. I don't think Jackson fully understands how much those words mean to me.

Especially coming from him.

Chapter Eleven

Jackson

We lost our home game last night 3-2, meaning the mood on the plane to Dallas early this morning was shit. We were all tired and achy, and the last thing any of us wanted to do was to get up at the ass crack of dawn to catch a flight to play a second game in twenty-four hours. But here we are, in the underbelly of the arena in Dallas, getting ready for game one of five on our eight-day road trip.

Something that my kids were *not* happy about and made sure to let me know yesterday morning, when my mom came to pick them up for school, by making things as difficult as possible. It doesn't get any easier. The guilt clawed up my throat, festering all day. I don't blame them for my piss-poor performance on the ice last night, but I can't deny my head was not in the game.

"Is everything okay?" Zach asks from my left, where he's getting his shoulder taped. "You've been uncharacteristically quiet the last few days."

I turn my head to face him, making sure I don't disturb Greg, who's currently working on my hamstring.

"Yeah, I'm okay. Just have a lot on my mind," I say quietly.

And isn't that the understatement of the year.

I haven't been able to get Hayden's words out of my head since Peyton's party. *He tried to end his life.* Every time it replays in my head, I get this sharp pain in my chest that takes over my entire body. I knew there was something he was hiding; I just never expected it to be that. It's shifted something inside of me, and I know there's a lot I need to consider. I can't be reckless and jump straight into something with him again. I need to make sensible choices. Not just for the safety of my own heart and for my kids but for Hayden too.

And like I told him, it's not as simple as saying yes or no. My heart sings for him like it has for no other, but it's bigger than the two of us now.

I've had so many questions running through my mind. Like what if I introduced him to my kids, and they fell in love with him, and he tried again? What if he was successful in his attempt that time? The kids haven't experienced loss in that sense, but they've gone through loss in the form of Laura's and my divorce, and look how well I screwed that up. Plus, I don't think *I* could cope with the loss of Hayden again, in any shape or form.

The fact he mentioned he's been—and still is—in therapy all this time tells me he's determined not to let this beat him. And from the sleepless nights I've lost reading articles upon articles, I know there isn't a cure for depression, but there is treatment, and the vast majority of those people who receive the appropriate help do go on to live full, healthy lives.

So, I need to focus on that and be there for him in any way he needs me.

Then there's the meeting I had with Isabela's school the other day regarding her behavior. I wasn't quite sure how to take it when they said they believe she might be on the autism spectrum. At first, I was shocked, and then I became kinda angry because I assumed they were trying to tell me she was a "problem child" and that there was something wrong with her. But once that initial shock wore off, I listened to their reasons, and it began to make a lot of sense. Her communication struggles, the way she always wants the same food, her need for control, her anxiety around new people or any form of change. Her separation anxiety with me.

I left the school with a handful of leaflets and feeling equal parts hopeful, guilty, and worried. Hopeful because I was in a privileged position where I had the money to put toward anything she needed. Guilt because I blamed myself. Was it something I gave her? Could I have picked up the signs earlier if I had been home more? Then also worried because I don't want her to experience any kind of nega-tivity from judgmental assholes.

I'm not able to take her to see the pediatrician until I get home from this road trip. My mom offered to take her, but I'm already absent for other important appointments, and I won't fail Isabela on this. I want to make sure the appro-priate support is in place to help her receive the best educa-tion possible while accommodating her and tailored to her learning styles, then I can ensure she has everything she needs at home.

She's still my incredible daughter, but now, I'll be able to educate myself to understand her better and give her whatever she needs in order to thrive.

"Wanna talk about it?" Zach asks. "I've been told I'm a good listener."

I smile over at my teammate.

Zach is one of the quietest guys I've ever met, and often, he gets shit on the ice because of his size. He's at least six foot six and weighs over two hundred and fifty pounds. Guys usually want to fight him because of it, but Zach doesn't fight. Isabela refers to him as a gentle giant because he is exactly that.

"There's been a lot going on recently. Like I had a meeting with Isabela's school because there's been a few... behavioral issues. They told me I should speak with her pediatrician about getting an autism diagnosis."

Zach's brows lift in surprise. "Ah, dude. Is there anything we can do to help out?"

"I can't help but blame myself, you know? I mean... Fuck. I'm away for eight days now. I'm their main guardian, and I'm not gonna be home for over a week. How can I give her the support she needs when I'm never fucking home?"

Greg gives my calf a reassuring squeeze, reminding me he's still working on my tight muscle. "Hey, it's not your fault. My son Ewan is autistic, and while it is really tough sometimes, once we found the right support for him and adjusted things to meet his needs, both at school and home, it became a little bit easier."

I glance over my shoulder at the Thunder's trainer and give him a grateful smile. "Yeah?"

"Yeah." He nods. "I'm happy to talk anytime, and I'll hook you up with a few of the specialists who work with Ewan, but I promise you, it's not because of anything you've done."

"Thanks, I appreciate it."

He gives my leg another squeeze. "Now, relax for me. This hamstring is going to give you shit all night if you keep tensing up."

I laugh and settle back on my front, resting my cheek on the back of my hands.

"We're here too," Zach chimes in. "I mean, I might not know what to do, but we're here for anything you need, even if it's someone to talk to or moral support at an appointment. You say the word, we'll be there with you."

Warmth travels across my chest at his genuine words. I'm so lucky to have these guys.

"Thank you. That means a lot."

But now, it's time to push all other thoughts to the back of my mind. Once Greg's worked out the tightness in my hamstring, I go through my usual pregame cardio and get dressed, ready for the game.

Dallas is all over us. I find myself battling in the corners, and whenever we make it into the offensive zone, their defense is rock solid.

Then again, so is ours. Elliot's stopped all Dallas' seventeen shots on goal, and Zach and Kendrick have been guarding that blue line like a brick wall during their shifts.

It's still a scoreless game when we go into the third period. Blaine lines up for a face-off in the offensive zone, and I take my position on the edge of the circle. Blaine wins the puck drop, passing the puck to Peyton, who passes to Zach. He hovers around the blue line, waiting for an opening, then passes to Kendrick, creating a diversion for Blaine and Peyton to position themselves better. I get myself into position, ready to take a shot on goal. Zach passes to Peyton, and when he dekes their winger, he flicks the puck to me, and I snap a wrister toward the net. It hits the crossbar with a loud *thunk*, and the goalie covers it with his glove the second it drops onto the ice.

"Fuck!" I grunt under my breath.

The official blows his whistle to signal the TV time-out, and I skate back to the bench in frustration as the ice crew comes out. Tension is coiling at the base of my neck, and I'm not the only one who's beginning to feel it. I jump over the boards and take a seat on the bench. Grabbing my water bottle, I squirt some into my mouth and watch as Elliot skates over. He removes his helmet, resting it on the edge of the boards in front of me, then pours water all over his face and hair.

"Did you see me out there?" he asks once he's finished shaking his hair like a wet dog.

"I sure did. You were on fire."

"I know! Fuck me sideways. I was like, *bam, pow, kapow!*" He mimics blocking shots with his glove and blocker. "I don't even know how I haven't let one in. I'm super impressed with myself. Five gold stars to me."

"Didn't you tell them to get off your lawn at one point?" Kendrick chuckles, squirting water into his mouth.

Elliot laughs. "Yeah. I mean, get outta my crease would've made more sense, but hey, same thing. The crease is my lawn, and they are not welcome on my lawn."

"You're doing a great job, Olsen." Peyton slaps Elliot on the shoulder pad. "Keep up the good work, dude."

"Will do, Cappy."

"Yeah, don't call me that."

"Why not? It has a cool ring to it. Captain Peyton. Cappy Peyton. Peyton Capybara."

Peyton slices his hand through the air. "Automatic veto. Denied. Rejected. Not a chance."

I snort a laugh, gaze bouncing between them. "Peyton Capybara. Wait until I tell the kids that."

Peyton whirls around, pinning me with a glare. "Don't you dare. I want to be the cool uncle."

"Too late!" Elliot calls out while skating backward toward the net. He's wearing a shit-eating grin and shimmying his shoulders to the music blaring over the speakers. "Peyton Capybara!"

I can't help but laugh. Their stupid banter alleviates some of my frustration.

But the feeling is short-lived. By the time there's five minutes left in the third period, I'm agitated again. I wonder if I'm like one of those cartoons with steam blowing out of my ears.

Please no overtime, I inwardly beg. I want to go back to the hotel, eat a load of food, and crawl into bed. Maybe speak to Hayden. I wonder if he'd be up for a phone call tonight. We've gotten into the habit of speaking at night, even if it's mundane shit like talking about our day. Just hearing his voice is becoming a favorite part of my day.

"Hey! Hey!" one of my teammates shouts as they skate past, snapping me out of my thoughts.

I shake my head. Okay, it's time to refocus.

I take to the ice again, and it's a fast-paced battle. The clock's ticking down, and the pressure is on. Blaine passes to me, and I quickly pivot on my skates, clearing the neutral zone. Dallas' defensemen are hot on me, but I skate up the right side and take another wrist shot. The puck sails into the top left corner, scoring the first goal of the game.

"Thank fuck, Jackie!" Peyton hollers, crowding me against the boards. "I was gettin' worried there, eh. Thought it was gonna be an overtimer."

I laugh around helmet pats and shoulder slaps, and I skate by the bench to accept the congratulatory fist bumps.

Lucky for us, Dallas fails to equalize the score, and the buzzer sounds 1-0 to the Thunder.

We trudge back to the visitors' locker room in high spirits. Zach hooks up the Bluetooth speaker. Elliot's the first to pick a song, seeing as he got a shutout, and seconds later, there are several guys dancing with their jerseys off in the middle of the room.

Coach Harris walks in, amusement flicking over his hard face. He claps his hands together to get our attention, and Zach turns the volume down.

"That was beautiful, you guys. When you play like that, beautiful things happen. The discipline you've shown so far this season is outstanding, so keep it up. Great fucking effort tonight. Let's get some rest and be ready to kick Colorado's ass in two days."

"Yes, Coach!" we shout in unison.

I strip out of my gear and hit the showers. My stomach is grumbling by the time we're on the bus heading to our hotel. We'll fly to Denver tomorrow morning, where we'll stay the night ahead of our game the following day.

"Bet you're looking forward to seeing Carter tomorrow," I say to my seatmate.

Zach turns to me and smiles. "Yeah, I am. I'm counting down the months until the football season ends."

Carter plays in the NFL for Denver. They've been doing long distance since they got together at the start of the year. I know Hayden is working hard on getting him a deal with Chicago because he's said if he can't play in Chicago, then he'll retire because Zach's more important than his career. And I admire that. Sometimes when you love someone so much and there's distance between you, nothing else matters except being with the person you love.

Something I know all too well.

At the hotel, we're shuffled into a conference room, where we load up on pasta and protein, and then some guys head to the bar. Not me, though. My phone has been burning a hole in my pocket since I saw Hayden's name flash on my screen during dinner.

I step into the empty elevator with my duffle bag in hand and press the button for the fourteenth floor. Just as the doors are about to close, Elliot jumps in and slumps against the wall with a tired sigh.

I frown. "You okay?"

"Yeah, I'm just so fucking tired," he says around a yawn. "Kinda hoping Lindy will be starting in Denver, but also, I don't because I like playing in Denver."

"You like playing everywhere," I laugh.

"True." He grins, and then it slowly slips from his face. "I know I need the rest, but being on the ice keeps my brain calm, and it feels very—" He shakes his hand around his head. "—chaotic, at the moment."

The elevator pings on my floor, and he follows me out. I have no idea if he's on the same floor as me, but I'm not going to kick him out if he needs someone to talk to.

"Are you still feeling low about what we spoke about in Boston?" I ask.

"Yeah." He stops in front of a door that isn't mine and lowers his voice. "Do you think I should talk to Blaine?"

I think it over for a minute before I reply. Since Hayden's and my relationship went up in flames over shit communication, I've always vowed that communication is a nonnegotiable. I had the same conversation with Zach when he and Carter were having problems at the beginning of their relationship. And obviously, Elliot's relationship with his twin brother isn't the same as mine and Hayden's or Zach and Carter's, but it still requires a level of communication surrounding emotions. And clearly, this change in their relationship since Blaine's marriage is impacting Elliot on a much deeper level than he realizes.

"Yeah, I do. He can't make something right if he doesn't know about it. He's still very much in the honeymoon phase. Not that I think he and Alex will ever be out of the honeymoon phase because that's just who they are, but you know what I mean. Having a husband is new to him. He's navigating a new path in his life, and maybe he's oblivious to how this is affecting you."

Elliot nods, a tired smile tipping his lips up. "Thanks, Jackson. You're a really great friend."

"Anytime." I slap his shoulder, then point to the door he's standing in front of. "This you?"

"Yeah. I think I'm gonna play one of my games to unwind, then try to get some sleep."

"Sounds good. You know where I am if you need me."

We say good night, and I head into my room. I pull my phone out of my pocket before the door's even closed behind me. My face splits into a wide grin when I read Hayden's text.

HAYDEN

You are fucking incredible, Jax.

You watched the game?

HAYDEN

Of course I did. Game-winning goal, baby!
You never cease to amaze me.

I feel my face heat at his compliment. Dropping my duffel on the luggage rack and shrugging out of my jacket, it takes me twice as long to get undressed and get into bed because I don't want to cut off this conversation with Hayden.

Big compliment coming from the iconic power forward.

HAYDEN

I was only good because of you.

You always made me want to be better.

I grin at my phone like a damn fool.

My instincts are telling me to respond with something flirty, but I haven't decided what to do yet, and I don't want to give him false hope. But if it happens naturally, there's no harm in that, right?

I always wanted to impress you.

HAYDEN

Yeah?

Yeah. I remember the first time I met you, and I thought, fuck, this guy is so hot.

HAYDEN

Do you still think I'm hot?

Fishing for compliments?

HAYDEN

Always <fishing emoji>

Yeah, I do. The gray hair suits you.

HAYDEN

<shocked emoji> I'm not going gray, fuck you very much.

Aging like a fine wine.

HAYDEN

Looks up the best anti-aging skincare

I'm kidding, but also not. You're still hot, Cas.

HAYDEN

Seems we had the same thought because I thought you were the hottest guy I'd ever seen.

Were? Ouch.

HAYDEN

Fishing for compliments, are we Jax?

Okay, okay. You got me.

HAYDEN

Yeah, that's what I thought.

And yeah, the thought still stands.

You're still the hottest guy I've ever seen.

But you won't be if you don't get some sleep. You've got an early flight tomorrow, and you know that altitude change is gonna kick your pretty peachy ass.

Oh, coming for my ass now too?

HAYDEN

<zipped lips emoji> I'm not falling for that bait.

I snort out a laugh into the pillow. Shit, my cheeks ache from grinning so hard. I hadn't realized how much I'd missed this until now.

Night, Cas.

HAYDEN

Night, Jax.

Chapter Twelve

Hayden

"I don't know what else I can do, man," Landon sighs, his frustration clear in his voice. "When is it gonna be my turn to be called up?"

I take a sip of my coffee, allowing time for my brain to find the right words.

"Without this sounding like some Yoda master type, but your time will come, kid. You're killing it right now. You're the second-highest goal scorer in the league for the third season running. You lead in ice time per game, and you have at least one assist in every game you've played," I reassure him, hoping my voice conveys my confidence in him. "They are some great stats. It's coming, I can feel it."

Landon Leroux is one of my newer signings. He's a twenty-two-year-old forward who has more talent in his pinky than quite a few guys who are currently playing in the NHL. He was a first-round draft pick for Toronto, and after finishing his freshman year at Michigan State, he joined Toronto's farm team in the AHL, where he's been playing since. His frustration right now is down to the various injuries Toronto has seen early into the season, and for him, it feels like everyone's being called up except for him. Which I know isn't the case, but it's easy to feel excluded in those situations.

It's clear he's chomping at the bit to play his first NHL game, and I genuinely believe it's only a matter of time until he gets the call to join them. And if my gut feeling is right, he will shine so bright they would be foolish to send him back down.

"Thanks, man. It just pisses me off. I don't want it to sound like I'm sucking my own dick—"

I let out a bark of laughter, which causes him to laugh too.

"Now, that's some talent. Don't know if you should promote that to the team, though," I joke.

He snickers.

"But seriously, I'm a great fucking hockey player. They would be lucky to have me."

This kid is definitely going to go places. He has belief in himself without being annoyingly arrogant about it, and that's a great trait to have.

"No need to thank me, I'm just speaking the truth. And I agree with you. *You are* a great hockey player, and they would be lucky to have you. You've just gotta keep doing what you're doing. Keep putting in the effort. Keep smashing it out on the ice. It's gonna happen one of these days, and when it does, you need to continue to hustle so you become invaluable to them and they won't want to send you back down."

A moment of silence passes through the line, and I start

to worry I've said the wrong thing. Was I too harsh? Too honest? Did he want me to say something else? Each one of my clients has different needs and expectations. I've had to learn how to handle all of them, molding myself to be what they need. Some like the tough love approach, but some don't. Some like more support, while some prefer the more businesslike approach where we only talk when there's information to share or offers to discuss.

I'm still figuring Landon out, though. I'm getting the sense he's the kind of guy who needs the support and reassurance. He also happens to be the youngest person on my roster.

And he has this uncanny ability to make me feel twice as old as I am.

"I knew you were the best guy to rep me," he says, and relief washes over me at the smile in his voice.

"I'm honored to rep you, kid. And I get it, truly. It's frustrating waiting for your moment. Wondering if and when it's gonna come."

"You spent a few years in Providence before you got called up, right?"

"Yeah, that's right. I played three seasons there. I was called up twice for a game or two, but it wasn't until my third season that I got the call and never went back down."

I remember how fucking ecstatic I was. Not that I wished any of the guys on the team harm. Usually when you got the call, it was to fill in for someone who was on the injured reserve list, but you have to be selfish in hockey. It's a dog-eat-dog world, and there are always other talented, eager guys out there, ready and willing to take your spot. I made sure that I gave it my all. Every time I stepped out onto the ice, my effort was maxed out. Two hundred and ten percent every time. And it paid off. I turned my two-way contract into a one-way NHL contract and stayed with Boston until that very last game.

And I want to help Landon get there. He deserves to be there, and I'm confident I'm the one to change his two-way into a one-way.

"I'm in my third season now, so maybe I'll follow in your footsteps."

I choke out a laugh and glance down at where I'm currently lying on the couch with ice packs on both my knees. "I mean this in the nicest way possible, I really hope you don't."

He laughs, and then his voice takes on a softer tone when he says, "Thanks, Hayden. I really appreciate it."

"Anytime, kid. I'm here to make your life easier, and that includes impromptu pep talks or if you can't decide between the Lucky Charms and Cap'n Crunch."

"Fuck you very much," he chuckles.

I've always vowed to be the agent I never had when I was Landon's age. I didn't get the supportive calls or the reassurance when I needed it. My first agent seemed to forget that I came into all of this when I was still a kid. I was playing in the OHL at sixteen, then moved into the AHL at twenty. I didn't know how to handle money or the pressures that came with playing at a professional level. It was only when I had been with Boston for a full year that I realized what an asshole he was. I fired him not long after that.

But now, I'm the one who's taking on young hotshots like Landon, and I won't let him down like my agent did with me.

I don't take as high of a cut as other agents do because I'm not doing it for the money. I'm doing it for the well-being of my players. And I know it's ironic because I bet if guys like Landon knew the state of my own mental health, they wouldn't be so eager to sign with me. But I've perfected the art of hiding and wearing confidence like a mask because I won't be a burden to them.

We hang up with the promise of keeping in touch. I rest my head back against the cushions and close my eyes. Today's pain is worse than my baseline chronic pain. I knew from the minute I woke up that it would be a write-off. I've ended up rearranging my appointment with Roberta and had to reschedule a business trip to Seattle because there's no way I can get on a plane and face people like this. Even wobbling the short distance from my bedroom to the living room was excruciating. I've spent the morning switching between doing some emails and snoozing on the couch to the sound of the waves outside while waiting for my pain relief to kick in.

I must end up drifting off again because I wake with a start when my phone vibrates on the coffee table. Stretching over, I glance at the caller ID, then prop myself up on my elbow.

Jackson.

We've been talking daily since that night at Peyton's party. I've been keeping to my morning texts that consist of a photo of the ocean and a random fact about jellyfish, but other than that, I've been letting Jackson take the reins. The number of texts and calls has gradually increased, and since his game in Dallas, he's been more… flirtatious. Not that I'm complaining. Not one bit. Hell, I'm happy with any kind of attention from Jackson, but knowing he's attracted to me, again, it's a high I never want to come down from.

I quickly answer and bring my phone to my ear. "Hey, Jax. What's up?"

"Hey, I'm sorry to call you out of the blue like this... I just..." He trails off and makes a frustrated noise. I'm instantly on high alert at how off he's sounding. "I needed to talk to you. I'm having a shit day."

"You know you can call me at any time. What's going on? Why are you having a shit day?"

"Both of the kids woke up with a fever, and it seems they've caught some kind of bug. I skipped out on practice this morning so I could stay at home with them, but I've just spoken to my mom, and it seems whatever the kids have, they've passed it on to my parents too." He sighs dejectedly. "I've got a game tonight, Cas, and I think I'm gonna have to call Coach and put me as a scratch."

Ah, shit. It sucks being a healthy scratch. It's not a fun feeling knowing you're not going to be dressing for the game, so I can understand Jackson's worries about it. I've seen guys spiral downward after being scratched, and sure, it wasn't for the same reasons as Jackson. It can be for roster management, or it can be strategic, but it still has implications on an athlete's mindset. It can take its toll on you mentally, knowing you're capable of playing, but you're unable to contribute.

"What about your sister? Is she around?"

"No, she's out of town. Fuck," he curses. "I've never had to do this before, but I can't leave my kids, Cas."

The panic in his voice has me getting to my feet. I've never heard him sound like this before, and the need to help outweighs my need to look after myself. I wince as pain ricochets through my body. But I push it down and try to ignore it. I head into my bedroom and glance at the clock on my bedside table. I work out in my head how long he has between now and the latest he needs to leave for the arena for the game. "Okay, you've got like… sixish hours, right?"

"Yeah."

"Have you eaten anything yet?"

"No."

I chuckle under my breath and fetch my duffel from the closet. "Okay, so first of all, you need to eat something, Jax. Then, go check on the kids and take a nap. It's going to be okay. We'll figure this out."

He makes another noise that sounds a lot like he's groaning into his hand. "Normally I'd ask Ethan or Jacob to help me out, but Ethan has his pre-op today, and I don't want to risk him getting sick."

"Oh, shit, I forgot about that. Knee, right?"

"Yeah, I think Jacob's more worried than he is."

I smile at that. Jacob has one of the kindest souls I've ever met. He's the complete opposite of Ethan, who's gruff and grumpy, but they fit each other perfectly.

"I'll bet." I throw clothes into my bag, along with my shaving kit and medication. Once everything is packed, I zip it up and head to my closet to grab a change of clothes. "So, I'm gonna make some calls while you go get something to eat and take a nap. We'll speak in a few hours."

There's a long pause, and when he finally speaks again, gratitude is palpable in his voice. "Thank you, Cas. You still have the ability to stop me from getting stressed-out."

A grin spreads across my face. "Don't thank me just yet."

He ends the call, and I change into jeans and a hoodie. I grab my laptop from the living room, putting it in my bag before going around and locking up the house.

Then, I'm dialing the number to the private jet company I use as the door closes behind me.

Chapter Thirteen

Jackson

I have to be at the arena in an hour, and I feel like shit. I haven't caught whatever bug the kids have come down with, but I am fucking tired. After I spoke with Hayden, I only managed to nap for forty-five minutes instead of my preferred ninety, and the stress of the day is starting to catch up with me. My neck and shoulders are stiff, and I'm pretty sure I'm dehydrated. If there was a recipe for how not to prepare yourself to play a game of professional hockey, this would be it.

Yawning, I head into the kitchen and begin to mix up some electrolytes. I guzzle down half when there's a knock at the door, and Isabela picks that moment to cry out for me.

I run an agitated hand through my hair and groan. Fuck. Maybe I should call Coach and get scratched for tonight's lineup. Consequences be damned. He won't understand fully because he doesn't have kids, but I like to think

Coach Harris is a pretty reasonable guy, and it's not like this is a regular occurrence. This is the first time.

Glancing up the stairs, I shout up, "I'll be there in a minute, peanut."

The knock sounds again, and I head toward the door, cursing the world under my breath. I swing open the door, and standing there is the last person I expected to see. Wearing dark-wash jeans and a cozy-looking zip-up hoodie, something I didn't think he owned, he gives me a tentative smile. Cautious, almost.

"Hayden?" I ask, raising my hand to rub the back of my neck. "What are you doing here?"

He shrugs slightly. "You called, so I came."

My mouth drops open. When I called him this morning in a panic, this isn't what I had in mind. I called him because I needed someone to vent to. Someone who would understand my hesitation around getting scratched without automatically thinking I'm a piss-poor father.

I called because I needed comfort, and he was the first person who came to mind.

"I… I didn't call expecting you to fly all the way from California."

His confidence slips as he lets out a nervous laugh, shifting his duffel to his other hand. "Yeah, I know, but I want to help. I wasn't doing anything, and I figured… why not. So let me help you. Let me be here for you."

I don't know how much time passes as I stare at him. I can't believe he did this. For me.

"Jackson?" he prompts when I still haven't said a word.

I shake my head, snapping myself out of the mental

cloud I disappeared into. "I'm sorry, I just... I can't believe you're here," I say with surprised laughter.

I step aside and open the door wider so he can come inside. He places his designer leather duffel on the floor and slips off his shoes, immediately placing them next to mine.

"What time do you need to be at the rink?"

I glance down at my watch. "I need to leave in about an hour."

"Did you manage to nap?"

"Yeah, but not for as long as I like."

"Daddy!" Isabela howls this time, and both our heads snap up toward the stairs.

Pinching the bridge of my nose, I take in a deep breath before exhaling. This wasn't how I wanted to introduce Hayden to my kids. Not just because they're sick but because it's going to be rushed. Isabela struggles with new people, and she gets very shy. The first time she met the team, she got so overwhelmed she became very emotional. Elliot came to the rescue, being the incredible guy he is, and sat on the floor with her to show her something on his phone. He's still her favorite, but Ethan and Zach are close behind.

"I need to warn you, Isabela is... She can find it difficult with new people."

Hayden's smile is patient. "Why don't you go see what she needs, then you can introduce me before you get ready?"

"Yeah." I nod a few times. "Yeah, okay. Make yourself at home. The kitchen's through there if you need a coffee." I point down the hall. "And the living room is through there."

"Okay." He waves me off. "Go see your kid."

Leaving Hayden in the hallway, I run up the stairs and

into Isabela's room. She's curled up under her blanket, flushed cheeks wet with tears.

"Daddy," she cries. "It's cold."

I sit down on the edge of her bed and place my palm against her forehead. She's not as hot as she was earlier, but she's still rocking one hell of a temperature.

"What do you need, peanut?" I look over to her bedside table; her cup is almost empty. "Do you want some more water?"

She nods, hugging her toy elephant closer to her chest.

Giving her a small smile, I brush her damp hair off her face, then bring her blankets back up over her and tuck her in. "Okay, I need to go check on Ryan, then I'll get you some more water. I've gotta go to work tonight, but my friend Hayden is going to be here because Gigi and Gramps are sick too."

Her eyes widen slightly in panic.

"It's okay," I quickly reassure her. "Daddy has known Hayden for a very long time. He'll even let you watch cartoons later if you feel better."

"*Bluey*?" she croaks.

"Yeah, he'll let you watch *Bluey*."

She slumps further into her pillow. "'kay."

"I'll bring him up to say hello when I bring your water."

Her eyes flutter closed, and she mumbles, "'Kay, Daddy."

Quietly, I head out of her room and into Ryan's. He's fast asleep with the covers kicked off to the bottom of the bed. I carefully place my hand on his forehead to check his temperature. His skin is still feverish, but he's not as warm or pale as Isabela. Hopefully with him resting, it'll help kick this bug. I bring his covers back up over him, then pick up his cup before heading back downstairs.

I wash them up, then wash my hands thoroughly with antibacterial soap. Hayden walks into the kitchen as I'm mixing up some Pedialyte to refill both of their cups.

"Is there anything I can do?" Hayden asks.

"No, it's all good. They haven't been sick for a few hours, so I'm hoping the worst has passed now, but they might want toast or something later. The bread is in the pantry." I show him where I keep the loaf of bread, then where anything else is kept that they might ask for.

"Ryan was asleep when I went up, but do you want to come with me in case he's awake now?"

"Yeah, let's do it."

Hayden's slow to follow me up the stairs, and when we reach the second floor, his face is strained like he's in some pain.

I frown and ask quietly, "Are you okay?"

"Yeah, I'm fine," he says quickly, but his smile is forced.

I stare at him for a second, waiting to see if he'll tell me the truth, but he doesn't.

Hm. Okay then.

Peering my head around the door to Isabela's room, I smile when I see she's still awake.

"Hey, peanut. This is my friend Hayden." He follows me into her room, and she watches him with big blue eyes. I place her cup on the side where she can reach it, then sit on the edge of the bed.

"Hayden's going to stay here while Daddy goes to work. You can sit with him and watch TV if you want, or you can go back to sleep."

She doesn't take her eyes off him as she nods.

"I hear you like *Bluey*." Hayden smiles. "Me too."

There's a flash of excitement in her eyes before she shyly hides half of her face under her blanket.

I grin, knowing the reason why Hayden likes *Bluey* lights something up inside me.

"I'm gonna go check on Ryan. Did you want to stay here or go downstairs?" I ask her, handing over her cup. She takes a drink, then lies back down, giving me her answer.

I tuck her back in and sit there for a few minutes while she falls back to sleep. When I look in Ryan's room, I'm pleased to see he's now awake.

"Hey, Dad," he says around a yawn.

"Hey, bud. How're you feeling now?"

"Okay," he says, then does a double take when he sees Hayden. "Who's that?"

Laughing softly, I look at Hayden before turning back to Ryan. "This is my friend Hayden. We played together in Boston many, many years ago. He's going to look after you while I'm at the arena because Gigi and Gramps are also sick."

"You make it sound like we're ancient when you say it like that," Hayden laughs.

"Well, we kinda are in hockey years."

Hayden's eyes glisten with the words he can't say. *Fuck off, I'm not that old.*

"Okay." Ryan's eyes flick back to Hayden. "You played hockey?"

"Yeah, I did. I played in the pros for twelve years."

Ryan nods approvingly. "What position?"

"Forward. Center."

"Me too. Well, I'm right wing, like my dad." Ryan points to me, and the pride that blooms in my chest threatens to crack my ribs when he says, "I wanna be just like my dad when I grow up."

I ruffle his hair. "You will be better than me, bud. I promise you that."

"I always wanted to be like your dad too," Hayden admits.

My head snaps to him. "You did?"

"Yeah, you were, and still are, magical out there. How many times have you won fastest skater at the All Stars? Pretty sure you'd still leave 'em for smoke if you did it now."

I dip my head, feeling my cheeks flame under his unexpected praise.

"What time have you gotta go?" Ryan asks.

"In about twenty minutes."

His assessing eyes take in my ratty old T-shirt and sweatpants, and then he raises an eyebrow. "You're going like that?"

Hayden laughs. "I knew it. Your kid is awesome."

Ryan's grin is sleepy.

"Obviously, I'm not going like this." I roll my eyes. "I was checking on you and your sister before I get ready."

"We'll be okay, Dad. I'll look after Iz."

"Hayden's gonna look after you both."

His gaze goes to Hayden. "Can we watch the game later?"

Hayden looks at me with questioning eyes. I give a small nod.

"Yeah, of course we can. Your dad better bring home the W for us, right?"

Ryan nods and looks back at me. "Yeah, you better win, Dad."

"Yeah, I will," I say, and I have to bite back my smile from taking over my face.

Fifteen minutes later, I'm dressed in my game-day attire and running down the stairs with my shoes in hand. I slip them on when I reach the bottom, then grab my car keys from the entryway table.

"Jax, wait."

I stop in the middle of the hallway, coat halfway on, and turn around to face Hayden. He stands there holding out a plate. I take it from him, and a choked laugh escapes me when I see he's made me a peanut butter and jelly sandwich with the crusts cut off.

My heart soars at the significance of a damn sandwich.

"You remembered."

He nods softly. "I've never forgotten anything about you, Jax."

I press my lips together, emotion clogging in my throat.

Fuck. I don't know how I can resist him any longer. He dropped everything for me and flew across the country because he wanted to help me. He's made me my favorite pregame snack, something he used to do for me all the time.

The twin flames are burning bright again, and the pull to him is stronger than ever. Maybe it'll be different this time. We're older. Wiser. We've learned from our previous mistakes.

Maybe before, it was the right person but the wrong time.

But now... Maybe this time, it'll be right, and we'll have

the kind of love story that's in the books I read to my kids at night.

"Thank you," I manage to croak.

He winks, then slips his hands into his pockets. "Go. They'll be safe here with me. Bring back the win and continue to make your kids proud."

"And what about you?" I find myself asking.

"What about me?"

"Will I make you proud?"

His eyes shine with so much adoration my breath hitches. "You've always made me proud, Jackson. You make me proud by simply being you."

Chapter Fourteen

Hayden

"So, let me get this straight," Zara says with a hint of amusement in her voice. "Jackson called you because he needed someone to talk to, and you took it upon yourself to call a plane and fly to Chicago so you could watch his kids?"

I wasn't quite sure what I was doing until I turned up on Jackson's doorstep earlier. All I knew was I hated the sound of panic in his voice, and I wanted to take away his stress. I wasn't thinking about how terrible I am with kids or how I can barely take care of myself when I'm sick, let alone two little humans. I haven't even booked a hotel room for the night. I kinda acted and figured I'd think about it later.

I've always been impulsive when it comes to Jackson.

"Well, when you put it like that, it sounds kinda desperate, doesn't it?" I groan.

I can hear the smile in her voice when she sighs, "No, Hayden. It sounds incredibly thoughtful and caring. I'm just... surprised, is all. You used to run away whenever babies or children were around. You never ran to babysit."

It's not a lie. When we lived in Boston, I would try and stay away whenever a teammate had a baby. I'd linger near the back of the room because what the fuck do you do with a baby? They just sleep. Or scream, and hell, I didn't want to drop it or make it cry. I would've felt like the worst person in the world if I made a baby cry. Even during the team hospital visits, it wasn't so bad with the older kids because I could talk hockey or whatever the latest superhero movie was, but otherwise, I was this awkward, robotic guy who didn't know how to speak to a child.

I mean, all I did when I was a kid was talk about hockey.

But now, I've willingly volunteered to take care of two sick kids. I've flown halfway across the country because the man I want more than anything needed help. He didn't ask for it, but I also don't want to let him down or make him regret this, so I've been on high alert since he left for the arena an hour ago.

"Maybe this was a mistake," I mumble, running a hand down my face. "What if they need something and I can't get up the stairs quick enough because I'm hurting?"

She ignores my panic and focuses on the last part. "You're in pain?"

"Yeah. I had to cancel my session with Roberta and my trip to Seattle to see that ball player."

"Hayden," she scolds. "If this was anyone but Jackson, I would be giving you so much shit right now. Please tell me you've taken your meds?"

"Of course I have. I'm not that dumb."

She curses under her breath. "I swear, you stress me out so bad."

While I know she doesn't mean it in a negative way, I can't help but take it in that sense. I stressed her out with my pain. With my depression. I stressed her out to the point we got a divorce because I was too much to deal with.

"I'm sorry," I say, barely above a whisper.

"Nope. Not doing that," she snaps. "You know I don't mean literally. I just worry about you."

Panic rises inside me when I hear the soft footfalls coming down the stairs. Maybe they just want toast or a drink of water. I can do that. I can put cartoons on the TV, and Jackson's game starts soon too.

"I've gotta go," I tell Zara. "The kids are awake."

"Good luck! Call me if you need me."

I hang up, and Ryan's voice comes from behind me. "Hayden? Can we sit with you and watch some TV?"

I glance over my shoulder to see him standing with Isabela in front of him. He's got a blanket under one arm and his other wrapped around his sister's shoulders. I can understand what Jackson means when he says Ryan acts so much older than eight.

"Of course you can. Do you want anything to eat? Or something to drink?" I push myself up off the couch and have to hide my grimace as pain jolts through me. Maybe I can take some more pain relief while I wait for their toast.

They climb onto the sectional in one corner, and Isabela watches me with wide eyes that are the exact same shade of blue as Jackson's. She's hugging a stuffed elephant to her chest, and she's got some color in her cheeks this time, which is good to see.

That *is* a good sign, right? That's what Google told me

earlier when I looked up how to care for kids with a sickness bug.

Ryan wraps the blanket over their legs, then leans back into the cushions. "Can we have toast and some water? Oh, can we put *Bluey* on too? That's Izzy's favorite."

"Yeah. Yes, I… uh…" I glance around, not knowing what to do first. I pick up the TV remote with shaky hands and end up dropping it. There's a light giggle, and I look up to see Isabela hiding her face behind her elephant. I can't help but grin.

Shit, I made her laugh.

I made her *laugh*!

I pick up the remote again and flick through the channels, then realize I have no idea what channel it's on, so I hand the remote to Ryan. "You can be in charge of this. I'll go make some toast."

He thanks me, and I head into the kitchen. I shake my hands out at my sides, trying to calm the nerves rippling through me.

I can do this. I can take care of them until Jackson gets home.

Retrieving the loaf of bread from the pantry, I quickly get to work making their toast and filling two cups with water, and when I carry it back into the living room, my breathing has started to steady.

"Here you go. Let me know if you want any more," I say, handing the two plastic plates over, then putting the cups on the coffee table.

"Thanks, Hayden." Ryan smiles, then takes a large bite into the slice of toast.

"Thank you," Isabela says quietly, watching me as I sit

down on the other side of the couch. She doesn't take her eyes off me while she eats, and I can't help but wonder what she's thinking.

Does she see all my flaws? Does she see that I'm pretty much shitting myself with anxiety because these two are the most important things to Jackson, and he's the most important thing to me?

There's a comfortable silence in the living room while they eat, and I find myself getting engrossed in the *Bluey* episodes. My phone chimes, and when I pick it up, it's the NHL app alerting me that the Thunder game is about to begin.

"Did you want to watch your dad's game?" I ask.

"Yes, please!" Ryan nods. "They're playing St. Louis tonight. I always like when they play St. Louis because it's usually fast."

I chuckle. "That's true. There's always been a great rivalry there."

He changes the channel, and the bright white sheet of ice fills the screen.

"Daddy!" Isabela puts her hands in the air when Jackson comes on the screen. "Go, Daddy!"

I grin.

She starts pointing out every player by name, gradually getting more enthusiastic. When the camera pans on Elliot sitting on the bench, as he's not starting tonight, she pouts.

"Is Elliot your favorite?" I ask her. I already know the answer, but I'm trying to keep her comfortable.

She looks at me out of the corner of her eye and nods ever so gently.

"He's fun." I smile at her, and the corner of her lips tip up in a small smile.

The first period goes scoreless, but it doesn't go without any action. The Thunder take twelve shots on goal but fail to sink one into the net. Blaine gets a holding penalty, which Ryan responds to with a roll of his eyes.

"He's always getting a penalty," he tsks. "The dude doesn't know how to be chill."

I bark out a laugh because being chill isn't something that's associated with Blaine Olsen. "It is one of Blaine's worst traits."

"Hey, Hayden. What's your full name?" he asks, changing the subject.

"Hayden Cassidy."

"I thought so." He nods thoughtfully. "Dad has some of your hockey cards."

My eyebrows must skyrocket off my face with shock. "He does?"

"Yeah, I wasn't allowed to put them in my folder. I've been trying to collect all the seasons since the year I was born."

Well, fuck. Jackson's kept some of my cards? To anyone else, it probably wouldn't mean anything, but to me, it means everything. It means he's still thought about me over the years. Thought of me enough to keep a piece of card for himself. I wonder where he keeps it.

His bedside drawer, maybe?

I have to hide my smile with my hand as the thought takes over.

Halfway through the second period, I take off my

hoodie and throw it over the back of the couch. There's a small gasp, and I turn to see Isabela pointing at my arms.

"You have pictures," Isabela says, voice barely audible.

I glance down at where my tattoos are now visible. "Yeah, I have lots of pictures."

Her eyes light up with glee.

"You like pictures?"

She nods, and then Ryan answers. "She likes coloring them in. Ethan and Zach let her color in their tattoos because Dad doesn't have any."

I look down at my arms. One sleeve is full color, whereas the other is black and gray, but there's plenty there for her to fill in.

"Do you want to color mine in?" I ask her.

Wordlessly, she nods softly, then slides off the couch, still hugging her elephant tight to her chest. She doesn't take her eyes off me as she walks around the couch and disappears down the hall, returning minutes later with a bag of markers. She climbs onto the couch next to me and unzips the bag, so I angle myself in the corner of the sectional, allowing her better access to my arm, and push my T-shirt sleeve up to my shoulder.

"Have at it." I grin.

She's quiet while she draws on my skin with gentle strokes of the marker, sometimes holding my arm with her tiny hand to move it to a different position. Ryan and I chat about the game, cheering when Peyton scores the first goal in the second period. By the time the teams take the ice for third period, Isabela has fallen asleep with her marker in one hand and her elephant in the other. I carefully take it from her, popping the lid back on and zipping the bag up. I lean over to put it on the coffee table, then glance over to Ryan. His eyes are heavy, like he's struggling to stay awake. Picking up the TV remote, I turn the volume down and settle back into the couch. It's not long before my eyes become heavy too, and I join the kids by falling asleep on the couch.

Chapter Fifteen

Jackson

The door closes quietly behind me, and I twist the lock. The soft sounds of the TV filter down the hall from the living room, and my heart soars at the reminder Hayden's actually here.

I still can't believe he came. Just rocked up with one thought in mind: helping me out.

If there was a sign to tell me I needed to stop fighting this—whatever *this* is—between us, then him turning up on my doorstep during my time of need was it.

The game was rough tonight. I don't know if it's because my head wasn't fully in it or if St. Louis brought their A game, but it's safe to say I was preoccupied. I couldn't think about anything except whether the kids were doing okay and if they were feeling any better or if they were worse. And whether Hayden was coping because despite him saying he was fine, I know he wasn't. He was in pain, and he was stamping it down to save face.

For me.

Shrugging out of my coat, I hang it in the coat closet and toe off my shoes. I try and keep my steps light against the wooden floor as I head down the hall to the living room. The TV is showing some infomercial selling some kind of food mixer, but it's the sight on the couch that has me stopping in my tracks. Hayden's asleep on his back with Isabela curled into his side. Her head rests on his shoulder, and her elephant is tucked close under her chin. There's a blanket over the two of them, and Ryan is fast asleep at the other end, his head tilting back against the cushions with his legs stretched out next to Hayden's.

Something swells in my chest at the sight of them. My kids are my everything. They are my entire world. And once upon a time, so was Hayden. Seeing him with them and how they must have been so comfortable with him to fall asleep... This means more to me than I can explain.

With an uncontainable smile on my face, I take my phone out of my pocket. I need to take a photo of this to give me something to look back on when this becomes a memory.

Picking up the remote, I switch the TV off, then move to scoop Ryan up into my arms. The movement must jostle Hayden because he wakes up with a stir.

"Jax?" he croaks, sleepy gray eyes blinking up at me. "What time is it?"

"Hey," I whisper. "It's just after eleven thirty. I'm gonna take Ryan upstairs, then I'll come back for Isabela."

At the mention of her name, he glances down at where my daughter is snuggled up against him, and a gentle smile spreads across his lips.

Guess she warmed up to him quicker than either of us expected.

"They fell asleep earlier, and I didn't have the heart to move them. I was trying to stay awake until you came home. I didn't mean to doze off."

"Don't worry about it. I'll be back down in a minute." I smile reassuringly.

I carry Ryan up the stairs, tucking him into his bed and turning on his night-light. When I get back down to the living room, Hayden has shifted slightly, allowing me to pick Isabela up more easily. Her head flops against my shoulder when I scoop her up, but she doesn't wake as I take her to bed and turn on her night-light. I carefully check their temperatures, and I'm pleased to see they are almost back to normal. Hopefully, this means they have nearly kicked whatever bug they had.

When I'm finally back downstairs, I find Hayden in the kitchen. His tired features are lit up by the refrigerator light. He's pushed his glasses up his face slightly to rub his eye with his fingers as he peers inside.

"Would you like anything to eat?" he asks, turning his head to me.

I step in close to him and breathe in his spicy cologne.

"I can make you—"

I don't let him finish. I cup his face with my hands and press my lips to his. His body goes stock-still for a brief moment, and then he relaxes into me. His hands land on my hips, rooting me in place, while my fingers sink into his hair.

I part his lips with my tongue, but compared to the kiss we shared in the bathroom at the party, it's tender when my tongue sweeps into his mouth. This isn't frantic or desperate.

I'm hungry for him, but in a way that I'm trying to tell him without words how much him being here means to me. Not just here in my house, taking care of my kids, but *here*. Literally. Living and breathing in my arms.

I swallow the small noise he makes, and then a jolt of pleasure rushes straight to my cock when he sucks on my tongue.

Fuck, I've missed this. I've missed *him*. I'll never regret my relationship with Laura. We had some great years together, and she's the mother of my kids, but what we had pales compared to the connection I have with Hayden. The strength of the pull between us is magnetic. He lights me up like nobody else. He knows my body better than I know myself.

I take another step forward, causing him to stumble backward into the refrigerator as I deepen the kiss. He drops his hands to my ass and gives my cheeks a squeeze. My fingers tighten in his hair, and I press my hips into his. There's no doubt he can feel how hard I am. I'm pretty much dry humping him, both of us groaning into each other's mouths. I fucking love the taste of him. I want to feast on him all night. Spend hours becoming reacquainted with every inch of his mouth with my tongue and the feel of his body against mine.

It's only when something falls out of the refrigerator and hits the floor with a thud that we pull apart. His gray eyes are hazy with pleasure, cheeks pink with exertion. My heart is thumping wildly in my chest, threatening to break out from behind my breastbone.

"Wow." He lets out a ragged breath. His voice comes out in a whisper when he asks, "What was that for?"

I loosen my hold, but I don't drop my hands from his head.

"I don't want to fight this anymore, Cas," I say, sweeping my thumb over his cheek. His day-old stubble scrapes against my skin, and it sends a shiver trickling down my spine that goes straight to my balls. "You've shown me how genuine you are about us. Like, *fuck*, Cas. You dropped everything and flew across the country to come take care of my kids without me even asking…" I shake my head. The back of my eyes sting with the magnitude of how much his actions mean to me. "Thank you."

His face softens. "I'll do anything for you, Jackson. I know I don't deserve it, but I—"

I quickly cut him off. "No, we're not doing that. If we're doing this, then this is a fresh start. What you did today means more to me than you'll ever know."

He chews on the inside of his lower lip and presses them together to try to disguise his smile, but the sparkle in his eyes gives him away. "Yeah?"

"Yeah." I nod. "I know we need to talk about it at some point, but I don't want what we used to have. What we used to have was toxic and unhealthy. So this time, it's a clean slate. We'll talk about it, then that's it. It's in the past, and it has to stay there."

"I like the sound of that."

"And I need you to talk to me. I know you lied to me earlier, telling me you were fine when you weren't. I want to help you, Hayden. I want to be there to support you in every way, but it means you need to be honest with me. Please don't hide your pain from me."

He scrunches up his face in a grimace. "I'm sorry. It's like a reflex."

"Don't be sorry, just be honest with me." I drop my hands to his waist and massage my thumbs into the soft flesh above his hips. "Can I help you with anything now?" I lower my head, and my breath ghosts over his lips as I say quietly, "I have an amazing waterfall shower. Will heat help?"

He smirks. "Is that an invitation, Jax?"

"It can be." I wink and press my lips to his in a fleeting kiss. "Stay the night. I've got a spare room. I'll cook you breakfast in the morning as a thank-you."

"Are you sure?" His brows pinch. "Will the kids mind?"

"Positive, and based on how comfortable they seem with you, they will want to see you too." I take a step back and head into the hallway to pick up his duffel bag from the floor where he left it.

I wait at the bottom of the stairs for him to follow. I can see the hesitancy in his eyes, but they're also full of want. I curve my hand around his waist and pull him closer. "So, how about it? Can I care for you?"

He answers by kissing me again and whispering, "Lead the way."

It's not long until we're both naked in my en suite bathroom and stepping under the warm spray. My hands find his waist, thumbs tracing circles over his hip bones. I'm silent as I take the time to really look at him. Under the harsh bathroom lighting, his face is thinner than it was before. The hollows of his cheeks highlight his high cheekbones and square jaw. I'm assuming he's lost thirty or forty pounds at least since he retired. There are fine lines around his eyes that don't just speak of his age but hint that there's a hidden story behind his slate-gray eyes. The silver strands around his temple blend into his dark blond hair, only catching in certain lights.

His hands land on my chest, smoothing over the hard muscle of my pectorals. His fingertips glide through the fine chest hair.

"You're covered," I whisper, referring to the tattoos that cover almost his entire body. "Will you tell me about them?"

He swallows hard, his eyes darting to a spot over my shoulder before focusing back on me. "I started to get them as a way to silence my brain when it got too much. A way to escape, I guess."

I trace my fingers over one of the pieces on his ribs. The water from the shower causes the vibrant colors to pop. "You really like jellyfish, huh?"

He huffs out a small laugh. "Yeah."

"What's the story behind it?"

"About the jellyfish?"

"Yeah. What started this fascination with these weird sea jellies?"

He diverts his eyes again, and his expression morphs into something akin to shame. It takes everything in me not to grip his chin and return his gaze to me. It's going to fucking hurt to hear about his struggles, but I need to remember not to push him or force him to tell me before he's ready. He needs to tell me in his own time, and I need to show him that I'm a safe space and I'm here to support him in whatever way he needs.

"My therapist, Roberta, has some moon jellyfish in her office, and the first time I was there, I must have spent a good twenty minutes just staring at them. I was jealous that they had it so easy. Just spent their lives swimming around this tank without a care in the world. Then I learned they have no brain, and I was even more envious because they wouldn't experience having their brain turn against them like I did."

I swallow down the lump in my throat and blink away the tears that form in my eyes. There's a deep-rooted ache in my chest, so visceral that I have to rub over it with my hand to remind myself that the giant chasm I'm feeling isn't real.

"They became a reminder to me that I am stronger than what my mind tells me. They say one of the hardest parts of having depression is asking for help, and for me, as long as I continue to see those jellyfish, I know I've already overcome one of the toughest hurdles, and I can keep doing it."

It's not until Hayden raises his hand and wipes over my cheek that I realize I'm crying. His smile is gentle as he takes my face in both hands and my lips in another kiss.

We stand there under the warm spray for minutes, just like that, exchanging tender, slow kisses. I wrap my arms around his waist and pull him close to me, needing to feel his heart beating against mine.

It breaks my heart knowing that there was a possibility I could've lost him. Sure, he wasn't mine then and hasn't been mine for a long time, but knowing there was a chance he could have been successful. That I wouldn't have gotten the chance to hold him again, to smell him, to kiss him...

I choke out a sob into his mouth and rest my forehead against his, tightening my arms around him.

"I know I've said this before, but I'm so fucking glad

you're here, Cas. I…" My voice cracks, and Hayden presses his mouth to mine again.

"I'm here, and I'll be here until you tell me otherwise," he whispers against my lips.

A few minutes pass by as we kiss, our hands roaming each other's warm skin and tongues exploring each other's mouths. I have to force myself to take a step back and pour some shower gel into my hands. I showered at the arena, so I can focus all my attention on this incredible man in front of me. I told him I wanted to take care of him, and that starts now.

I press light kisses to his skin as I move down his body, taking in his tattoos up close. Each one is incredibly beautiful. Not just for the artist's sheer talent of creating these impressive images but for how each one tells a story. He endured the pain of getting these pieces of ink in order to shut down the pain in his mind. Each one represents how Hayden chose life.

There's also evidence of my daughter on him, where she's colored in one of his arms.

By the time I drop to my knees in front of him, my throat is thick with emotion, and my chest aches so much it hurts to breathe. Water clings to his eyelashes as he watches me rub my hands over his thighs to his knees. The scars from his surgeries are healed, but it causes another wave of… something to rush through me. Guilt? Fear? Pity? I don't know, but all I know is I will do anything I can to ensure he doesn't suffer. If it means carrying him up and down my goddamn stairs, I'll do it. I'll do anything.

I stand up, and Hayden immediately takes me into his arms. Our mouths collide with urgency and hungry sweeps of our tongues. My cock hardens, becoming a steel pipe between us. But I ignore it. Because tonight, it isn't about sex. It's all about reuniting with the man I once loved more than life.

He drops his head to my neck, trailing kisses under my jaw and dragging his teeth over my Adam's apple.

"I hear you've got some of my hockey cards," he murmurs.

I laugh softly, hands skimming his ribs.

"Who told you that?"

"Your son."

I snort. Of course Ryan told him. "The little shit. I told him to keep that a secret."

He lifts his head to look at me with one eyebrow raised. "You wanna know a secret?"

"Yeah," I croak.

"I have yours too. I keep them in my office."

"You do?"

He kisses one corner of my mouth, then the other. "Yeah. It's always been you, Jax."

And I know, right there and then, while we exchange tired kisses and gentle strokes of hands over skin, that it's always been Hayden for me too.

Chapter Sixteen

Hayden

I wake up in Jackson's spare room the following morning. The sheets smell like him, all clean and fresh.

I would prefer to be waking up in Jackson's actual bed, but after we made out in the shower and I bared yet another fracture in my wing to him, he explained that his kids have a habit of climbing into his bed during the night. And while he really wanted to continue our epic make-out session in bed, it was best we slept separately for their sake, which I fully understood. They've literally just met me. I can't imagine the shock they would experience if they found me in bed with their dad. So after we managed to tear our mouths away from each other, I had the best sleep I've had in a fucking long time.

I still can't quite believe he wants to give things a try again. Yeah, we have a lot to talk about, and that's going to be a tough conversation, but it's needed. We need to clear the air in order to move forward.

I'm grinning into the pillow as I slowly roll over to grab

my phone from the bedside table and pull up the text thread with Roberta. She was understanding yesterday when I had to reschedule our appointment because she knows how it is with my pain. Sometimes we swap to video call, even though I don't find them as personable. I know it's very much a me thing, but like I said yesterday to Jackson, I've trained my brain to use those jellyfish as a marker, and I can't see them when we video call.

> I don't want to alarm you. I may have done something reckless yesterday, but it had the best payoff.

ROBERTA

> Do I want to know? Do you need bail money? Because I hate to break it to you, while you pay me very well, I don't know if I can stretch that far.

I let out a bark of laughter.

> No, it's nothing like that.

> Jackson called me sounding very stressed out. His kids were sick, and he was spiraling. I may have gotten on a plane and flew to Chicago to help him out. And he may have kissed me late last night and agreed to give us a try.

I hold my breath and watch as those three dots bounce across the screen.

ROBERTA

Wow, this is great news, Hayden. How do
you feel about it all?

Amazing! I can't stop smiling, my face kinda
aches. We're going to talk about what
happened before, which I know is needed
for us to move forward, but I feel like
everything is coming together, you know?

I feel like I'm being rewarded for the hard
work I've been putting into myself.

ROBERTA

I can sense your smile through your words.
Let's catch up next week. I look forward to
hearing about it.

There's a light knock on the door, and then Jackson pokes his head through the gap. When he sees I'm awake, he comes in, a soft smile on his face. He's wearing plaid pajama pants and a worn T-shirt. I lock my phone and place it on the mattress beside me.

"Hey, I've brought you coffee."

I sit up against the pillows, wincing slightly when my hip pinches. I haven't taken my meds yet today. He sits on the edge of the bed and hands over the steaming cup. I take a sip, letting out a satisfied "ah" as the delicious caffeine hits.

I wet my lip with my tongue, and Jackson's eyes zero in on the movement. It was like no time had passed when we were making out last night. Like I had been transported to our bathroom back in Boston after a game when we would shower together. We'd exchange lazy kisses and stroke each other's hard cocks before tumbling into bed, where we'd fuck for most of the night.

"Did you sleep okay?" he asks.

"Like a dream." I smile, taking another sip before placing the cup on the table. "Did you?"

He dips his chin, and his cheeks flush slightly. "Yeah, I, uh… had to see to something, then I slept better than I have in a while."

The thought of him touching himself on the other side of the wall sends warmth down to my groin.

"Damn, I wish I could've helped you out with that."

"Me too." He smirks. "Maybe next time."

A beat of silence passes between us as our eyes remain locked, a silent promise of what's to come when the time and place is right. I have to trample down the urge to grab the back of his head and slide my tongue into his mouth because now isn't the time. And Jackson's next words solidify that.

"There's two kids waiting downstairs who haven't stopped asking about you since they woke up."

"Yeah?"

"Yeah, they're very excited that you're still here. Isabela's drawn you a picture too."

I grin. "You have two amazing kids, Jackson. You must be so proud."

"I am." He nods, his smile full of pride. "Do you need to head back to California for anything?"

"No, only a therapy session, but that's not until next week. Other than that, I have nothing going on that I can't do from here. Why?" I lean closer. "What are you thinking?"

His hand lands on my thigh over the comforter, giving it a gentle squeeze.

"I'm hosting Thanksgiving here this year. My parents

and some of the guys from the team are coming. I'd love it if you could stay and spend it with us."

My eyes widen slightly, not expecting him to say that. I usually go to Zara's for Thanksgiving because she refuses to let me sit around on my own, but I'm sure Connor would love to not have his girlfriend's ex-husband around. "I mean… I'd love to. Is there anything I can help with? I'm not good at cooking, but I can help chop veggies?"

"My mom's pretty much got it covered, but thanks." He smiles, and then something in his eyes flickers as he tugs his lip between his teeth. "Also… we're playing in Los Angeles next week…" His hand inches higher as his words trail off, and my cock doesn't fail to notice. "We're staying the night before heading down to San Jose."

"What are you thinking?" I ask huskily.

"Maybe you could come stay the night."

I beam. "You want me to be your booty call, Wilde?"

"Fuck off." He laughs. "We're limited on what we can do while the kids are here, but fuck, Cas. I want to get my hands on you so bad." My cock is half-hard by the time his fingers coast over my lap. His tongue darts out, swiping over his lips. "Wanna taste you so bad. Wanna feel you on my tongue."

I let out a sharp gasp, and my hips automatically press up into his touch. "I'm sure I can make it happen."

"Good." He moves in closer, taking my bottom lip in his mouth before kissing me hot and fast. But before it can go any further, he pulls away, stands up, and adjusts himself. "I think we both need a minute, but are you ready to be welcomed into chaos?"

My grin almost splits my face in two. "I'm more than ready."

⚔

"Hayden?" Isabela appears at my side, peering up at me with her wide blue eyes that are an exact match to Jackson's. "Can I have a drink?"

"Yeah, of course," I say with a smile. I take her cup from her and refill it with water from the fridge. I slowly crouch down and hand it over. "Do you need anything else?"

She shakes her head and whispers a quiet "thank you" before running back into the family room with her cup.

Any nerves I had about being around Jackson's kids have vanished because these last few days have been incredible. Jackson wasn't kidding when he said the kids were excited to see me that morning. From the moment I got downstairs, they were back to full energy and smothered me with attention. I didn't quite know what to do with myself. Ryan was asking me a million questions about my time in the NHL, and Isabela had been so obsessed with my tattoos, Jackson had to force her coloring book in front of her to give my skin a break.

I'd let her do whatever she wanted as long as she felt comfortable with me, but it turns out she can get obsessive, and Jackson doesn't want to enable that behavior.

He had an away game in Philadelphia last night, so his parents had the kids to keep to their routine. It was the first night we had alone together, but by the time he got home, I was fast asleep in his bed, and we didn't have time for anything this morning as the kids came back early when his parents arrived to help with dinner.

And that's another thing. I wasn't anticipating this many people to come for Thanksgiving. I thought maybe Peyton, considering he's now single, and possibly Zach, as Carter is in Denver because he has a game tomorrow.

Jackson's parents, Peyton, and Zach are both here, along with Elliot, Blaine, and Alex, and Ethan and Jacob are on their way. If they think it's weird that I'm here, they haven't said anything, but I wouldn't be surprised if when a certain Mr. Ethan Parkes turns up, there will be some questioning looks. Especially after he caught us sneaking back downstairs at Peyton's Halloween party. The only person who's missing is Jackson's sister, but she's spending the day with her husband's family.

"What is *that*?" Elliot points to a dish with slight disgust.

I follow the direction of his hand, then swallow down my laughter. "Sweet potato casserole with marshmallows."

His eyes widen. "With *marshmallows*?"

"You've never had it before?"

"No!" He practically lies on top of the counter and takes a deep inhale. "It smells fucking awesome, though. Like my teeth are gonna fall out."

"Whose teeth are falling out?" Blaine appears with a beer in hand.

"Mine when I eat that." Elliot points to the casserole. "Have you ever had sweet potatoes with marshmallows?"

"Uhh, no? Who would put marshmallows with potatoes?"

"It's a holiday classic, you dingus." I grin at the twins' puzzled faces.

"I thought you were Canadian?" Elliot frowns.

"I was born in Maine, but I grew up in Nova Scotia." I roll my eyes. "You two were clearly deprived as children if you've never had this."

"Maybe." Blaine shrugs. "Do you know what time the old man is getting here?"

I arch a brow, urging him to elaborate.

"Ethan," he clarifies.

"Old man? He's the same age as me."

Blaine looks me up and down, then shrugs again. "Yeah, do you know when he's getting here?"

My mouth drops open. "You asshole."

"Hey! My husband had a crush on you, I'm allowed to be mean to you."

"It doesn't work like that." Alex appears, patting his hand on Blaine's ass. "I was a teenager when I had a crush on Hayden. Plus, I married *you*, remember."

Blaine grins and wraps his arm around Alex's neck, pulling him in close to kiss his temple. "Damn right you did."

"I believe they're due any minute now," I say. And right on cue, the door opens, and Isabela's loud shriek causes me to flinch.

"Ethan!" she squeals.

Jackson's on his feet in an instant as the sound of her little feet pounding against the wooden floor echoes down the hallway. "Iz, be careful! He's had sur—"

"Whoa there, kiddo," Jacob says around a laugh. "We've gotta be slow around Ethan. He's not too steady at the minute."

I peek my head around the corner and see Ethan's on

crutches after his recent knee replacement. I scan his expression, looking for any sign of pain or regret, but there's nothing. His usually stoic face is soft as he smiles down at Isabela, allowing her to take a look at his crutches.

"Hey, Hayden." Jacob smiles when he spots me.

Ethan's head snaps up, and his eyes narrow behind his glasses.

"Hey," I reply and tilt my chin, motioning to his leg. "How are you holding up?"

"All good," Ethan grumbles, and Jacob rolls his eyes.

"He's fine, just grumpier than usual because he doesn't like being told to rest."

"I don't like sitting still and doing nothing," he argues.

"Well, tough shit. Now, go be a good boy and sit down in the living room." Jacob points in the direction of the living room.

A flash of heat crosses Ethan's expression. He bends forward, and whatever he whispers in Jacob's ear causes him to shiver. Jacob rises on his toes to kiss Ethan, and then Ethan makes his way into the living room with Isabela at his heels.

"Is there anything I can help with?" Jacob asks.

"No, I think we're all set." Jackson looks over at me, and I nod.

Dinner is chaotic, but Jackson's mom seems to revel in it. She beams as every dish is emptied and bellies become fuller. Jackson takes the kids upstairs after they fall asleep on the couch, and the rest of us settle in the living room to watch the football game before having dessert.

He sits next to me and gives my thigh a gentle squeeze.

"You okay?" he asks quietly.

"Yeah." I smile, resting my head back against the cushions. I want to kiss him so bad. "Thanks for inviting me."

He winks, making the urge to kiss him even stronger.

Elliot returns minutes later, wearing pajama pants covered in cartoon otters holding a slice of watermelon.

"What are those?" Peyton asks from where he's slouched in an armchair with the button of his jeans undone.

"Dude, I'm so full my stomach might explode. Jeans make me feel constricted." He gets on the floor and lies on his back. He bends his knees and grabs hold of his feet, pulling his knees toward the floor, and lets out a groan. "That feels so good."

Shock filters through Peyton's face. "Goalies are fucking weird, yo."

"I'd like to see you try that." Blaine grins.

"I don't think I'd be able to get back up. You'd have to roll me out the door."

We all burst into laughter.

By the time the others begin to head home, I'm happy and content and full of dessert. I'm loading the dishwasher when Jackson comes into the kitchen. He glances over his shoulder, then wraps his arms around my waist. He ducks his head, pressing his lips to the delicate skin over my pulse point.

"Did you have a good day?" I ask, tipping my head back to give him better access.

His kisses travel up along my jaw before he slants his mouth over mine.

"Mm," he murmurs against my lips.

We're both on high alert for the sound of footsteps as he pushes his tongue into my mouth, and I let out a quiet moan. There's something so hot about stealing kisses from him. A high ecstasy that we might be caught. Not that I want us to be caught because that'll cause a lot of confusion, but the thought of it goes straight to my balls.

"Wanna shower again when the kids have gone to bed?" I whisper.

"You bet." He lifts his head, and his blue eyes are dark with heat. "I cannot wait for LA. I hope you're ready for it."

And while I'm so ready to get my hands on Jackson's naked body again, there's a pool of dread in my stomach at the conversation we'll need to have before we do anything.

Chapter Seventeen

Jackson

The tension is palpable as we trudge down the tunnel for the first intermission. LA are holding no punches tonight, and I mean that quite literally. Peyton ended up dropping the gloves four minutes into the first period after Zach was cross-checked and it went uncalled by the refs.

It seems they've come out with a point to prove tonight, and we're the unlucky suspects because we're currently down by three goals.

We take a seat in our designated stalls, and Coach Harris stalks into the locker room. He paces the floor, biting on the side of his thumb. The hard set of his jaw tells me he's struggling to rein in his frustration.

"What the fuck happened out there?" he spits, but we all know not to answer back. We don't have any acceptable excuse for our piss-poor performance. "They took eighteen shots on goal. *Eighteen.* And we had fucking six." He turns slowly, making sure to look every single one of us in the eye. "Our rebounds are sloppy as fuck. We don't look like the team who won the Cup last year. We've been on a three-game losing streak since we came back from the holiday, and I don't want tonight to be a fourth. We need to stay out of the box—" He gives a pointed stare to Blaine and Peyton, who have already taken three penalties between them so far. "—and we need to get pucks into the back of the net. I'm so fucking tired of losing, so when we get back out there, you better bring your A game. Be the team I know you are, and don't give them something to laugh about."

At that, he storms out of the locker room, door slamming shut in his wake. Nobody dares to speak. The mood is sullen, and we keep our eyes down. Some retape their sticks, and I head to the bathrooms to do my business.

I can't believe Hayden is witnessing this game. He flew back to LA a few days ago so he could attend his appointment with his therapist, and it's felt like weeks since I've seen him. Weirdly enough, the house feels empty without him in it. To the point the kids have noticed it feels different without him. They adore him, more than I could've imagined, and they've asked when he's coming back multiple times a day since he left.

And as much as I love them, I'm glad I get to have him to myself tonight. Even if I am going to be full of embarrassment if we don't sort ourselves out and start scoring some goals.

When we head back onto the ice for the second period, it's a hard battle to take possession. Elliot stops shot after shot. I manage to get my stick on a few following the rebound, hitting it away from the net. Zach dumps the puck into the offensive zone, and it's a quick race to beat LA's D-man to reach the puck first. I curve around the net, slapping the puck to Blaine, who passes it to Peyton. He takes a shot, but their winger intercepts. It goes on like that for several minutes. The boys try desperately to take possession. So much so that Zach ends up with a two-minute penalty for tripping, and the penalty kill is painful to watch from the bench. We're like sitting ducks as an LA forward gets on a breakaway. Elliot's eagle eyes track the puck, but the forward sinks it into the net with a lightning-fast move, giving LA the advantage at 4-0.

"These guys are pissing me off," Blaine grunts as he drops down onto the bench beside me. He picks up his bottle and squirts some water into his mouth before slamming it back into the holder. "Like, fucking stop with the fucking poke check, fucking ding-dongs."

Normally I'd laugh at his frustrated outbursts, but I'm getting pissed off too.

I manage to score a goal before the buzzer, and when we head out for the third period, Coach pulls Elliot and puts Lindholm in. I glance over to Elliot, who's slumped on the bench and removes his mask. No goalie likes to be pulled, and defeat is written all over his face. It's not his fault, but he won't see it that way. He'll see that he let in four goals, and he's the reason we're losing the game.

But the real reason is us. There's more than just him out there.

"Come on, boys." I slap the boards, hoping to gear up some momentum. "We didn't come here to lose. The shit streak ends here."

There are some grunts in agreement, but I don't let it faze me.

The whistle blows with a penalty on LA for holding, and I jump over the boards for the power play.

"Let's fucking do this!" Peyton shouts.

My teeth clench in frustration as I watch for the puck drop. Blaine wins the face-off, slapping the puck over to me. I take the puck into our defensive zone and around the back of the net before passing it over to Peyton. We make our way up into the neutral zone. Peyton passes to Blaine, and I angle myself to the right of the net, watching out of the corner of my eye as one of LA's defensemen tries to guess my next move. The pass from Blaine connects, and I raise my stick, making it look like I'm about to take a shot, but instead, I poke the puck between my skates, then take a backhander. The puck flies past the waiting defenseman and into the back of the net.

Fucking *finally*!

I don't feel like celebrating because we're still down by two, but I accept the back pats and cheers and head back toward the bench.

When there are two minutes left in the third, Coach pulls Lindholm for an extra forward, and Blaine puts another on the board with a stellar Michigan goal. Lindholm remains on the bench for the final thirty seconds, and desperation is pouring off us in waves. Zach manages to close the gap. I'm ready, waiting by the crease. An LA defenseman shoves me in the back, but I hold my ground so I'm not on the blue. Zach takes a risky slap shot from the blue line and sinks the puck in the bottom left corner, sending us into overtime.

"Holy fucking shit!" Peyton beams as we skate back to

the bench to get ready for overtime. "Reidsy, that was a beauty. I think I have a boner."

Zach chuckles quietly under his breath, squirting water into his mouth. But my attention latches onto Elliot, who's sitting silently in the corner. I skate over with my bottle in hand and tap my gloves on the board in front of him.

He lifts his head. There's so much emotion swirling in his green eyes, but he doesn't say a word. I give him a small and what I hope is reassuring smile. *This isn't a reflection of you*, I try to say with my eyes.

He shrugs and drops his gaze again.

Fuck, I hate that he's feeling shit over this. But I don't have time to do anything as we get the signal to skate to center ice for the face-off.

Blaine takes the face-off, with me on the right of the circle and Zach by the blue line. Blaine wins, passing it back toward Zach. He skates into the defensive zone and around the back of the net, eyes assessing my and Blaine's whereabouts.

We change lines, and neither team gets a decent shot on net. But it all changes when LA gets called for hooking, and now it's four on three. I'm back on the ice with Blaine, Peyton, and Zach.

Peyton drags it into the offensive zone, and I'm hot behind him. The two of us battle with one of LA's forwards in the corner, and I manage to get the puck out from the boards with the toe of my stick. Blaine's ready and waiting, and with a flick of his wrist, the puck bounces off the post and into the net.

He thrusts his arms up in victory, a wide grin spreading across his face.

Holy shit, talk about a fucking comeback.

My heart rate is through the roof as I slam into him, wrapping my arms around him. Peyton and Zach join us seconds later, and then we skate back to the bench. This time when we enter the visitors' locker room, it's buzzing with excitable energy.

Zach plugs in the post-W playlist, but unlike every other time, Elliot isn't on his feet. I frown, watching in concern as he changes and heads into the shower without joining in on the activities.

Glancing over to Blaine, I'm pleased he's picked up on it too.

I head into the showers and get changed into my game day suit, but before I head out to the bus, I grab Blaine's arm as he passes.

"I know you're eager to speak with Alex, but spend some time with him." I jerk my chin toward Elliot.

Blaine's brows furrow.

"He's beating himself up pretty bad about tonight, and the last thing he needs is to be on his own. All I'm saying is, when you've spoken with Alex, spend some time with your brother. Make sure he's not blaming himself for the way we failed him earlier."

Because we did fail him. Yeah, he got pulled, but it was because we folded like a house of cards both offensively and defensively, and we weren't there to help him protect the net.

Blaine looks in the direction of where Elliot's disappeared toward the bus, then nods. "Yeah… Yeah, I will."

I give him a tight smile and return to lacing up my shoes.

"Thanks," he says after a beat, and I glance up, waiting for him to elaborate. "For looking out for him. Sometimes I get so carried away and in my own bubble that I forget to look in front of me."

I smile. Glad he's aware of it.

"Don't sweat it."

"Hey, maybe you can be the new team dad now Ethan's retired," he chuckles, and I laugh.

"Sure, but don't expect me to pick up after you. I have enough trouble trying to pick up after my actual children."

He gives my shoulder a squeeze and heads out of the locker room.

By the time we're all seated on the bus, I'm a mix of exhaustion and excitement over the thought of seeing Hayden. I pull my phone out of my pocket and bring up our message thread. A small smile appears on my lips to see he's already texted.

HAYDEN

Well, fuck me! I haven't been on the edge of my seat watching a game for a long time. What a game!

I'm heading to the hotel now. I'll hide out in the bar until you give me the all clear.

I can't wait to see you.

I have to duck my chin to hide the face-splitting grin.

I'm glad it was fun watching it because it didn't feel fun playing it. We're just leaving the arena now, should be there in ten mins. I'll text you my room number as soon as I have the key.

We're in the hotel lobby in less than ten minutes. Something warm fills my chest when I see Blaine and Elliot head toward the elevators with their bags in hand. Blaine has his free arm wrapped around Elliot's shoulders, their heads tucked close together as they disappear. Hopefully, our goalie won't be beating himself up too badly, especially with his twin taking the time to spend the night with him.

I accept the paper card slip with the key inside from our travel coordinator with a quick thanks and make a beeline for the elevator. I hit the call button, then take my phone out of my pocket to text Hayden.

HAYDEN

The elevator ride up to the fourth floor seems to take an eternity, and when the doors finally ping open, I'm practically jogging to my room. I scan the key card and push open the door as soon as the little green light flashes. Dumping my bag near the desk, I quickly unzip it to find my toiletry bag and head into the bathroom to brush my teeth. Then like a creeper, I stand by the door and peer through the peephole. My pulse increases at the sound of footsteps, and the moment Hayden appears, I swing open the door before he can raise his hand to knock.

His eyes widen slightly in surprise, but before he can say anything, I pull him inside. The door closes behind him, and then I curve my hand around his neck and slant my mouth over his. He stumbles back against the door, dropping his bag at his feet, and wraps his arms around my waist. His hands smooth over my dress shirt at the base of my spine, then travel up, stopping between my shoulder blades. I slide my tongue into his mouth, tasting the hint of whiskey.

My cock is a steel pipe pressing against my zipper when he pulls away, breathing heavily. I duck my head, nipping and sucking along the column of his neck as my hands travel up into his hair.

"Mm," he murmurs, tilting his head back to grant me better access. "This is the kinda hello I can get behind."

I lift my head and steal another kiss from his swollen lips. "Hi."

"Hi," he whispers. "Great game tonight."

"Thanks." I smooth my hands down from his head and down his chest. He's wearing an impeccable navy blue three-piece suit and white shirt. I flick the buttons open on his waistcoat, then start on his shirt.

He leads me backward into the room, a wicked grin on his face. The back of my knees hit the bed, and I drop down to sit. I undo the final button and spread his shirt open, revealing inches of smooth, inked skin. Leaning forward, I press an open-mouthed kiss just below his belly button, then kiss a path up toward his nipples. I flick my tongue over one brown disc, smirking against his warm skin when he shivers, and then I move to the other one. The sound of his soft gasp causes my cock to throb more. He cradles my head with both hands, fingers tangling into the strands on the back of my scalp.

I graze my teeth over his nipple, and he moans.

"Fuck, Jax."

I push off his jacket, tossing it on the nearby chair, then slip off his waistcoat and shirt. I'm about to make a move on his belt when he stops me with both hands on my wrists.

"Hey, slow down." He chuckles softly, looking down at me with so much affection in his eyes it makes my chest ache.

"I'm sorry, I'm just… I've been dying to get my hands on you. Being under the same roof as you, sleeping on the other side of the wall to you and not being able to touch you, has been a torture I never knew existed."

He smiles and leans down to kiss me.

"I know, but there's something I need to tell you before we carry on." He swallows roughly. "Because it might change your mind about me."

My brows furrow in confusion. "What do you mean?"

He sucks in a deep breath, and that's when I see it. He's nervous. Whatever it is he's about to tell me has most likely been eating at him, and here's me ripping off his clothes like an unhinged animal.

"What is it, Cas?" I whisper, feeling my own anxiety beginning to spike.

"The medication I'm on… it has some side effects."

"Okay… I mean, I'm not going to change my mind about you because you're on medication?"

He worries his bottom lip between his teeth. "I… How

do I put this… I don't perform as well as I used to, and I understand if that makes you rethink all of this."

It takes a while for his words to fully sink in on what he's trying to say.

Oh. *Oh.*

I stand up, shaking my head softly. "I promise you I won't rethink this. Tell me what you need from me." I kiss him gently. "Tell me what I can do to make this be good for you."

Chapter Eighteen

Hayden

This is so fucking embarrassing. I know it needs to be said, but fuck, I'm going to kill the mood big-time. Because how can I say, "Oh, hey, so I struggle to get hard sometimes, please don't take it personally," without killing his boner?

Jackson smooths his hands along my shoulders, then rubs his thumbs into the muscle between my neck and shoulders.

"Talk to me," he says gently.

"This is really fucking embarrassing." I scrub my face with both hands. "My medication means sometimes I can't get hard or stay hard, or when I do, I struggle to come."

I drop my gaze, focusing on his designer belt buckle. The imprint of his semi-hard dick is still visible through his dress pants, and I make a mental note that I did that. My broken, fucked-up self made this incredible man hard.

"Hey." He tilts my chin up until I'm looking into his blue eyes. "This doesn't change anything, okay? I still want you.

I'm not going to be jumping ship because I can't jump on your dick like I used to."

I snort at his choice of words, and then we both burst into laughter.

"I mean it," he says between laughter, then sobers. "If anything, I want to know how I can make this good for you. I've already been looking up how to make things comfortable for you with your arthritis, but now I want to know how I can make this good for you regardless of whether you get hard or shoot your load. I want to show you there's no pressure from me. I just want you to be comfortable and satisfied."

The back of my eyes burns at his earnest expression.

This has been something that's been plaguing me for a long time. Four and a half years, in fact. Zara and I stopped having sex long before we filed for divorce, and the times I tried to bring someone home from a hookup app, they left disappointed because I couldn't get hard. After that, I stopped trying.

But I'm not going to tell him that.

I've gotten by with my hand, some lube, and a whole heap of frustration. I don't want him thinking that he might be able to cure me or some shit.

"Thank you," I whisper, then decide to lay my vulnerability on the table. "I don't want to disappoint you."

He takes my face in both hands and presses his lips to mine in a kiss that's brimming with emotion. His tongue slides perfectly against mine. Our chests slot together just right. I can feel the gentle beat of his heart, almost in rhythm with mine.

"You won't disappoint me, Cas," he promises against my swollen lips. "I mean it."

And that's all the validation I need to push my embarrassment down and take the lead. With my hands on his chest, I push him down onto the bed. He sits willingly, then spreads his legs for me to step between them. His hands glide up the back of my thighs to my ass and give both cheeks a squeeze.

I start by removing his shirt, uncovering his strong, rounded shoulders and muscular torso. Carefully placing his shirt on the chair alongside mine, making sure it doesn't crease, I bite back a smile at the fact he's going to smell my aftershave on him tomorrow.

Without a word, I motion for him to lie back on the bed and let out a strangled moan as his abs ripple.

"You're so fucking hot, Jax."

His pupils flare, darkening with heat. "Says you. You look like a ripped, tattooed god. Take your pants off already."

I grin down at him.

"Soon."

I unbuckle his belt and pop open the button of his dress pants. I tap his hip with my fingers.

"Lift."

He raises his hips, and I tug down his pants, folding them neatly on the chair next to his shirt. When I return to stand between his legs, I take in the sight of him lying on the bed. Thick thighs dusted in dark blond hair are spread wide. His hard cock strains against his gray boxer briefs, and my balls tingle when I see the small wet spot near the head of his leaking cock.

I continue my visual exploration, trailing up his V-cut, over his abs and wide chest. His hands fist the bedspread underneath him like he's trying so hard not to touch himself or me. The small smattering of chest hair between his pecs has my tongue darting out to lick along my bottom lip.

How is it he's even hotter now than he was when he was in his early twenties? If anything, he's stronger now. Bigger. And I want to explore every inch of his incredible body with my tongue.

"If you're done feasting on me with your eyes, take off your damn pants, Cas," he growls.

A shuddering breath escapes me when I catch his molten eyes.

My hands tremble on my belt buckle and pants. I toss them aside, then hook my thumbs into the waistband of my boxers. I'm half-hard, which tends to be the furthest I can get, but Jackson's heated gaze doesn't change as I pull down my boxers. He sits back upright and runs his hands up my thighs to my hips. He leans in, nuzzling his face into the juncture of my groin, and takes a deep inhale.

"Fuck, I've missed how good you smell," he groans, then laves his tongue on the delicate skin near my pubes before he takes my cock into his mouth and gives me one hard suck.

My hands find his hair, combing through the soft strands to anchor myself. I allow him to explore my body with his mouth and hands before I press a knee onto the mattress and straddle his lap. Strong arms wrap around my back. I swallow down his moan and slide my tongue into his mouth.

"I want you so bad, Cas," he murmurs against my lips.

"You can have me." I suck on his tongue and flick my thumb over his nipple, causing him to gasp. "Own me like you used to. Own me like we've only been apart for days, not years."

I land on my feet when he stands abruptly. He shucks off his boxers, and my mouth waters at the sight of his long, engorged cock springing free.

"Lie back," he rasps. His voice is all rich and husky.

I climb onto the bed and prop my head up against the pillows as he crawls over me. My eyes roll to the back when he licks a hot, wet stripe up my semi-hard cock, then straddles my chest.

I wish I could take a mental snapshot of how Jackson looks right now. All heavy-lidded eyes, swollen lips parted. His expansive chest rises and falls with his labored breathing, and his cock points proudly, only inches away from my mouth.

I look up at him from beneath my lashes and smirk. "Do you want something from me, Jax?"

"Yeah, I do. Open up." He grips the base of his cock and angles it in the perfect position for me to lean my head forward and wrap my lips around him. I place my hands on his thighs, digging my thumbs into the solid muscle, and suck him deeper into my mouth. I keep my eyes fixed on him, watching his head tilt back on a moan. He rocks his hips slightly, and I relax my jaw and throat, taking him as deep as he wants to go.

"Fuck," he gasps, pulling himself back. He shifts down my body until he can take my mouth in a heated kiss.

I can feel my cock thickening as he grinds himself against me, but I put it to the back of my mind, accepting that if it happens, it happens, but I'm in this moment, wholly.

"Roll over," he demands when he finally pulls away. He gets off the bed, and I roll onto my front while he retrieves lube from his bag. He throws a leg over mine, then takes one of the pillows and slides it under my hips.

"Is that okay?"

I bite back a smile. "Yeah, it's all good, Jax."

He kisses the side of my head, then sits back on his haunches. I watch over my shoulder as he pours lube onto his fingers before he spreads my cheeks. He runs a lubed finger around my hole, and I shiver from my head to my toes.

"Holy shit," I moan.

The sensation is heady. I haven't been touched so intimately in such a long time. He works me open with his fingers, and my body melts into the mattress. I'm an incoherent, mumbling mess by the time he's three fingers deep and stroking my prostate like a dream.

"Jax," I say with a gasping breath.

"What is it, Cas? What do you need?"

"You. I need you."

Without a word, he slips his fingers from inside me, and I whimper at the loss. I curl my arms around the pillow beneath my head, and the click of the lube bottle sounds throughout the otherwise silent room, along with the telltale rip of foil. Moments later, Jackson's warm body blankets my back, his hot breath fanning against my ear. My eyes fall closed at the feel of his blunt cockhead pressing against my hole. He slowly inches inside of me, and we both moan in unison once he passes the first ring of muscle. Then with small, shallow thrusts, he sinks in further until his balls rest against my taint.

"Fuck," I grunt, feeling fuller than I have in over a decade.

He's always had the ability to make it feel like I'm levitating. To light up every single nerve ending in my body and make them sing.

He tucks his arms under mine and laces our fingers together. His cock grazes over my prostate with every thrust, and I moan into the pillow. The friction of my cock rubbing against the pillow sends electricity down my spine. Yeah, I might not be hard enough to pound nails into a wall, but this is the most alive I've felt in years. Even more alive than the time Jackson kissed me in Peyton's bathroom.

"I want to hear you," he whispers in my ear.

"Jax," I moan.

"That's it. Say my name, Cas." He thrusts his hips deeper. "I love it when you say my name."

My toes curl and abs tense as heat sizzles down my spine.

"Jackson."

I'm panting hard. My heart is thumping wildly in my chest. His hips falter, and he lets out a loud curse when I clench around his pulsing cock.

"Hayden." His moan is almost feral as his hot release fills the condom. He collapses on top of me, both of us gasping for air and skin sticky with sweat. My entire body tingles, like I've been zapped by a million tiny shocks.

I might not have come, but holy fucking shit, it was like I had an out-of-body experience.

After a few minutes, Jackson gently eases himself off me,

and I listen to his soft footfalls as he enters the bathroom and turns on the tap. He returns a moment later with a warm washcloth and cleans me up. I roll onto my back and search his expression for disappointment when he realizes I didn't come, but the only expression on his face is lust and affection.

"Is there anything you need? Or is there anything I can do for you?" he asks.

I shake my head. There's a puck-sized lump of emotion lodged in my throat.

"No, that… That was more than perfect for me."

Jackson smiles and gives a small nod. He ditches the washcloth, then slides into bed next to me. He wraps his big body around mine and presses a tender kiss to my temple.

"Jax?" I whisper.

"Mmm?" he murmurs sleepily.

I swallow roughly because there are so many things I want to say. Like *I've never stopped loving you* is on the tip of my tongue. But there's something holding me back from saying it. Maybe it's because I only used to speak of that four-letter word when we were lying in bed, bodies covered in sweat and drying come.

I don't want it to be like that this time. I want him to know how I feel about him outside of being high from orgasms.

He'll soon get bored of you, the voice tries to convince me, but I squash it down.

After everything I've told him, he's still here. That has to mean something, right? That maybe I'm not as broken as I think I am?

"Thank you," I say instead.

I cringe when he doesn't reply because it sounds so pathetic. But he answers by squeezing my torso and nuzzling his face in my neck.

"Night, Cas," he mumbles against my throat.

"Night, Jax."

I don't know how many hours pass as I lie there watching him sleep. His lips are parted slightly. His steady breaths come out in warm, soft puffs of air. His thigh rests heavy over mine, and his arm is draped loosely over my waist. I lift my free hand that isn't caught beneath his arm and gently brush the hair away from his face. He looks so fucking peaceful and beautiful that I choke on my breath, and my eyes burn with tears.

Fuck, I almost didn't get this. I almost didn't get this opportunity to watch him sleep again. To have him in my arms or the memory of how he felt inside me.

I blink away the few tears that threaten to fall.

"I won't fail you a second time, Jackson," I whisper, carding my fingers through his hair. "I swear to you, I'll be loving you every day for the rest of my life."

Chapter Nineteen

Jackson

"Daddy?" Isabela tugs on the collar of my jacket. "Get ice cream now?"

My mom chuckles. "See? She's going to be perfectly fine. I mean, yeah, it helps that you have the money for therapists and specialists, but still. You've been worrying yourself for nothing. These are the best people in Chicago to give her everything she needs."

She's not wrong, but what am I earning seven figures a year for if I'm not going to spend it on my kids?

We've just come out of the final appointment in regards to Isabela's diagnosis. Over the last few weeks, we've met with various specialists, such as developmental pediatricians, child psychiatrists and psychologists, and neurologists, and had meetings with her teachers on how her school can provide the appropriate support. I've come away with more information than my brain can process right now, but I feel more confident that Isabela is going to get the support she needs, especially when she goes into first grade. But it's been a hard process. Having to watch as your child is visibly uncomfortable around all these strangers doing various different tests and assessments on her and not being able to do anything about it because it's necessary for her development. It fucking sucked. But I'm glad it's done now, and we can move forward with a suitable plan.

"Of course we can, peanut," I say to Isabela while I carry her back to the car, then turn to my mom. "Are you coming for ice cream?"

She shakes her head. "No, you go. Remember, Ryan has hockey practice after school, so you'll need to pick him up at six."

I raise my hand and give her a salute, which causes Isabela to giggle. We wave my mom goodbye, and I strap Isabela into her seat.

"So, do you want ice cream or cupcakes?" I ask her.

Her face lights up, and she shakes her fists in excitement. "Cupcakes!"

"Okay, you got it." I kiss the top of her head and hand over her iPad, then climb into the driver's seat.

I'm pulling away from the curb when Hayden's name appears on the dashboard with an incoming call. Grinning, I hit the green Answer button.

"Hey, Cas. I'm in the car with Isabela," I say quickly, giving him the heads-up.

There have been a few close calls where he's called me and was about to spill some filthy talk until I let him know the kids were in the car. We've both learned our lesson.

"Hey, Jax. Hey, peanut."

I glance in the rearview mirror to see Isabela hiding her toothy grin behind her elephant.

"It's Hayden. You gonna say hi?"

She shakes her head, but she's still smiling.

"She's gone all shy," I chuckle.

His laugh is like a smooth caress through the car speakers. "I was just calling to see how the appointment went."

I relay everything the specialist told us about the changes we need to make at Isabela's school, the additional support groups I need to enroll her in, and the changes we need to make at home.

"They recommended I create visual aids to show her when I will be home because I don't have the most structured home environment, especially during the season, and establish some clear routines."

"What does that mean?"

"Well, when I'm home, it's usually chaotic because I'm just happy to be home with them. My mom is the one with the structured routine, and that goes out the window as soon as I'm home with them."

That was something that was hard to hear. That I might have been doing more harm than good. But I'm ready and willing to do whatever's necessary.

"That's doable. Even if you apply what your mom does, then add in some extra dad time."

"True, and they mentioned a behavioral chart. Like stickers or tokens to reinforce positive behavior."

"Which will be hard for you," Hayden laughs softly. "You know you'll need to do the same for Ryan so she doesn't feel singled out."

I pull up to a stop light and scrub my face, thinking about the conversation I need to have with Ryan too. "Yeah,

I know. It's a good thing he's such a good kid that he won't bat an eye."

He hums. There's a small beat of silence. I can hear Isabela murmuring to herself in the back, and I quickly glance in the mirror to find her fixated on the iPad that's playing an episode of *Bluey*.

"Is there anything I can do?" he finally asks, and my smile is instant.

This man.

He never fails to make me feel like I'm nineteen all over again, feeling giddy when my crush first spoke to me in the locker room.

"Not that I can think of right now, but honestly, my brain feels like it's overflowing. I'll probably need a few days to figure everything out, and I'll have to fill Laura in on everything."

And that's a conversation I'm dreading the most. No doubt she'll blame me for something.

"Okay, well, you know where I am if you need me, and I'll see you in a few days anyway."

"We can't wait." I catch Isabela's eyes in the rearview mirror. "Can we, peanut?"

She hides her giggle behind her toy.

"I'll take that as a yes." I can hear his smile in his voice. "Are you doing anything fun this afternoon?"

"Just heading to Jacob's shop, then we'll probably get hot dogs before we pick up Ryan."

"Wow, watch you don't go too wild with that. Coach might have you doing bag skates."

"If I could flip you off right now, I would," I warn, but my cheeks are aching with my wide-set grin.

"I'll let you go and speak to you later."

"Okay." I swallow and lower my voice, even though it won't make any difference because Isabela will still hear me regardless. "I miss you."

"I miss you too, Jax. Later."

We hang up with the promise of speaking later and I pull up outside the front of Jacob's Delicious Desserts. The bell rings when we walk inside, and I let go of Isabela's hand. She runs to the glass cabinets and places her hands flat on the glass to peer in.

"Hey, Jackson." Alex smiles, then rests his elbows on the counter and leans across. "Hey, Isabela. Is your Daddy treating you to a cupcake today?"

She nods silently.

"She was brave today, so I said I'd treat her to either cake or ice cream, and she chose cake," I say, running my hand over her head.

"Good choice." Alex stands back upright and props a hip against the counter.

"Hey, Jackson!" I hear Jacob shout from the kitchen. "I'll be with you in a sec!"

"He's mid-decorating a custom order," Alex explains. "So, how's things? I haven't seen you since Thanksgiving."

"All good. Did Blaine tell you we're going on a toy drive next week?"

"Yes," he chuckles. "Well, I didn't find out from him, I found out from Elliot, who is *very* excited about it. Did you ever have those baby harnesses for the kids when they were little?"

I furrow my brow at the change in topic. "Uh, yeah, why?"

"I think you might need to bring them for Elliot because you'll lose him based on how much he's looking forward to it."

I huff out a laugh. "I'll keep that in mind."

"Daddy, I want this one." Isabela tugs my hand for me to follow. She points at a vanilla cupcake covered in rainbow sprinkles. When I look up at Alex, he's already on it.

"This one?" He points, and Isabela nods. He puts it on a plate and slides it across the counter. I pull out my wallet, but he waves me off. "You're family."

"Alex," I argue.

"Nope. We don't charge family." He waves his hand in the direction of the booths. "Go take a seat. I'll bring you a coffee over."

I stuff a twenty in the tip jar when he turns his back, then lead Isabela over to the booths. I help her peel the cupcake wrapper off and grab a handful of napkins because no doubt we'll end up in a mess. Alex joins us with a steaming hot cup of coffee and a cream-cheese-filled bagel.

"We're trying something new," he says, sliding the plate across the table. "If you don't want it or don't like it, I won't be offended."

"Oh, wow, thanks."

It's not until I take the first bite that my stomach rumbles loudly. Shit, I think I skipped lunch.

"So, how's Hayden?" Alex asks.

I swallow down my bite of bagel and glance up. His eyes sparkle with a knowing look. I'm about to open my mouth, ready to play dumb, when Jacob comes rushing out of the kitchen.

"Wait! Don't answer that without me!" He quickly walks

over and nudges Alex with his hip to move up so he can sit down.

My gaze darts between the two brothers. Both of them are wearing matching bright expressions.

"How is Mr. Tall, Blond, and Handsome?" Jacob asks. He lets out a happy sigh and props his chin on his hand.

"Don't think we didn't notice the tension between you at my wedding." Alex smirks.

"Or how you came downstairs pretty much together at Peyton's Halloween party," Jacob adds.

"*Or*—" Alex's lips tip into a wicked grin as he continues. "—the way you kept making heart eyes at each other at Thanksgiving."

I shoot my gaze down at Isabela. She's not paying any attention to us as she's too engrossed in eating her cupcake.

"You two are hellions," I grumble under my breath. "We might be seeing each other."

Jacob lets out a loud "whoop," and Alex fist bumps the air.

"I think Hayden's great. He's done so much for Blaine over the years. And let's be honest, he's really easy on the eyes."

"Don't let Blaine hear you say that," I chuckle.

Blaine's oddly possessive over Alex, something I know Hayden likes to wind him up about whenever he can.

"Eh, it's all part of the fun. But seriously, I'm happy for you both."

"Me too," Jacob agrees. "And I'm assuming this is on the DL?"

I nod, lifting my hand to rub the back of my neck. "Uh, yeah, it is."

Alex mimics zipping his lips. But Jacob scrunches up his nose. "Ethan's the one who pointed it out, so I can't exactly stay secret. But he's the only one who knows!"

This doesn't surprise me in the slightest. Ethan has always been so observant.

At the mention of his partner, I seize the opportunity to change the subject. "How's his recovery going?"

"It's all going well, except he's bored. I think with this being his first season in retirement and having to spend it resting, it's been a bad combo, but he's getting there."

"Daddy," Isabela whines quietly and holds up her frosting-covered hands.

While I'm wiping her hands clean with a napkin, Jacob must have gotten up and boxed up a few more cupcakes because he slides a box in front of me on the table.

"One for Ryan and yourself and another one for Isabela." He smiles.

"Thank you."

He gives me a wink, then lowers his voice. "Let me know when Hayden's next in town. I'll make sure you have some more of those and let you in on a little secret that'll bring a whole new meaning to if you use too much frosting, it won't fit in your mouth."

My jaw drops open.

Is he implying what I think he is?

Alex drops his face into his hands and lets out a strangled groan.

There's a flurry of heat sizzling in the bottom of my stomach at the thought of indulging in Hayden in a different way.

The next day, I decide to pay a visit to my old captain after practice. Ethan was the first guy to welcome me to the team when I was traded from Buffalo. Of course, with him being the captain, it was only natural he was the one to welcome me into the fold, but he went that one step further than my previous teams. He made sure I knew that he was there if I needed anything, and that included watching my kids sometimes.

Isabela and Ryan adore him too. So much so that they like to FaceTime with him on a weekly basis.

I fired off a text to Jacob asking if he was home when I left the rink, and he let me know that while he was at work, Ethan was—or should be—at home and to let myself in. But despite the open invitation, I still rasp my knuckles on the door before I let myself in and kick off my shoes.

"J?" Ethan calls out from the living room. "You're home early. Something up?"

"Wrong J." I round the corner and flash a wide smile.

"Jackson, hey. What's up?"

"I thought I'd come see how my old captain is holding up."

I sit down next to him where he's sitting on the couch with his leg propped up on the coffee table, crutches resting at the side.

"Less of the old, thanks," he grumbles. "It's okay. I'm fucking bored out of my brains, though. Who knew TV was so shit, eh?" He waves a hand at the wall-mounted TV that's showing a sports talk show. "These presenters don't know squat either. Have they always been this shit?"

I laugh. "I've gotta hand it to you because I don't think I'd cope with daytime TV. It's *Bluey* in our house, all day, every day."

He grunts and turns the volume down.

"So, how's the knee? What have the doctors said?" I ask.

"Not a lot. Just that it's healing as it should be, and I'll hopefully be done with them soon." He points to the crutches. "But I've gotta admit, I'm glad I waited to do it now and not while I was still playing because I think I would've pushed myself to be back on the ice sooner than I was ready. Though, now I hate that Jacob's waiting on me."

"Maybe he wants to wait on you. You ever thought of that?"

"He's too good." His lips tip into a small smile beneath his scruff. "Anyway, enough about me. Jacob mentioned you're dating Cassidy."

I lean back into the cushions and huff out a laugh. "Wow, news spreads fast, huh?"

He gives me a bored look. "Don't act like it was some big secret. If you were trying to keep it under wraps, you did a shit job."

I let out a choked laugh. It's not like I can deny it.

"Yeah, it's fairly new, but we… uh…" I run a hand through my hair. I might as well be completely honest about everything now. "We actually used to date when I was playing for Boston."

This time, he doesn't try to hide his surprise. His eyebrows lift, and his mouth drops open. He blinks at me for a beat, then shakes his head slightly. "Wow, okay. Well, I didn't see that one coming."

"That was kinda the point. We worked hard to keep it a secret because we didn't want anyone to know."

Ethan's brows furrow as his expression turns thoughtful. "Huh, you know, that makes a lot of sense."

"What does?"

"I've known Hayden for a long time. I don't know him well enough to consider us friends, but enough that we'd acknowledge each other whenever we were in the same place." He rubs the scruff on his jaw. "He always seemed like he was running from something. I'd heard some talk that he dabbled in drugs, which wasn't my scene at all, but it seemed like he had some demons he was fighting. And now that I think about it, it kinda happened after you were traded to LA."

I drop my gaze. There's a cold, hollow feeling in my chest. Did my trade trigger his downward spiral? We haven't had the conversation yet on what truly happened between us, but was it the beginning? He never touched drugs when we were together, despite a few of our teammates doing the occasional line or two.

I struggle to swallow from the heavy lump forming in my throat.

Fuck. Did I fail him? Did I give up on us too soon? Did I miss the signs that he was hurting and was pushing me away to protect himself?

"He was running from himself, I think." My voice cracks slightly.

When I look back up, Ethan's smile is sad.

"It makes sense. Sometimes our biggest demon is our own minds. I mean, *hell*, I spent a long fucking time allowing my fear of history repeating itself to rule my life. We're conditioned to believe that we're strong, and emotions are for the weak, but ultimately, the only people we're hurting by doing that is ourselves."

Ethan told me all about how he fell in love with Jacob while on summer break in London but was too chickenshit to show his underbelly and take what he wanted because he had been burned in the past. It almost cost him Jacob. But he managed to pull his head out of his ass and go for what he wanted, fear be damned.

Maybe I need to take a page out of his book.

"I guess I'm just scared," I admit.

"Because you've got more than just yourself to think about now?"

I nod.

"Eh, kids are more resilient than you think, but I get it. It's natural to be cautious, given you've gone through a divorce and moved states, but if everything in you is telling you this thing between you and Hayden is right..." He shrugs. "Sometimes you've just gotta go for it because life's too short for regrets and questioning the 'what could have been.'"

Ethan's right. Everything inside me is screaming that this is it. That he was my first love, but it was the wrong time for us back then. Hayden has slotted back into my life better than he did before, and I would be a fool to ignore the magnetic connection between us. He's proved himself tirelessly. My heart yearns for him, and I know it could go one of two ways. It could be the best thing, or it could destroy me more than it did before.

"You're good at this, you know."

He arches a brow. "What's that?"

"Being the one who gives good advice. Carter mentioned the talk you gave him when he and Zach were figuring things out, and Alex and Blaine adore the shit out of you."

He rolls his eyes, but it doesn't do anything to dampen the smile that appears on his lips. "I'm gonna start charging you all for my time."

"Hey, I should get it for free, considering I've taken on the role of team dad, apparently."

He snorts. "Good luck with that."

We pass the time chatting about the season and our plans for the holidays. Before I leave, I fetch him a coffee, then slip on my coat.

"Oh, I know what I was going to ask you. Jacob mentioned letting him know when Hayden's back in town and something about if there's too much frosting, it won't fit in your mouth?"

For the first time ever, the top of Ethan's cheeks turn pink. He blushes. Fucking *blushes*.

I bark out a laugh. "Holy shit! Are you telling me that he was on about something sexual?"

"Fuck off," he grunts, but it's only half-hearted. "Get out of my house."

I hold my stomach and bow over with laughter. "I never knew you had it in you."

"I didn't. I had it on me." His eyes widen, and then he blanches, realizing what he said. "Don't you dare tell the guys. They won't let me hear the end of it."

I hold my hands up in surrender, but I'm still struggling to breathe. "It's in the vault, I swear." I take a deep breath, trying to calm myself down. Once I've stopped wheezing, I ask with a smirk, "But you recommend it, yeah?"

He shoots me a glare with his dark brown eyes, then gives the slightest of nods.

I slap him on the shoulder. "You're a good man, Ethan Parkes."

He huffs in response. I turn and head toward the door, stopping when he calls out my name.

"Talk to Hayden. Be vulnerable, and go for what you want."

"I will. Thanks."

I say goodbye and head back into my car, feeling a lot lighter than I did before.

Chapter Twenty

Hayden

I wince from the bitter wind coming in from the lake. I pull my hat further down over my ears before stuffing my hands in my coat pockets. When I lived in Boston, the winters were brutal for me after my injury. It was almost like my bones had become meteorologists and could sense the change in weather before it happened. But as the years have gone on, it's only become worse, which is why I now call California my home.

Sure, sometimes the winters there can get cool, but it's nothing like this.

I've only been out of the car for less than two minutes, and already my knees are beginning to feel stiff. The wind is making it feel like mid-twenties.

"It's just a short walk," Jackson tells me while he unbuckles Isabela from her car seat. We had to park near Millenium Park as the first parking lot we tried was full. Ryan stands next to me on the sidewalk, decked out in a Thunder hat and scarf, and the sight makes me smile.

"Where we going, Daddy?" Isabela asks, holding on to his shoulders when he lifts her out and sets her on the sidewalk.

"To a Christmas market," he replies, shutting the car door and locking it. "No running off, okay? Either of you. There's going to be a lot of people, so you need to hold my hand at all times."

"You got it, Dad." Ryan nods, stepping next to Jackson, ready to take his hand once Jackson's finished putting his gloves on.

Isabela looks up from beneath her hat. It's white with the Thunder logo on and a big fluffy pom-pom on top. But it's so big on her that it's fallen over her eyes. She pushes it back with her mitten-covered hands and shocks me when she asks, "Can I hold Hayden's hand?"

Wait, *what?*

My head snaps to Jackson as his gaze immediately meets mine. I must not be doing a good job at hiding my surprise because his lips twitch, breaking out in a smile. "If you want to, peanut. As long as Hayden doesn't mind."

I have to swallow hard as emotion gets stuck in my throat. Shit. Am I going to get all emotional because a four-year-old wants to hold my hand?

It's because she's his *four-year-old.*

I look down at her and smile. "Of course you can." I hold my hand out to her, and my heart swells in my chest as she takes it with an excited squeal.

Is this what it feels like to be chosen? Like when a dog picks you out of a room full of people for a cuddle?

Ah, hell. Now I'm comparing Jackson's daughter to a dog. I didn't mean it like that.

Jackson's expression is filled with pride as we make our way toward Daley Plaza, one of the locations for Chicago's annual Christkindlmarket. Our hands brush against each other, and I sneak glances at him. I want to grab hold of his hand so badly, but I understand that he doesn't want the kids to be confused before he's had a chance to talk to them. Something he doesn't want to do until *we* have spoken, but we're both dancing around it. Digging up the past sucks, even if it's necessary for us to move forward in our relationship. He deserves to know that I was the reason our relationship ended, and it wasn't because of anything he did or didn't do.

My steps falter when we turn the corner to Daley Plaza, and I notice the line to enter the market wraps around the corner.

Standing still in this cold weather is hell for me.

"Uh, Jax. I don't suppose you can use your Thunder pro-athlete status to jump the queue?"

He chuckles. "I'm afraid it doesn't work here. Maybe if I played baseball, it would be a different story."

The image of Jackson in tight baseball pants and an unbuttoned shirt appears in my mind. His golden chest glistening with sweat. His round ass threatening to split the seams of his pants.

Fuck. Maybe I need to make this happen, like a one-man strip show.

I suppress a groan. And because he knows me so darn well, he arches a brow and throws a smirk my way. "You okay over there?"

"Mhm," I hum, mentally stashing the thought away to bring up later.

He laughs, and we join the end of the line.

It takes twenty minutes by the time we get into the market, and my body is aching. I'm trying to hide my discomfort because Isabela is also crabby at having to wait. Jackson had to carry her for a bit, all while she hid her face in his neck and grumbled, but now she's back to holding my hand, leading me toward the hut that sells mini Dutch pancakes.

"Look!" She points at the menu board and jumps excitedly. Then she looks up at me with big, innocent blue eyes and asks, "Buy me some?"

I practically melt into a puddle on the floor, but Jackson swoops in before I can pull out my wallet.

"Isabela, that's not how we ask for things, is it?"

"It's okay—" I stutter.

"No. She knows that's not how she asks for things."

She sticks out her bottom lip and lets out an almighty sigh like she's just worked a seventy-two-hour shift. "Can I have some, please?"

"That's better."

"I'll get these." I glance over to Jackson, looking for his approval.

He shakes his head. "No, I can't let you do that. They're twelve dollars for some pancakes."

"Jackson," I scoff. "I earned eight million a year. I'm pretty sure I can buy your kids some pancakes."

We end up in a stare-off as he has an internal war with himself, but eventually, he caves with a sigh. "Okay, but only this once."

"Noted." I wink, but hopefully, this won't be the first and last time we get to spend the day together like this.

Like a family.

I order three trays of the mini pancakes with strawber-ries and melted milk chocolate. We find a table to sit and eat next to some outdoor heaters, and the warmth is an instant relief. I slide the tray in front of her, and Isabela beams up at me. Her soft "thank you" makes me want to run back to the stall and buy her twelve more.

"These are so good. Thanks, Hayden," Ryan says between bites. Somehow, he's managed to get chocolate all around his mouth.

"So good you had to shove your face in them?" I tease.

Sighing, Jackson picks up a napkin and hands it over to Ryan.

"Jesus, can't take you anywhere," he murmurs, causing Ryan to laugh.

I dig my fork into a juicy strawberry and mini pancake, making sure to get plenty of chocolate, and then I hold it out in front of Jackson. His blue eyes sparkle as he eyes the food, then back at me.

"What?" he asks.

"Try it." I edge the fork forward. "Tell me how good it is."

The tip of his tongue darts out to wet his bottom lip, and then he leans forward and opens his mouth. Just as he's about to take a bite, I raise my hand and get chocolate on his nose. Both kids burst into giggles, and I grin wickedly.

"You sh—" he curses, but I cut him off before he can finish.

"Hey, the kids are present. You've gotta be nice to me."

His eyes darken with heat. He grips his hand around my wrist and brings the fork to his mouth. Keeping his eyes locked on mine, he wraps his lips around the fork and pulls the food into his mouth.

"Mmm," he moans while he chews. "So good."

"You've still got some…" I motion to my nose with my fingers.

"Daddy," Isabela giggles. "You got chocolate on your face."

With a roll of his eyes, he picks up a napkin and wipes it off, but the corner of his lips is tilted up.

"That was funny," Ryan chuckles, and I lean over the table to give him a high five.

Jackson and I finish our tray in a more civilized manner. There are no more chocolate incidents, but he doesn't stop with the heated glances and brushing of his knee against mine under the table. Ryan fills me in on how his hockey training is going, and once the kids have finished and their faces have been cleaned up of chocolate, we make our way around the rest of the market.

When we line up for the specialty hot chocolates that come in souvenir mugs, his hand finds the base of my spine beneath my coat. I lean back into him, loving the warmth of his hand over my sweater.

"What can I get for you?" the woman asks when it's our turn.

"Three hot chocolates in the souvenir cups and one child-size hot chocolate," Jackson says.

"They have gingerbread cookies!" Ryan points to the menu board.

"And two gingerbread cookies," I chime in, earning another high five from Ryan.

"Yes!" Isabela chants, clapping her hands.

I shift to pull out my wallet, but Jackson drops his hand to curve around my hip and squeezes. He gives me an *I don't think so* look and taps his phone on the card reader.

"Why don't you and Iz grab that table," Jackson suggests, pointing to a high-top table to the left. "Ryan can help me carry the drinks over."

I hold my hand out to her, and she grabs hold of it, marching me over to the empty table. She twirls around the table post, then stops in front of me and beckons with her mitten-clad hand.

I try to hide my grimace as I crouch down, my hips and knees protesting the movement. Fuck, it's like my bones are grinding together.

"What's up?" I ask her quietly.

She eyes me for a moment, suddenly turning all shy. I catch Jackson's eyes the second she wraps her arms around my neck. His eyes widen in surprise, but his broad smile hits me square in the chest. My breath hitches. I wrap one arm around her, not quite sure how to take this sudden burst of affection. My eyes burn despite the frigid weather, and I quickly wipe at them when she takes a step back, then returns to twirling around the table as if she didn't just shift my world on its axis.

All the pain that spikes through my body when I stand back upright is ignored because holy fucking shit. I'm stunned by the realization of how significant this is. Jackson has told me all about how Isabela doesn't take too well to new people, and here she is, openly offering her affection to me after a couple of weeks.

It's not just Jackson's heart you're at risk of breaking by being a fuckup. It's theirs too.

I squeeze my eyes shut, trying to push the negative voice away. I know I can't think like that. I've worked too hard to allow the voice to win when I'm finally in a good place. I can't allow the doubt and the anxiety to ruin what could possibly be the most perfect thing I'll ever have.

Jackson and Ryan carry the hot chocolates over to the table, and he must sense that I'm struggling to keep my emotions in check.

"You okay?" he asks quietly, brushing his hand over mine when he hands over my drink.

"Yeah," I croak. I give a shaky nod and clear my throat. "Yeah, I am. Wow, these look great."

"Did you know they use a special whipped cream, so it cools it down a lot quicker than an ordinary hot chocolate?" Ryan tells me.

I glance at Jackson, silently asking, *How is he so grown-up?* But he answers with a shrug.

"Daddy!" Isabela appears from under the table and jumps up and down at Jackson's side, tugging on his arm. He scoops her up with ease, holding her up in one arm, and takes a sip of his hot chocolate. It has a scoop of homemade whipped cream and a small gingerbread cookie. She plucks the cookie from his mug and takes a huge bite, then proceeds to spray crumbs everywhere when she bursts into a fit of giggles at his shocked expression.

"Did you just steal my gingerbread?" He mock gasps. "Isabela Wilde, you little thief," he tsks, which only makes her laugh harder.

"Can't take her anywhere." Ryan rolls his eyes, echoing Jackson's words from earlier, and I snort with laughter.

As I watch the three of them laugh and joke over the

stolen gingerbread, I make a silent oath that while I'm on this earth, I'll never do anything to risk hurting them. I'm still a work in progress, and I'm never going to be truly fixed, but they are quickly becoming my entire world.

And I'll do anything to protect their happiness.

Chapter Twenty-One

Jackson

I gently close Ryan's bedroom door behind me and pray that my kids will sleep through most of the night. They were pretty wiped out from being outside all day at the market, and they fell asleep the second their heads hit the pillow. I purposely kept them awake for as long as possible in hopes they will sleep in their own beds tonight.

Because I *need* some alone time with Hayden.

I need to touch him without the worry that one of my kids will wake up and need me to lie with them.

And I need to taste him more than I need my next breath.

When there's no sound coming from either of their rooms, I rush downstairs as quietly as I can. I find Hayden in the kitchen, chopping up the leftover strawberries we had to buy on the way home because Ryan wanted to recreate the pancakes we had earlier.

"They go to sleep okay?" he asks, tilting his head to look at me. His hands are covered in juice from the strawberries.

And when he raises his hand and sucks his thumb between his lips, my eyes zero in on his mouth.

Is he trying to kill me?

"Yeah," I say absentmindedly and stalk toward him. I take hold of his wrist, bring his hand to my mouth, and suck each of his fingers into my mouth one by one.

"*Jackson*." His breath hitches, and a visible shiver travels down his body.

Our eyes lock in a heated stare. I swirl my tongue around the tip of one finger, loving the fruity taste and the taste of *him*. His lips part on a shaky breath, and his eyes flutter closed.

With his wrist still in my grip, I pull his finger from my mouth, then duck my head to his neck. I run my nose along his throat, then flick my tongue over his pulse. A low moan escapes him as he tilts his head back.

I trail open-mouthed kisses up his neck, grazing my teeth over his jaw before taking his lips. His moan is muffled when I slide my tongue into his mouth. He tastes like strawberries and a hint of the whiskey I poured him at dinner. My cock thickens in my briefs at the sound of his low mewls.

"How about we put those in a bowl and head up to my room?" I murmur against his lips.

He gives a jerky nod. I let go of his wrist, and he hastily tosses the strawberries into a bowl with shaky hands, causing some to bounce out of the bowl.

"Cas," I say softly. I step up behind him, curving my hands around his hips and kissing the back of his neck. "There's no rush."

"What if they wake up?" he whispers.

"They won't. They're out for the count. We've got a few hours at least."

He presses back into me, pushing his ass against my groin. "Then take me upstairs, Jax."

We pick up the bowl of strawberries, and I fetch the left-over melted chocolate. I let Hayden head up the stairs first, admiring the way my sweatpants stretch over his ass. When we're in my room, I lock the door and flick on the bedside lamp. I had already closed the curtains earlier, so I waste no time pulling my sweater off and tossing it onto the floor. Next goes my jeans, then my socks. Hayden watches me under hooded eyes the entire time.

"What are you thinking?" he asks, voice slightly raspy.

"I'm thinking—" I take a step closer and twirl my finger through the drawstrings on his sweatpants and pull him toward me. "That I do some coloring of my own." I close the gap between us and nip his bottom lip. "Take off your clothes, Cas. Let me see your sexy-as-fuck body."

He shudders and shoves the bowls at me. I take them willingly. He removes his clothes with trembling hands. I let out a hot breath when I see his cock is fuller than normal. He's not fully hard, but he's harder. I've had to remind him a million times since that first night that him getting an erection isn't my goal when we get naked. My goal is for him to feel immense pleasure and enjoy himself, and so far, I've succeeded.

I place the bowls on my bedside table. The strawberries are so juicy there's a pool of juice at the bottom of the bowl. I glance at my white bedsheets, then head into the bathroom. Grabbing a towel, I lay it on top of the duvet.

"Lie down. On your back," I demand.

With a smirk, he presses a knee on the bed, then lies flat on the towel. I waste no time straddling his thighs, then hook my fingers into the waistband of his boxers. Searching his eyes for approval, he gives a subtle nod. I toss his boxers on the floor and bend down. I run my nose along the underside of his shaft, inhaling his musky scent, and brush my lips over his tip.

"*Fuuuck*," Hayden hisses. His hand grips my hair as his hips arch off the bed.

I make my way back down, nuzzling his sac before sucking one of his balls into my mouth. I give the other a hearty suck, then lick a path up his semi-hard shaft until I reach the tip. I wrap my lips around him, bringing him into my mouth. He bites down on his fist and thrusts his hips up. It's easier to take him deep because he's not fully erect, and I don't pay no mind to the fact he's not getting any harder. But that's okay because the way he's writhing and moaning beneath me tells me he's feeling every ounce of pleasure.

After several minutes of reveling in the taste of him and the feel of him on my tongue, I release him with a pop. He's breathing heavily, chest rising and falling quickly as he catches his breath. I kiss him, deep and hard, before reaching over to grab one of the strawberries. His chest is covered in delicate linework, and I start by tracing the outer edges with the berry, leaving a trail of juice.

"Ho-ly shit," Hayden gasps, watching me with dark eyes.

My lips tip in a smirk. When I'm done with the outline, I take a bite out of the end, causing the berry to drip with juice, and begin to fill in the rest. I do the same with a few other tattoos, then bend down and lick the strawberry juice from his skin in slow, teasing sweeps of my tongue.

"Fucking hell, Jax." He shudders beneath me.

I work my way down his torso to the top of his thighs, alternating between using the strawberries and melted chocolate. I shift so I'm lying on my stomach. He spreads his legs, making room for my wide shoulders. The move gives me a perfect view of his hole, and the need to be inside him becomes a desperation.

Bringing my fingers to his mouth with my free hand, I rasp, "Suck. Get them nice and wet."

He sucks three fingers into his mouth, and I stifle a moan. While he's sucking and working my fingers with his tongue, I run the strawberry over his thigh, drawing over one of his tattoos with the berry before licking the juice with my tongue.

He releases my fingers with a hot gasp. "I'm ready."

I don't need to be told twice. I throw the berry into my mouth and trace his rim with my spit-dampened fingers before slipping one inside him. He takes me with ease, his body relaxed and satisfied. I add a second, then a third. Without removing my fingers, I sit on my haunches and pick up his leg with my free hand. Bending his knee, I rest his ankle on my shoulder and angle my head. I press gentle kisses over the scars on his knees then spread the berry juice over his calf. I catch a wayward drip with my tongue, all while pumping my fingers inside him.

"Fuck me, Jax," he begs. "Please. I—" He moans when I curl my fingers against his prostate. "I need you."

I let go of his leg and halt my hand, fingers buried deep to the knuckle. Popping the strawberry into my mouth, I place my free hand on the pillow beside his head. I hover over him, loving the feral look in his eyes. His need is palpable, and it's taking everything in me not to devour him like the starved man I am for him.

I bite into the berry, and the sweet flavor bursts in my mouth. I let the juice trickle down my chin as I chew then swallow, and the fire in his heated gaze only grows. He grabs the back of my neck and smashes his mouth against mine.

My fingers move in time with the glide of my tongue against his. We swallow each other's groans, and it's not long until I'm grinding my hard cock against his thigh. Hayden drops his hands to my hips and tugs my boxers down under my ass.

"Off," he murmurs. "Need you."

Reluctantly, I pull my lips off him and slip my fingers free. I quickly discard my boxers and grab a condom and bottle of lube from my bedside table. I sheathe myself and lube up, then curl my hands underneath Hayden's knees. I watch his expression for any kind of discomfort or pain as I bring his legs up to my ribs, but there's nothing except brazen heat radiating in his eyes. I line up my cock at Hayden's entrance, but I don't push inside right away.

"You're so fucking hot," I tell him, skimming my hands over his thighs and up his flank. They end their journey in his hair, and my lips hover devastatingly close to his, but we don't touch. "I want to spend an entire day where you're naked the entire time. Where I can touch you whenever I want. I can kiss every inch of you. Trace your tattoos with my tongue. Feast on your cock and spend hours tasting your hole, loosening you up so good so I can slide my cock inside you."

I thrust my hips, and he bites back a moan as the head of my cock breaches the first ring of muscle.

"Yesss!" he breathes. "I want that. I want that so fucking bad, Jax."

"I want to ravish you until you're begging for me. And when you're too spent for more, I want you to watch me fuck myself with my dildo so you can see exactly how I'll ride you when the time is right."

"Fuck, Jackson." He squeezes around my cock, and I hiss through gritted teeth. "You have no idea how badly I want to be inside you again."

I pump my hips in shallow thrusts, sinking deeper with every stroke.

"Is that right?" I ask in a horny rasp.

"Yeah. I dream about you riding me. Straddling me with that big body of yours." He bites my lower lip hard, and the shot of pain sends heat down my spine.

"Tell me more."

"Sometimes, I'm waiting in your hotel room after a game—*ahhh!*" he moans when my cock tags his prostate. "And I'm already naked and hard when you come in and strip out of your suit."

"Then what?" My voice is gravel.

"You climb onto the bed and sink down on my cock. Your hard body ripples as you bounce on my dick, and you don't care about the goals you've just scored because the only goal you care about is my come filling your ass."

The picture he's painted is vivid in my mind. It's exactly how we used to spend our nights on the road. Sneaking into each other's hotel rooms, being prepped and ready to fuck because we were at risk of being caught. And I can't deny it made sex on the road all the more hotter. I was hungry for him all the time.

"Fuckin' hell, Cas," I growl. "I want that too."

His arms wrap tightly around my shoulders. His fingers curl into the hair on the back of my head while the others dig into my traps. My hips piston inside of him, picking up pace as I chase my release. The noises he makes are the sweetest sounds I've ever heard, and I have no doubt he's feeling this same intense sense of pleasure like I am. His semi-hard dick is trapped between our stomachs, and I roll my hips in a way that makes my happy trail brush against the underside of his dick.

"Gonna come," I warn him, and seconds later, I'm filling the condom with my release. I drop my head to hide my face in his neck, his name a feral cry on my lips.

Unable to hold my weight up any longer, I carefully lie on top of him, my spent cock still inside the warmth of his body. His hands soothe over my skin, trailing over the taut muscles in my back and massaging my scalp.

My heart is so fucking full for this man. His gentle love, his kind heart. The way he's so good with my kids. His slow smile when he catches me watching him.

I want to tell him I love him. And that I don't think I ever really stopped. I want my soul to be next to his for the rest of my life. I want to be with him through everything. The ups and the downs, the good and the bad. I want to be the one to wait on him and to care for him on the days he struggles.

I want to spend every day showing him how much he's loved. How he's worthy of every good thing and that he's the most incredible person I've ever known.

I want it all with him. I just hope he wants the same.

Chapter Twenty-Two

Hayden

"This is nice," Jackson says sleepily, his fingers lazily drawing the shape of a heart on my back. "I could get used to this."

"Mmm," I hum because I'm unable to form actual words. I'm feeling spent and languid after our second round in twenty-four hours. The pleasant ache pulsating throughout my body is a reminder that it isn't anywhere near as fit as it used to be. But I'm not complaining because it means I get to be next to Jackson.

His mom, Christie, came to pick up the kids and take them to school this morning while Jackson headed off for an early practice. He got back a little over an hour ago, and as soon as he finished the brunch I prepared for him, we hopped in the shower together before ending up in his bed. We haven't moved since. He's got a game tonight, so the kids will stay at Christie's house, and that means we have the house to ourselves until tomorrow. A whole night together. It's like Christmas has come early.

It should be embarrassing how much I'm looking forward to waking up next to him. Although I haven't told him just *how* excited I am to spend the night in his bed. I didn't want to risk him thinking I don't want his kids around, but I also haven't wanted to admit that something fractures inside me every time I have to make the silent walk across the hall to the guest room at night.

I get why I have to do it. I really do. But it doesn't make it sting any less.

We've been dancing around the subject of the old us for weeks now. Every time I'm about to bring it up, he changes the subject. And when I see that thoughtful expression pass over his face like he's about to bring it up, I distract him with my mouth. But we need to talk about it. Even if it's just for the old version of us to heal and not allow it to impact us as we grow into the new version of us.

Gathering up the courage, I suck in a steady breath and hope for the best.

"I guess we should talk about what happened between us before," I begin.

As much as I want to stay nestled into the side of his warm body, I push myself up and sit back against the headboard. Jackson does the same, tugging the sheet up to cover our naked bodies.

"Yeah, I guess we should."

My skin suddenly feels hot and tight. Fuck, I can do this. We've come so far, and this is what I've been working toward all this time. I need to own my mistakes and make sure he knows it's not going to happen again.

"I wanna start off by saying nothing I'm going to say excuses what I did to you or my behavior. I regret it deeply, even now. If I could go back and change it, I would." I instinctively start picking at the skin around my thumbnail as my heart rate begins to spike.

He places a hand on my thigh and gives it a reassuring squeeze. "I know."

"I'm not gonna lie, I was a fucking disaster when you were traded. I felt like the rug had been ripped out from beneath my feet, and I didn't know what to do." I rub my face with my hands, then tip my head back and stare up at the white ceiling. "I got it into my head that when you'd get to LA and meet all these new people, you'd realize that I was a waste of space. That you would realize you'd be better off without me."

There's a moment of silence, and the sadness in Jackson's voice when he speaks is like a stab to the heart. "What hurt was I kept telling you I was willing to do the long distance, Cas, but it was like you didn't seem to hear me. Or you didn't want to listen to what I had to say."

I pick up my glasses from the bedside table and slip them on as I turn to face him. His brows are furrowed deep over his nose, the corner of his lips tipped in a frown. I smooth my thumb over the crease on his forehead, and his face relaxes under my touch.

"The voice that gets into my head wouldn't let me hear you. I had spiraled so low at that point. You could've asked me to marry you, and I wouldn't have believed you."

"Do you think…" He swallows hard, seeming to contemplate his words carefully. "Do you think that's when your depression started? When I was traded?"

I shake my head. "Roberta doesn't believe so. She's been my therapist for six years now. She said it stems from before that. Maybe even to my teen years and the pressure I was under from a young age. You know I didn't have the most stable upbringing. I spent more time with billet families than my own, and I developed some unhealthy coping mechanisms along the way."

Jackson takes hold of my hand and interlaces our fingers, resting them on his thigh. "I wish you would have talked to me about it. We could have figured it out together."

"I know, but I was so scared of losing you, Jax. I wasn't thinking clearly. I thought that if I ended things first, it would save me the heartbreak when you inevitably left me. Like if I hurt you, then you couldn't hurt me." I let out a strained noise. "I was such a fucking coward. God, I was so immature and such a fucking coward, and it took me a long time to come to terms with that."

He gives my hand a squeeze. "Maybe. But maybe I was too. What would have happened if I didn't give up so easily? If I had noticed the signs that you weren't yourself instead of turning my back on you with my tail between my legs…" He trails off.

"You wouldn't have had those incredible two kids," I point out, giving him a small smile. "There's so many things I wish I had done differently, but all I can do is make sure I do the right thing going forward. Maybe in some fucked-up way, this is how it was supposed to be for us. Right person, wrong time, and all that, you know? Except now you've got two awesome mini yous, and I'm in a lot better place than I was. But the thing is, Jax, I'm never gonna be perfect, and I'm never gonna be 'fixed.'" I air quote with my fingers. "I'm gonna have bad days."

"I don't want to try and fix you, Cas. Plus, being perfect is overrated."

I arch a brow. "I'll remember that next time you have a tough game and you're overly critical of yourself for not being *perfect*."

He huffs a laugh and rests his head back against the headboard. Those blue eyes are still locked on mine, his thumb skimming over my knuckles in a soothing caress. "I want to be here to help you. Through the ups and the downs. I know it's going to be tough some days, so I don't want you to hide your struggles from me."

And that's something I'm going to need to unlearn. I've spent so many years putting on a facade that everything is okay. Wearing a mask to shield how I was really feeling. But if we're going to do this, I need to be open. From what's going on in my mind to the extent of my pain. I've only had two people in my corner for the last six years. Zara and Roberta are the only ones who I've allowed to see the real, raw struggles, and it's going to take wading through an ocean of anxiety to let Jackson in.

And hope that he doesn't change his mind about me when he realizes how shit it can get.

"Will you always be honest with me if I get too much?" I ask in a whisper.

He sits up and raises his hand to cup the side of my face with his palm, his thumb tracing the shape of my lips. "You will never be too much, Hayden, but yeah, I'll make sure I communicate better this time around."

It was never your fault, I want to tell him, but I'm already feeling more emotionally drained than I was expecting to be having this conversation. Instead, I close my eyes and kiss the pad of his thumb.

"Will you tell me about Zara?" he asks, dropping his hand back into his lap.

I blink at him, not expecting him to bring up my ex-wife.

"What about her?"

"How did you meet? And what happened between you two? Last I heard, she cheated on you with Connor Dubinsky?"

I let out a small, surprised laugh, which only causes him to raise his brows in surprise.

"We're probably breaking every divorced couple code because as exes go, she's pretty awesome. I met her at a fundraiser in Boston. It was something for the foundation. You know how they are. Lots of booze. Everyone is wearing suits and dresses showing a lot of skin. We got chatting, and things went from there. I thought if I could have the picture-perfect life on the outside, then somehow, it would fix me on the inside, but it didn't. It didn't stop the emptiness that seemed to thrive inside of me."

His thumb runs over the back of my hand again, reminding me he's there like a gentle anchor.

"But she didn't cheat on me. Our relationship had fizzled out long before I retired, but we decided to file for divorce once I was in therapy. But I was so afraid of people seeing me differently. I wanted them to continue seeing me as the golden boy of the NHL or whatever the fuck they used to call me. I didn't want them to see me as this weak, pathetic person that I was. I was still clinging on to a narrative that had died along with my career, but Zara… She came up with the idea to divert the attention away from me when news of our divorce got out. I hated the idea, and I didn't want her to be seen in such a bad light, but she pleaded for me to go along with it. As long as I continued to get help. She was dating Connor by that point, so it was plausible."

Jackson's watching me with a sense of understanding and sadness in his brilliant blue eyes.

"She was protecting you," he says softly, and I nod.

"Yeah, she was. Even now, she's fiercely protective over me, which is nice, you know? She and Roberta have been all I've had, but I want her to live her life for her now. She and Connor want to get married and have kids, and I don't want her to be worrying about me."

"It sounds like she's the type of person who's going to worry about you regardless of where she is in her life."

I give a thoughtful hum. It does sound about right for Zara.

"Thank you for opening up about it. I know we can't do anything to change the past, but I think we both had a lot of growing up to do." He leans over and captures my lips in a tender kiss. "But we're here now, and I'm really glad to call you mine again."

My eyes widen a fraction. We haven't spoken about labels or discussed what "we" are. In my mind, we're together. Boyfriends. Partners. But hearing him call me "*his*," putting that claim on me like we used to… It's everything.

"You mean that?"

"Yeah, I do." He grins. "You've always been mine in one

way or another. Maybe I just loaned you to Zara for a while."

I snort out a laugh. "Loaned me?"

"Borrowed, I dunno." He shrugs, still grinning. "Better than saying I lost you."

"You never lost me, not fully. I was still there emotionally, I just… took the wrong path." I take his face in my hands, sifting my fingers through the blond strands on the side of his head. "But it ended up putting me exactly where I needed to be."

Chapter Twenty-Three

Hayden

To say I was surprised when Jackson asked if I wanted to take care of the kids this afternoon would be an understatement. He had a full day of team obligations, and Christie had an unexpected appointment she needed to attend after she did the school run. I've been a nervous wreck all day because this is a big deal.

Yeah, I took care of them when they were sick while Jackson was at his game, but this time, they're healthy. They're running around, making a lot of noise—and also a lot of mess—and it means I have an even bigger chance of fucking things up.

"Hayden! Check this out!" Ryan calls out from the family room.

I round the table to where he's got his mini goal set up, but he's not using his mini sticks. No. He's using his full-sized stick and a real puck.

Christ. I can just see it now. How will I explain a broken

window to Jackson? He'll never leave me unsupervised ever again.

"Whoa, no. No pucks in the house," I quickly say, reaching down to pick it up. "Where are the foam ones? Or the foam balls?"

"In my room," he says with a sigh. "But it's such a long way."

I scoff. "Ryan Wilde, you're telling me you want to be a professional hockey player, but you can't run up a small flight of stairs to get a puck? What's your dad gonna say when he comes home to the Lake Michigan wind blowing a mess in the family room 'cause you broke a window?" I raise a questioning brow.

Isabela giggles from where she's sitting in the corner of the couch, iPad and elephant in hand.

Ryan rolls his eyes and sighs again defeatedly.

"Okay," he drawls. "I'll go get them."

I take the hockey stick from him, and he runs upstairs. Turning to Isabela, I sit on the edge of the couch. She's warmed up to me a lot, but sometimes she still gets overly shy, so I always let her do things on her terms.

"What do you wanna have for dinner? Your daddy says you like mac and cheese."

Her eyes light up, and she nods.

"Okay, we can do mac and cheese, and then maybe we can have ice cream cookie sandwiches after."

"Yay!" she cheers.

Ryan comes back downstairs with a bucket of foam pucks, and I show him a few different stick-handling techniques until it's time to start dinner. They busy themselves by doing some coloring, and then I sit with them in the living room while they eat and watch *Bluey*.

"I'll wash up, then I'll make us some ice cream cookie sandwiches," I say, taking their bowls into the kitchen.

I'm rinsing up the saucepan when the front door opens, and I make quick work of drying my hands. Jackson's home a lot earlier than I was expecting.

"Hey!" I call out, but when I round the corner, I freeze.

Because it isn't Jackson standing in the hallway.

"Mom!" Ryan jumps up from the couch and wraps his arms around Laura.

"Hello! Surprise!" She beams, catching Isabela when she throws herself at her mom's legs.

She does a double take when she spots me, eyeing me curiously between greeting the kids and responding to their mile-a-minute questions. All I can do is stand there.

Well, this is awkward.

"Oh, hi. Christie mentioned you were with the kids. Where's Jackson?" she asks, glancing around as if he'll pop out from under the stairs.

"Uh, he's doing a toy drive with the team. He should be back soon."

This is the first time we've ever met, and I'm not sure whether she knows who I am. Judging by the friendly smile on her face, I'm guessing Jackson didn't tell her about us.

"Oh, cool. Sorry, I'm being rude. Hi, I'm Laura," she says when she untangles herself from the kids. She walks over to me with an extended hand. "I'm their mom."

"Yeah, I know," I reply dumbly and shake her hand. "I'm Hayden."

"It's nice to meet you." She smiles.

Yeah, she has no idea who I am.

"I'm…" I motion to the kitchen over my shoulder. "I'm about to make ice cream cookie sandwiches for the kids. Would you like one?"

"Sure!"

"Why don't you, uh, take a seat and spend some time with the kids? I'll bring it out."

She flashes me another dazzling smile and heads into the living room with the kids, who are talking her ear off.

Taking the ice cream from the freezer and cookies from the pantry, I scoop a serving of ice cream, placing it on one cookie before placing another on top, squeezing it gently so the ice cream spreads out in the middle, then place them in a bowl. My hands are trembling from the anxiety beginning to brew inside of me.

Is she going to tell me to leave? Tell me that I have no right looking after the kids or tell me that she doesn't approve of Jackson's and my relationship?

Fuck. What if she makes his life hell because of me?

You're overthinking things, my conscience says, sounding a lot like Roberta's voice.

Maybe, but I'm not sure how I'm supposed to play this. One side of me wants to tell her she's too hard on Jackson. How she needs to give him more credit, considering he's the main parent. How she doesn't really have the authority to criticize him when she's the one who comes for a few days every couple of months. But then the other side of me wants to keep my lips sealed tight. To just nod and play nice because I don't want to make things more difficult for him.

Sighing, I slip my phone from my pocket and text Jackson to let him know Laura's here. He responds almost instantly to say he'll be home within the hour as they're finishing up.

Okay. I can do this. I can survive an hour with the love of my life's ex-wife.

Taking a deep breath, I pick up the bowls and carry them into the living room, where Isabela's showing Laura some pictures she painted at school and Ryan's showing her his recent math test results.

"Here you go!" I say, handing over the bowls. The kids take them from me with an enthusiastic thank-you, and then I hand the other to Laura.

"Thank you, this looks great," she replies.

I sit down in the chair, letting Laura and the kids take the couch, and quietly eat my dessert. Episodes of *Bluey* play on a continuous loop, and I end up so engrossed in the show I don't realize it's gone eerily quiet.

I glance over to where Laura's standing behind the couch, hands resting on the back of the cushions.

"The kids wanted to watch a movie on the big screen," she clarifies, pointing to the open door that leads down to the theater room.

"Oh, yeah, that's a good idea."

Silence falls again, and it's so fucking painful. I subtly look at my watch. Where the heck is Jackson? Doesn't he know I need saving right now?

"So, how do you know Jackson?" she asks, clearly not picking up on the awkward tension radiating from me.

"We used to be teammates. Played together in Boston."

Surprise flicks over her face. "Oh. I know Jackson loved his time in Boston. Well, until it was all ruined after he was traded."

Ruined. You ruined it.

I ruined his memories of his time in Boston.

I ruined the joyous moments he had.

I ruined it.

There's a numb sensation between my ears, like time is slowing and being dragged under a metaphorical wave. And Laura continues talking, completely oblivious to the dark pit I'm falling into.

"He was seeing someone there, I'm sure you know. But Jackson genuinely thought they were going to spend the rest of their lives together. He was thinking about where he would propose, where they would get married. He had planned out how they would spend their retirement. The whole thing. He was completely in love with them. Then he got the call he was traded."

My throat closes up. Fuck. I can't breathe.

He was going to propose to me?

You ruined his life. You don't deserve him.

Numbness travels up my legs and my arms.

She throws her arms up in the air and shakes her head, disgust written all over her face. I'm not sure whether the disgust is aimed at me or, well… me. Because clearly, she has no idea that she's referring to me.

"It was like he was just… abandoned! He had to move to this strange city where he didn't know anyone."

My chest becomes impossibly tight at the thought of Jackson, confused and alone and hurting over the trade. Over leaving me.

Over how you ruined his fucking life.

"He was screwed over, big-time. I know we're divorced, and while I'm not in love with him anymore, he's still the father of my kids, you know? I still care for him. But if I ever meet the person who could do that to Jackson… I'll be sure to give them a piece of my mind. Who *does* that to someone? Just cut them off like they meant nothing? And to say they never really loved him?" She exhales a sharp breath. "What a fucking asshole move. They never deserved him."

You didn't deserve him then, and you don't deserve him now.

I stand up in a rush. Dizziness washes over me as all the blood goes straight to my head.

"Yeah," I manage to croak out. "Excuse me, I need to… uhhh…" I point toward the stairs and hastily make my way up to the spare room where I've been staying.

The pain in my knees and hips is like fire as I take the stairs as quickly as I can. I need to get out of here. I need to go before I ruin Jackson's life again. I don't want to be weak. I don't want to make the same mistakes that I made before, but Laura's right.

I didn't deserve him then, and clearly, I don't deserve him now because the voices in my head are louder than my conscience.

Once I'm inside the bedroom, I fumble for my phone, and my voice is shaky as I send a voice message to Roberta.

"Roberta, I need to see you. Tomorrow. Please. I…" My voice cracks. "I'm… I'm not as strong as I thought I was… I…" I gasp for air and squeeze my eyes closed. "Tomorrow. Please."

I hit Send, knowing she'll be there waiting for me.

Like she always has been.

Dropping my phone on the bed, I fetch my bag and

begin throwing in my clothes and toiletries. Then my phone vibrates on the bed with a text message.

ROBERTA

I'll be here, but Hayden. You're stronger than what your mind is telling you. You are worthy. You are deserving of goodness. You are loved.

She follows it up with a video of her jellyfish tank, and I don't know how many minutes pass while I watch the video on repeat. It's only when I hear the front door closing that I snap back to the present.

He's home.

Glancing to my bag on the bed, tears well in my eyes, and I let out a choked sob.

Maybe this time was all we were supposed to have. I just hope he can forgive me for what I'm about to do.

Chapter Twenty-Four

Jackson

I'm working with one of the rookies and Peyton on some passing drills when Coach Harris blows his whistle so loud we all wince.

"Fuck, I hate when he does that," Peyton groans, rubbing his ear dramatically with his glove.

"Tendy Olsen, let go of my forward, or get off my ice," Coach calls out.

I glance up the other end of the ice to see Elliot's holding on to Blaine's waist from behind, in full goalie getup, while Blaine drags him around the ice.

"He's taking me on a tour," Elliot replies. I can hear the smile in his voice. "I've carried him on my back through a majority of my career. It's only fair that he returns the favor."

Coach blinks at him as Blaine continues to skate around, and then his head whips toward me and Peyton. "Am I having some kind of weird caffeine dream, or have I been around them for so long that it makes sense?"

I snort a laugh. "Probably the latter."

Blaine's skate blade gets caught, and he topples forward, causing Elliot to fall on top of him. They burst into laughter. Blaine pushes Elliot off, and then they both lie on their backs.

"Someone spin me!" Blaine shouts, his arms and legs out wide.

"Me too!" Elliot adds.

Kendrick is the first to skate over and uses his stick to push Blaine. Then, once he's spinning around in a circle on the ice, he does the same to Elliot.

"Sometimes I wonder if I run a daycare," Coach grumbles under his breath.

I look at Peyton. "You wanna join in, don't you?"

"I really do," he laughs. "It sucks being the responsible adult—" I choke a laugh. "Hey! I am!"

"If you say so, bud."

But before Peyton can skate over, Coach blows his whistle again. "Hit the showers. Don't forget, we're heading out on the toy drive this afternoon. So be out by the bus in thirty minutes." He taps his stick on the ice before leaving the ice.

I head into the locker room to shower and get dressed in jeans and a team-branded hoodie. The Chicago Thunder Foundation does a toy drive every year where we buy gifts for children in the Chicagoland area who are spending the holidays in the hospital. We're split into groups and given a list and an age range, and then we have to fill our carts with gifts that fit the demographic.

It's one of my favorite things to do. Knowing we can put

a smile on kids' faces. I always donate outside of the foundation too, but I do that away from the team.

Forty minutes later, we're wearing fresh jerseys, and I'm paired up with Zach. We have our list, and we're buying for ages five to seven.

"I didn't realize there were so many Barbies," Zach announces, gaping at the entire aisle filled with Barbies.

"Oh yeah. I'm pretty sure Isabela has more than this. She likes to leave them on the stairs sometimes."

He laughs. "And I bet you find them early in the morning when you're half-asleep and bare-footed?"

"You got it."

We take a side each and pick out the listed amount of Barbies and place them in the cart.

"What are your plans for the holidays? Are you able to see Carter?" I ask.

"Yeah, he's flying in on the twenty-third. He has a game the night before, then he needs to be back on the twenty-sixth, but I'll take any time I can get with him." He shoves his hands into his pockets. "How about you? What have you got planned?"

We're less than two weeks away from Christmas, and I haven't done any shopping. My mom has picked up some gifts for me, but I haven't had the chance to go anywhere. Or even buy a tree.

Jesus. I'm really slacking this year.

I want to ask Hayden to stay for Christmas. We can put up the tree together with the kids. Maybe decorate a gingerbread house together. We can head downtown and go gift shopping, as long as he isn't in too much pain. Then, we can wrap them up in front of the fire with a glass of wine. Maybe the wrapping turns into kissing.

An image of Hayden's face appears in my mind, lit up by the soft glow of the tree lights, making his gray eyes sparkle. My heart does a flip in my chest. Fuck, I love him so much. If there was a Santa in here, I'd ask if I could sit on his knee, and my one wish would be, *Can I keep Hayden?*

But there is no Santa. Just my teammate watching me with a perplexed expression, waiting for me to reply.

"I, uh, haven't figured it out," I say, running a hand through my hair. "Haven't really had a chance to think about it with hockey and sorting Isabela's support groups out."

We chat as we make our way around the store, stopping to pose for photos and film clips for the team's social media. Then we round the next aisle and almost collide with the twins. Elliot's sitting in the cart, toys piled on top of him.

"I fuckin' love doing this!" He beams, then holds up a *Star Wars* Darth Vader mask. "Hey, Zach, look!" He holds it up to his face and quotes the iconic Darth Vader *"I am your father"* line.

"I'm terrified," Zach deadpans, but his lips twitch with a smile.

"I know, right!" Elliot grins. "I love shopping for gifts."

"It's true," Blaine chimes in, passing a few more things to Elliot to put inside the cart. "If you ever need someone to get you a gift, ask this guy."

"I'll keep that in mind," I chuckle.

"You guys almost done?"

"Yeah, just a few more things to get." Zach waves the laminated sheet we were given.

"Cool. Us too. The cart's getting heavy." Blaine goes to push it, but he ends up having to push it with his chest to get it moving.

"Maybe because you've got a goalie in there. I don't think the kids will want that at Christmas," Zach jokes.

"Oh, that was mean!" Elliot throws a stuffed toy and hits Zach in the face. It falls onto the floor, and both Zach and I stand there, not moving to pick it up. "Noooo! Save the unicorn!"

I'm about to open my mouth to tell him maybe he should get out of the cart and pick it up himself, but Coach Harris rounds the corner and beats me to it.

"Get out of the cart, Olsen," Coach pipes up from behind us, his own cart overflowing. His eyes land on me. "Daycare. Seriously."

I smother my laughter with my hands, but I wouldn't have them any other way.

By the time I pull up to my house, there's a sense of unease in the pit of my stomach. While I told Laura what happened between me and Hayden, I never told her who he was. I wanted to protect us, protect him, even though we were no longer together. Maybe I broke our vows by keeping it a secret from her, but it was a choice I made, and I don't regret it.

The house is quiet when I go inside. I can hear noise coming from the theater room in the basement, but the TV in the living room is off. There's no sound of chatter, and something about it causes my spine to stiffen.

"Hey," I call out, hanging my coat in the closet.

Laura appears from the kitchen, her eyes wide with worry. "Hi. I, um, I think you need to go check on your friend. I think he might be sick. I didn't want to go up and see if he was okay, but we were talking, and he went really pale and started sweating. Do you think he's sick? What if he passed it on to the kids?"

I pinch the bridge of my nose, trying to take in everything she just said.

"He's upstairs?"

She nods, wringing her hands in front of her.

"Okay, I'll go see him. Are the kids okay?"

"Yeah, they're watching *Inside Out*."

I nod and head up the stairs. I don't bother knocking on the door to the spare room because we're beyond that. And while him sleeping in this room is only temporary, he's still the man I love.

The first thing I notice is his bag on the bed. It looks full, like he's packed, and then my eyes land on him sitting on the edge of the bed. He's staring aimlessly at the wall. His eyes are red and puffy behind his glasses. His hands are in his lap, and his nails are short, bitten down as far as they'd go, along with the skin around them. Some look to be bleeding.

I've never seen him like this before. So completely... broken.

"Hayden," I say cautiously. I don't want to spook him, but I need him to know I'm here for him. Especially if he's spiraling.

I step in front of him and break his vacant stare with the wall. My heart falls to the pit of my stomach when he looks up at me.

"*Cas*," I croak, reaching up to cup his face with my palms, but he flinches. "What's going on? Talk to me."

His gaze is distant when his eyes meet mine.

"I ruined your life."

What?

"No, you didn't. Where is this coming from?" I furrow my brows, my panic rising.

"Have you ever been so scared of failing someone that you question whether they would be better off without you in their life at all? That you love them so wholly, so fucking completely, that you would give up your life, just to spare them any ounce of pain you might cause them?"

My eyes start to burn. I blink quickly, trying to fight off the tears that are close to falling.

"Hayden, what's happened?" I ask, but he continues.

"Because that's how I feel for you, Jackson. I would do anything for you, absolutely anything, and hearing I ruined your life..." He shakes his head as tears begin to fall down his cheeks. "I need to make sure I'm worthy of you, Jackson, because you and your two kids..." He sucks in a ragged breath. Each word is pained when he speaks. "You're everything I've ever wanted. A family. And I don't know if I'm too broken to ever make this work."

My mind is reeling. Did Laura say something to him? That's the only thing I can think of. He was okay this morning. He seemed happy with the kids this afternoon when I checked in on him after practice. The only thing that could have caused him to spiral was Laura.

"You didn't ruin my life, Hayden." I curve my hands around his neck. "I need you to listen to me. We put the past in the past. I'm not hurting over that anymore, Hayden, because you know why?" I squat down between his legs until we're at eye level. "You've shown up for me. You've shown up for my kids. You've shown me that you have a big fucking heart and that you care. You've shown me that you're fucking strong because despite whatever lies your mind is telling you, you were strong, and you got the help you needed."

Tears fall down my cheeks, but I refuse to wipe them away. I need him to see I'm serious about this. About us.

"I love you, Hayden Issac Cassidy. I've always loved you, and I will continue to love you. I'll love you so fucking hard you won't ever question it."

He drops his head and lets out a pained sob.

"I... I need to see Roberta." His eyes are full of agony when they meet mine again.

"Do you want me to come with you?" I say automatically. Because I will. I'll drop everything. The kids will be okay with my mom, or maybe Laura can even step up. I'll call Coach and tell him I can't play and to scratch me. Fuck the team. Fuck hockey.

But before I can suggest any of it, he shakes his head. My throat is lined thick with emotion. I swallow hard, trying to push the weight down.

"I need to do this on my own, Jax." His voice is hoarse. "I need to see Roberta. I need to work on some things so I can make sure I'm worthy of you."

How can I deny him this? He's telling me what he needs, and that's to see his therapist. How can I stop him from doing that when he's clearly in a dark spiral I'm unable to pull him out of? I feel helpless, but I love him too much to let him suffer for my sake.

Taking in a deep inhale through my nose, I dig my teeth into the inside of my lip and angle his face to look me in the eyes. "If this is what you need to do, I will support you with whatever you need. But you're not giving up on me, Hayden. You're not giving up on *us* because it's not just my love you have now. It's Ryan and Isabela's. They fucking adore you to the moon, and maybe I'm being a jackass by mentioning how fucking upset they'll be if you don't come back, but it's the truth. You have a family here who love you, Hayden, and you have a home. Here. With us. And we'll be waiting for you, whenever you're ready to come home to us."

"I'm sorry," Hayden whispers before letting out a heart-wrenching sob.

I catch him in my arms, holding him as tightly and closely as I can. I wish there was something I could do to take away this excruciating internal war he is battling.

My own heart is breaking as I kiss the side of his head over and over, telling him I love him repeatedly while holding him as he crumbles.

By the time I follow him down the stairs to the door, I'm feeling hollow. My eyes are tight from shedding my own tears, and I'm lucky the kids are still in the theater room and won't witness me about to lose it when the love of my life walks out the door.

I have to trust that he's coming back. I have to trust that all he needs is to see his therapist and this isn't him saying goodbye for good.

I have to because I won't be able to cope if I think otherwise.

I wait while he puts on his shoes and coat, and then I grab him by the lapels and pull him close.

"You're not giving up on me, Cassidy. I won't allow it," I say quietly. "I fucking love you, and I won't let whatever your head is telling you, get the better of us. Of what we've got."

His gray eyes fill with tears again. He gives a jerky nod and presses a fleeting kiss to my lips before slipping out the door to where a car is waiting for him.

I let out a heavy exhale, running my hands through my hair while I stare at the closed door.

"It was him, wasn't it?"

I turn around at the sound of Laura's voice. She looks genuinely distraught, hands wringing in front of her like she always does when she's worried.

"Your first love. The one from Boston," she says when I haven't responded. "The one who broke your heart."

I nod.

She grimaces. "I'm so sorry, Jackson. I had no idea it was him, but I stand by the things I said."

"What did you say to him?" I ask, and then she tells me everything.

"I told him the truth, that you were heartbroken and felt abandoned. I thought he knew because you were teammates."

"Fuck!" I squeeze my eyes closed. I'm not going to tell her he's been spending the last six years working on himself to believe he is worthy of me because it's not my story to tell.

"Just because we're not married anymore doesn't mean I don't care about you. He hurt you. Badly."

"It was fourteen years ago!" I bellow. "And I don't think you have the right to come in here, into my house, and preach about what you think *I* deserve."

She startles at my outburst, but I'm vibrating with so much emotion. Heartbreak, fear, anxiety. I'm scared, and I'm so fucking pissed that Laura caused him to spiral.

"That man has shown up for me, and for our kids, when I never asked him to. He has proved time and time again that he is *worthy*. He has shown more love to our kids in these last few months than you have. You make me feel like *I'm* not good enough of a father for our kids. It's *my* fault Isabela has separation anxiety. It's *my* fault she needs additional support."

My voice gradually gets louder, and I'm thankful for the soundproof basement because the kids don't need to hear this.

"Jackson—" she goes to argue, but I don't let her interrupt.

"I will do anything for my kids. Anything. I will make sure they have everything they could possibly want or need in life, all while having the job I do. I don't even know who I am anymore outside of being a dad and playing hockey. I've let go of everything to be the best dad I can be for those two kids."

I take in a deep breath, trying to calm the war inside of me but feeling relief pour out of me with every word as they get off my chest.

"I'm not perfect. I know that, but I'm damn well trying my best, Laura. You made your choice clear when you chose your career over the kids, and I accepted that. I didn't judge you, or belittle you, or make snide remarks about how you barely spent time with them. No. I let you live *your life* how you decided it."

I take a step toward her, and with a calm voice, I say, "Those kids love Hayden, and I'm pretty sure he loves them too. Now, let me live my life the way I want to and in a way I believe is best for my kids and get the fuck out of my house."

Chapter Twenty-Five

Hayden

"Can I get you something to drink, Mr. Cassidy?" the flight attendant asks. Her name badge reads Mona.

This is probably the easiest flight she's been on tonight because I've been too numb to do anything except sit here and disassociate from the fact I'm a fucking asshole.

"No, I'm fine. Thanks, Mona." I force a smile.

She returns to the galley, and I go back to staring out at the dark sky. Rain splatters against the window.

I regret the way I handled everything with Jackson. I allowed the darkness in my mind to take control and cause me to spiral. Because holy shit, did I spiral. I haven't had a moment like that in a long time, but the things Laura said triggered something inside me. Something that I worked hard on healing, but hearing the things she said about me, even inadvertently, just tore through all the progress I thought I'd made. And I'm ashamed of myself for letting it happen.

I'm going to be so lucky if Jackson gives me another chance.

I fucking love you, and I won't let whatever your head is telling you, get the better of us. Of what we've got.

His words from before I left have played on a loop in my mind since the door closed behind me. He might say that now, but once he's had time to calm down and think clearly, he might not feel the same. Though, there's nothing I can do right now. I'm on my way back to California, and Roberta will be waiting for me at 9:00 a.m.

I will work through this. I won't let this beat me.

I just hope he meant it when he said they would be waiting for me.

The plane jolts when it hits some turbulence, then again a few seconds later. I glance over to Mona. She holds on to the countertop and carefully makes her way toward the cockpit. The door slides open, and I hear the captain say we're going to hit some rough air and she needs to take her seat.

Spine stiffening, I double-check my seat belt before looking back to Mona.

"Mr. Cassidy, the captain has requested for you to keep your seat belt on. We're expected to experience some heavy turbulence," she says, just as the plane shudders.

She stumbles backward, and I quickly reach out to steady her, stopping her from falling back.

"You got it, Mona. Don't worry about me. Go take your seat."

She holds on to the counter again for support while she makes her way back to her seat and does up her seat belt.

Minutes later, the entire plane vibrates as we hit it. I'm

bouncing in my seat, thankful I'm secured with the seat belt, otherwise I'd most likely be on the floor right now.

My heart drops into my stomach like a brick. I shoot a panicked gaze back to Mona. Her eyes are closed, lips pressed in a thin line. Her hands are clutched tightly in her lap like she's trying not to show that she's uncomfortable.

If a flight attendant is nervous, then this can't be good.

The dark part of my brain tries to take over again. The shadow that resides permanently in my head since I fucked up my life, but I won't let it win again. Not for a second time today.

I know, logically, nothing bad is going to happen. I've experienced turbulence several times over the years, but with how my anxiety is heightened right now, I can't help but think negatively. And unlike those times when I'd stand in the ocean and wish for the waves to take me away, I don't want this to be it. No matter what happens, I won't let go of the tiny glimmer of hope in my chest that this isn't how our story ends.

I need the opportunity to make things right.

Taking out my phone, I unlock it and tap on Jackson's name. My heart wrenches on the last text I received from him.

JACKSON

Let me know when you get back to California. I love you, Cas.

Then I take a deep breath and hit the button to begin recording a voice message, trying to keep my voice steady as I speak.

"Hey, Jax. I know you're sleeping right now, and I hope

the kids don't wake you up too early. I wanted to say I'm sorry for how I left things tonight. I hate the fact you saw me that way, and I hate that I allowed that part of my mind to win." I swallow roughly and turn my head to focus on the rain pattern on the window.

"I'm ashamed of how I reacted. I shouldn't have let Laura's words get to me the way they did. She didn't say anything I didn't already know, but hearing her say it out loud… It fucking hurt, Jax. And I know we said we were going to put the past behind us, but I'm so fucking sorry for what I did to you. But if I get the chance to make things right… I've been thinking… Maybe I could look for a place in Chicago. Somewhere nearby because I don't expect to move in with you, especially when you're working hard to establish stability and structure for the kids. I can keep my house in California. Maybe we can stay there in the off-season. We can take the kids to Disneyland and spend our days on the beach. I could teach Ryan to surf. I think he'd really like that."

I smile at the memory of showing Ryan and Isabela the photos of the beach outside my house. Their excitement had me looking at it through a different lens. They peppered me with questions about the wildlife and whether I've seen any sharks.

"But most of all, I'd like to spend every day with you. I want to spend the rest of my life waking up next to you and falling asleep in your arms. I'd like to spend Christmas mornings with you, watching the kids open their gifts with so much excitement they don't know what to open first. I'd like lazy Sundays with you, making pancakes and stealing kisses whenever the kids aren't looking. I'd like to grow old with you—well, *older*, because fuck, Jax, that day we went to the market made me feel about one hundred and three."

I let out a choked laugh, then bite down on my bottom lip, digging my teeth into the flesh. Just so I can feel something other than the fear lacing through every fiber of my being. I know he can most likely hear the shuddering of the plane that seems to only be getting louder. "I hope I'm not too late, Jax. I hope that you can forgive me for the pain I put you through, both tonight and all those years ago. I hope that you'll let me make it up to you by loving you every day for the rest of my life. I love you, Jackson Wilde. I love you so fucking much," I confess, my breath hitching on those last few words.

I release the button to stop recording and blink away the tears in my eyes before closing them tight. Digging my fingers into the soft leather of my chair, I grip onto the armrest and imagine Jackson's smile and the sweet sound of the kids' laughter and hope we can get through this storm so I can hear it again outside of my imagination.

We land safely in LAX several hours later. Both Mona and I shared worried glances throughout the flight, and I tried to distract her by asking her questions about what she did outside of work and where her favorite places to travel were. It seemed to help both of us, and soon enough, we were out of the worst of it. She told me all about her nephew and how he plays hockey. He's around Ryan's age, only he lives in Oregon. We joke that maybe they'll face off against each other in the future.

As much as I enjoyed talking to her, I'm glad the flight is over. I'm exhausted. Physically, mentally, and emotionally. My hips and knees ache to the point I'm unable to walk smoothly to the front of the plane.

The captain smiles as I shake his hand. "I apologize for the bumpy ride."

"You must have nerves of steel because I sure didn't back here," I chuckle. "But thank you for getting us all here safely."

"It's my pleasure. Hopefully, it didn't stop you from flying with us again."

"Of course not," I say truthfully, then turn to Mona and offer my hand. "Thank you for your company tonight. And make sure to email me, and I'll get you some signed merch for your nephew."

She gives me a soft smile. "Thank you, Mr. Cassidy."

"It's Hayden." I wink, giving her hand a small squeeze. "Take care," I say to them, then duck my head through the door.

I tense instantly, unprepared for the cold wind. I take the first few steps and wince. My joints feel like they're grinding together, and then it hits me. With everything that's happened tonight, I forgot to take my medication. I'm going to be paying the price tomorrow.

I go to grab the handrail, forgetting my phone is in my hand. It slips free, and I watch, wide-eyed, as it bounces off the tarmac.

"Fuck," I mutter and continue to make my way slowly down the steps. When I pick it up, the screen is completely smashed. I guess I'll be making a stop by the mall after I meet with Roberta in the morning because I don't want Jackson to be worrying about me.

The following morning, 9:00 a.m. on the dot, I'm sitting on Roberta's aqua-blue couch, locked in a daze watching the jellyfish bob around the tank. The light is currently purple, and it's almost like the tension from the last twenty-four hours is seeping out of me, limb by limb as they float around in such a gentle ease.

Roberta sits in her chair, feet tucked beneath her, notebook in hand. There's a coffee on the table in front of me, and she sips on a matcha.

Minutes go by while we sit in silence. She knows I need this time watching the jellyfish to come back down. I wish I could own some of my own. Maybe that would help keep the bad days to a minimum. I looked it up once but then convinced myself that I would only kill them because I travel for work, and I'd be useless, but I don't think that now.

"Are they easy to keep?" I ask, pointing to the tank.

"Yeah, they're relatively easy. They require regular water changes. I usually change weekly, but not a full change. And as they require a certain temperature environment, you need to check often that everything is as it should be, but other than that, they're pretty maintenance-free."

I hum my approval. Okay. That's not so bad. Maybe I can get some when I find somewhere in Chicago.

"Thank you for reaching out to me yesterday, Hayden. I can imagine that was a difficult thing to do."

I sit forward to pick up my coffee and take a sip before replying. "Yeah, it was. I handled it all wrong, though."

"In what way?" she asks.

"Well, I shouldn't have let Laura's words get to me, first of all. She didn't say anything that wasn't true, but it still hurt to hear it. Then I just surrendered to the voices in my mind emphasizing everything she said."

"Can you tell me what she said to you?"

I suck in a deep breath and relay everything Laura said, including what went through my mind.

"I can understand that would be very upsetting to hear. Sometimes hearing the impact of our actions from someone else can feel a lot more significant." She takes a sip of her drink and makes a note in her book. "Did you speak with Jackson before you left?"

"Yeah, I did. He…" The vision of him with hurt in his eyes and tears falling down his cheeks is something I never want to see again. "He was really upset, but he said he understood why I needed to come back to see you."

"You told him your return to California was purely to see me?"

"Yeah."

A small smile appears on her face. "That's great, Hayden. You allowed him in. You communicated your needs and allowed him to support you."

Oh, I never thought of it like that. I thought I was running away. Taking the coward's way out.

"He said he'll support me in whatever I need to do, but he's not going to let me give up on them."

"Them?"

"Him and the kids."

She gives me another smile, and this time, I can't help but smile too.

"And are you? Going to give up on them?"

I shake my head vehemently. "No. Never."

"Good, I'm glad to hear it. It's important to remember that you're not a burden for asking for help or expressing what you need. I'm not going to say you're not going to have bad days, but you've widened your support system now. And when you have those bad days, they may become easier to manage."

"They did become easier while I was there. It didn't feel so… heavy, sometimes." I interlock my fingers together in my lap and massage my thumb into my palm. "It was like the storm cloud was there, but being around them kept me dry."

"That's good. I'm glad they could provide that for you."

I take another sip of my coffee and glance over to the jellyfish. The lights turned pink, and it makes me wonder what Isabela would think of them. Would she find them as calming as I do? Maybe we could go to the aquarium when I'm back in Chicago.

Only when I'm living in Chicago, I won't be near Roberta, which brings me to my next topic of conversation.

"I… I was wondering if we could revisit the option to have our sessions via video call."

Her eyebrows lift slightly in surprise. I think this might be the first time I've ever surprised her.

"Of course. Can you tell me what has made you change your mind about doing video call sessions?"

"On my flight back last night, we had some pretty bad turbulence. The worst I've ever experienced, and I don't know if it was because I was already so emotionally charged, but I felt scared. My mind was already in overreaction mode, and I ended up sending Jackson a voice message." I swallow thickly, wondering what he must be thinking after hearing that voice message and not being able to get hold of me because of my broken phone. "I said if I get another chance to make things right, I'd like to move to Chicago so I could be near him and the kids. And that would mean…"

"You wouldn't be close by to have in-person sessions," she says with a smile. "You know that's always been an option, Hayden. I'm happy to adjust to suit you. You being comfortable and safe is the most important factor for me, and if that means we meet via video, I'm perfectly happy with that."

A relieved breath whooshes out of me. "Thank you."

"Anytime." She sips her matcha, then places it on her knee. "Is there anything else you'd like to discuss today?"

There is, but I'm not quite sure how to bring it up. It's not something I've had to mention before because when I was trialing the different medications, having sex was at the back of my mind. But now, I have Jackson. He has reassured me no end of times that being able to get an erection isn't a deal breaker for him, but I don't want this to be my life. *Our* life.

Don't I deserve to remember how it feels to be overtaken with euphoria when you're having sex with the love of your life?

I smile at myself. I do deserve it.

And isn't that a fucking milestone moment?

"I…" I take a deep breath and remind myself, *I deserve*

this. "I have an embarrassing question, but it's something that I'm hoping you might be able to help put a recommendation forward to my psychiatrist."

"Okay. You know there are no embarrassing questions, Hayden. This is a safe space for you," Roberta says softly.

Even though her words bring me a sense of ease, I still shift my gaze to the jellyfish. The lights are green, and they're back to looking like mini aliens.

"I've noticed since I've been on this medication, I… uh… struggle to get an erection sometimes. I ended up doing what you told me not to do and looked it up online. And apparently, it's common for a lot of people, which made me feel a little better because it wasn't just me, but I also saw there's some other medications out there which don't have those same side effects…" I trail off, hoping she will get my ask without me saying the words.

"Yes, it's common to experience side effects such as a reduced sex drive, erectile dysfunction, and/or ejaculatory dysfunction. There are other medications out there, which I can discuss with your psychiatrist, but one thing I'd like to ask first is, how would you feel if we suggested you weaned off the medication?"

My head snaps back to her, my eyes widening in surprise. "No. I'm not ready for that. The thought of not having them makes me really nervous."

She bobs her head a few times, making more notes. "Okay, thank you for being honest. But yes, I can give him a call and let him know what we've discussed and go from there."

"Thank you." I wipe my hands down the front of my pants. "Jackson said it wasn't a problem, but it is for me, you know? It might sound ridiculous, but I feel like I'm not pulling my weight in the relationship. He's okay with it for now, but it's only been a month. Forever is a long time."

Her eyes crinkle at the sides as she smiles widely.

"What?" I ask her cautiously.

"Hearing you talk about forever… Yeah, there's still a negative tone to it, don't think I missed it, but when you walked through those doors six years ago, you wouldn't have looked forward even a day, let alone the rest of your life. I'm pleased to see you have this belief in yourself because you deserve forever."

The back of my eyes burn at the kindness pouring out of every word. She's right. The person I was six years ago wouldn't have even considered being in the position I'm in right now. I would have laughed at the suggestion of being back in Jackson's life. But I'm here. He loves me, and he wants to be with me. Bad days, bad knees, and all.

"Thank you, for everything," I say to her on a shaky breath. "I wouldn't be here without you, and I'll forever be grateful for your faith in me."

"You're welcome, Hayden, but you're stronger than you give yourself credit for."

We finish up our session, and this time, I give her a hug goodbye. It might be unprofessional, but after the last twenty-four hours, I feel like it was necessary.

And as I get in my car and head to the mall to replace my phone, there's only one thing on my mind.

Jackson Wilde.

Chapter Twenty-Six

Jackson

I don't know if it's true what people say about kids being able to pick up on things or whether my kids decided to be tiny saints this morning because holy shit. When they both climbed into my bed at 3:00 a.m., I had to stop myself from crying. I had Isabela curled up against me on one side and Ryan on the other. They wrapped their little arms around me and didn't kick me in the balls once.

But now, there's no possible way of holding back my tears. My hand trembles as I finish listening to the voice message for the third time.

Why... Why did it sound like he was saying goodbye?

I press call on his number again, but it goes to voicemail. All of my texts have gone unanswered. I've sent so many messages on Instagram too, but they're still marked as unread.

What the fuck is going on? He said he wasn't going to give up on us. He said he was coming back for us.

Resting my forearms on the kitchen counter, I bend forward and bury my face.

"Dad?"

I snap my head up at the sound of Ryan's voice, quickly wiping away the tears from my cheeks.

He frowns up at me. "Dad? Are you okay?"

"Yeah, I, uh—" I clear my throat and give him a shaky smile. "Just had a message which upset me, that's all."

I try not to hide my emotions from my kids, especially when I'm upset and vulnerable. I want them to grow up knowing it's okay to be upset and not to bury it down.

Ryan doesn't say a word. He closes the distance between us and wraps his arms around my waist, pressing his head into my stomach.

"It's okay to be sad, Dad," he tells me, and fuck, does it hit me right in the heart.

Shielding my eyes with one hand, I wrap the other around his shoulders as I let out a choked sob.

"Daddy?" Isabela comes running in. She takes one look at us before barreling over to us, clinging onto my leg like a koala. I lean down to scoop her up, sitting her on the kitchen counter. She moves to stand up and wraps her arms around my neck. I hold on to her tight with one arm and Ryan with the other, and I cry.

I cry for the man that I loved fourteen years ago, and I cry for the man I love today. I wish I could make it all go away for him. The pain he experiences as a result of his injury. The self-sabotaging thoughts and the anxious spirals. I wish I could help take it all away for him so he can see how fucking special he is. How fucking loved he is.

"Where's Hayden?" Ryan asks, resting his chin against me as he looks up.

"He…" I clear my throat. "He had to go back to California for an appointment."

"Is he okay?"

Ryan's question startles me. I don't want to lie to my kids, and if things work out the way that I hope they do, they'll be around Hayden when he has his low days. I don't want to shield them in that sense because I believe it's important to show kids that it's okay to ask for help when they're feeling down or to show their emotions when it gets too much. But I also don't want them to worry about him because I will do enough of that for all of us.

"He's going to be okay," I tell him, smoothing my hand over his unruly blond hair. "Sometimes our minds can say mean things to us, and it gets us upset. Sometimes Hayden's mind can upset him, and he's gone to speak to someone who will help him."

Isabela twirls the hair on the back of my head around her finger, head resting on my shoulder as Ryan seems to contemplate my words.

"There were some days that he seemed sad. It was like he was trying not to let it show, but when he thought we weren't looking, he looked sad," he explains, and then he manages to knock me speechless when he adds, "Hayden knows we love him, right? Me and Isabela."

My eyes sting, filling with tears again. Ryan goes blurry, and when I don't answer, the two of them squeeze me again in a hug. It takes me several long minutes to be able to stamp down the lump lodged in my throat and blink them into focus.

"He knows," I whisper with a jerky nod. "And he loves you too."

✕

Hayden's phone still isn't connecting by the time I get to the practice facility. I confided in my mom over the phone after I dropped the kids off at school, and she tried to put me at ease by suggesting maybe he turned it off so he could get some sleep, but I don't think it's that.

Yeah, he would turn off his phone at night while he was with me, claiming he didn't want our time to be interrupted, but there's something in my gut telling me something happened.

And I don't think I can carry on until I know what it is.

I stop by the kitchen lounge first, picking up a granola bar and bottle of Gatorade, then head into the locker room without saying a word. I sit in my cubby and try Hayden's number again.

"Hey, you've reached Hayden Cassidy. Sorry I can't come to the phone right now."

FUCK!

I press the End Call button so hard my knuckle cracks. In all the time we've been together, I never got his address. It never came up in conversation, and it didn't cross my mind to ask him. All I know is he lives in Hermosa Beach.

But there are people in this room who have contracts with him. He and Peyton used to be tight; maybe he's got it noted somewhere.

"Hey, Blaine, do you have Hayden's address?" I ask.

My teammate lifts his head to look at me, his hands

poised midair as he tapes his stick. "Uh, no, I don't think I do. It might be on my contract, but that's somewhere in my apartment. I'd call Alex to check because he did all our wedding invites, but he's at the bakery." He turns to call out to his twin. "El, do you have Hayden's address?"

"No." Elliot shakes his head. "I know it's somewhere near LA, like Malibu? I dunno. Sorry, man."

"I thought it was Santa Monica?" Zach adds.

I can feel my blood pressure beginning to spike. These guys have been in his life for years, yet they don't know where the fuck he lives?

"You're all wrong. He lives in Hermosa Beach," I snap, getting to my feet. "I thought you all considered him a friend, yet in a time of need, you'd be fucking useless."

I know I'm being an asshole, but my emotions are heightened from the lack of sleep and having my heart broken less than twenty-four hours ago. I'll apologize to them later, but right now, my only focus is Hayden.

There's only one other person who can help me, but at this point, I'm not holding on to hope. I head out of the locker room and down the hall to the gym.

"Peyton!" I call out to our captain. I round the corner to the gym and find him on one of the stationary bikes.

"Yeah?" he answers in a breath.

"Do you have Hayden's address?"

His brows furrow as he thinks. "Maybe somewhere? Katy did all the holiday cards and shit. Why can't you text him and ask?"

"Because I fucking can't get hold of him!" I bellow. Why is it so fucking difficult? "He left me a voice message late last night, and I haven't been able to get hold of him. My calls are going to voicemail, and he's not reading my texts." I drop onto the weight bench, my body trembling. I rest my head in my hands, willing my heart to calm down before it beats out of my chest. My voice is so quiet when I speak again it's barely recognizable. "I'm worried something's happened to him."

The familiar whirl sound of the bike's belt comes to a halt, and seconds later, Peyton's dropped to a crouch in front of me. When I lift my head, worry flashes through his blue eyes. Blaine, Elliot, Zach, and Kendrick walk into the locker room wearing matching concerned expressions.

"In what sense? You think he's in danger?" Peyton asks.

Sighing, I shrug. "It's not my story to tell, but potentially. We…" I glance up at the ceiling, unable to meet his gaze. We haven't had the conversation on what we're going to say to people. I mean, I haven't even told my kids, but judging by this morning, I think they already know what Hayden means to me. But these guys standing around me are like family. We support each other through everything. We're there for each other through the highs and lows, both on and off the ice. And if there's a time where I need their support, it's now. Because I'm a whisper away from falling apart. "We've been seeing each other for a couple of months now. We've been taking it slow because it's not the first time we've dated."

Someone gasps. I think it's Elliot.

"You met someone in your rookie year at Boston," Zach states, recalling the conversation I had with him last season while he was figuring things out with Carter. "But it all crumbled when you were traded to LA… That was Hayden?"

I nod. "Yeah, it was."

"Wow, plot twist because I didn't see this coming," Blaine admits.

"I did," Peyton says, surprising me.

"You did?"

"Yeah. I didn't think about it until now, but he's always admired you. He wouldn't let anyone chirp you on the ice or go near you, really. He was pretty reckless when we went out, but he was always more… I dunno, broken, I guess, whenever we played against LA. Then there was how you both behaved at Blaine's wedding." He throws a thumb over his shoulder to where our teammate stands.

"True. Alex mentioned it seemed odd," Blaine agrees.

"Then there was my Halloween party. You two came in matching costumes, then you both disappeared for a while, then you were gone."

"And Thanksgiving," Elliot adds. "You were all heart-eye emoji at each other." He makes a heart with his hands and puts it in front of his face.

I scrub my face with my hands. I guess Ethan was right. We did a shit job at keeping it quiet.

"I don't know what to do. I've been getting his voicemail all morning, and he's not answering any of my texts."

"Mitchy! Get our phones, will ya?" Peyton shouts, and moments later, the young forward comes rushing in carrying all four phones.

"Here you go, Peyton Capybara." Mitch grins.

Elliot hoots and smacks his hand in a high five.

"Fuck you both." Peyton throws up his middle finger over his shoulder and taps on his phone with the other. They take it in turns trying to call Hayden, but as expected... "Voicemail." Peyton frowns.

"What's going on here? Some kind of secret society?" Coach Harris appears in the doorway, arms crossed over his wide chest.

"Jackson has an emergency, and we need to get him on a flight to California," Elliot announces, then practically shouts, "Hermosa Beach!"

"We have time to call someone up from the farm team for tomorrow night's game," Blaine interjects.

"Or we can shuffle the lines around," Peyton suggests, standing up to nudge Blaine. "We can take some extra ice time if needed."

Coach's expression turns puzzled. He holds his palms up. "Whoa, whoa. Slow down. Let's start at the beginning because I feel like I've missed a crucial part of this conversation."

I stand up and step in front of the guys. "Coach, I understand the implications that come with this kind of request, but I wouldn't ask if it didn't come from a place of desperation." Taking a deep inhale, I do something I haven't done in a long time. I put myself first, above being a hockey player and being a dad. "I need to skip today's practice. I'll be back for our game tomorrow night, but I need to go to California and bring the love of my life home with me."

Chapter Twenty-Seven

Hayden

"Do you need anything?" Zara asks, placing a cup of coffee on the bedside table.

"No, I'm okay." I glance over at my new phone on the dresser, where it's plugged in next to my old, beat-up phone. "Has it still not updated yet?"

She shakes her head, sitting down on the edge of the mattress. "No, not yet."

I groan. The guy in the store said it could take a few hours to transfer everything, but it seems to be taking forever. Doesn't it realize I have calls to make?

Zara's been coming over to check on my house while I've been in Chicago and collect my mail, and she showed up as I got home from the mall. I didn't know how much I needed to see her until I did because it was like the moment I stopped, the weight of everything that's happened came crashing down, hitting me with a wave of exhaustion. I told her everything that happened with Laura, and what Jackson said when he got home, and about my flight last night. I proceeded to get worked up while trying to sort my smashed phone, and she responded with one of her tight hugs, something that's always surprised me because she's a petite woman, but damn, she's strong. Then she told me to take a nap while she sorts out my phone and prepares some lunch.

"I need to get hold of Jackson," I say, moving slowly into a seated position, trying to hide the throbbing ache that blooms in my hips.

I can't begin to imagine what he must be thinking right now, especially if he listened to the voice messages and has been unable to get hold of me. He's bound to be worried, probably angry.

"Is he on social media?" she asks.

"Yeah, he's on Instagram."

"Should I send him a message? Let him know what's going on?"

"Yeah, that would be good." I smile. "Thanks."

She leaves the room to get her phone, but before she can come back, the doorbell chimes. I strain to listen to the murmur of voices as she answers, but my bedroom is at the back of the house, overlooking the beach. Reaching over, I grab my coffee. I zone out, staring out the window at the waves crashing against the sand. The anxious part of my brain begins to think up seven hundred different scenarios.

Maybe I need to start keeping a note of my emergency contacts in my wallet in case something like this happens again.

In my disassociated state, I'm vaguely aware of the sound of footsteps against the hardwood in the hallway, but nothing could prepare me for the sight of Jackson appearing in the door. Relief flashes through his eyes the moment those gorgeous blue eyes settle on me.

"Hey," I croak, and the second I put my cup of coffee down, he's moving toward me.

Placing a knee on the bed, he engulfs me in his arms, hiding his face in my neck. The tightness of his embrace could rival Zara's, but I melt into him. Wrapping my arms around his wide shoulders, I pull him closer. His scent grounds me. The warmth of his soft breath against my skin brings me a sense of peace.

"You scared the shit out of me," he mumbles into my sweater.

"I'm sorry, I didn't mean to," I whisper.

He shakes his head slightly, the move causing his blond hair to brush against my cheek. I press a kiss to the side of his head.

"I'm just glad you're okay. I thought you were saying your final goodbye in that voice message. Then I couldn't get hold of you…" He trails off. His unspoken words are loud and clear. He thought the worst, and I hate that I caused that fear.

He lifts his head, letting me go to cradle my face with his palms.

"I was really scared." He swallows roughly. "I thought something really bad happened, that I'd lost you."

Fuck, I'll never forgive myself for putting him through that. I thought I was doing the right thing, and I still managed to fuck it up somehow.

He's still here, my conscience reminds me, sounding a lot like Roberta. *He still came for you.*

"I ended up breaking my phone. We had really bad

turbulence, and my mind started to catastrophize, and by the time we landed, I was so shaken up that I dropped my phone going down the stairs. I got a new phone this morning after I saw Roberta."

I take his hand in mine. His skin is warm and familiar. I run my fingers over the calluses, memorizing how each one feels scraping against my skin.

"It's okay. I'm just glad you're okay." He smiles. "Did everything go okay with Roberta?"

"Yeah, it did. I spoke to her about possibly changing or adjusting my medication so I can..." I wave my hand in front of my lap. "You know, get it up."

"You know it doesn't bother me."

"But it bothers me, Jax. I realized this morning during the session that I'm a lot stronger than I give myself credit for, and I do deserve good things in life, and those good things include getting hard and coming all over your chest."

He grins so widely his eyes crinkle at the corners. "You do deserve good things, Cas. You deserve all the good things, and I can't wait to contribute to that."

He leans in and kisses me. My free hand finds its way to the back of his head, sifting through the strands. He traces the seam of my lips with his tongue, and I open willingly, groaning at the taste of him. We've kissed thousands of times since we met, but this one feels different. It feels like a thousand I love yous. It feels like I can't breathe without you. It feels like a turning point for better things to come.

It feels like the start of forever.

The sound of Zara clearing her throat causes us to pause mid-lip lock. She's wearing a wide, toothy grin when I reluctantly pull away from Jackson's mouth.

"I hate to interrupt, but I'm gonna go. Do you need anything?" she asks, looking pleased as hell.

"No, I'm all good. Thanks, Zara," I say with a half smile.

"Anytime. And Jackson?" She turns to my man. "I'm so happy to finally meet you! Make sure you look after this one, okay? His phone is almost done transferring everything, and lunch is in the fridge for whenever you guys want it."

"You got it, and thank you." He clears his throat. "For taking care of him when I couldn't. Not just today, but before… You know. Thank you for being there for him."

Recognition dawns on Zara's face, and her eyes fill with tears. We don't talk about the *before*, choosing to keep focused on the future. She wets her lips and nods, her voice soft when she speaks again. "I'd do it all again in a heartbeat for him. We might not be married anymore, but he's still important to me." She turns her gaze onto me while still addressing Jackson. "He's one of my best friends, and I'd be lost without him."

I give her a grateful smile, and she gives us both a hug before she leaves.

Jackson kicks off his shoes and crawls into bed next to me. I take my glasses off, placing them on the bedside table. We lie down, and I curl into him, my head on his chest, his arm wrapped around my shoulders, his fingers lazily drawing a heart against my back.

"Did you mean it about getting a place in Chicago?" he asks quietly.

I tilt my head up to look at him, resting my chin on his firm pec. "Yeah, I was going to look today to see what was available."

"Move in with us."

My eyes widen, his words completely unexpected. "What?"

"Move in with us. The kids love having you around. I love having you around. There's a room upstairs you can convert into an office. I want everything you said in your voice message. Waking up next to you, falling asleep in your arms. I want lazy Sundays with you. I want to come home from a game, knowing you're at home waiting with the kids."

"Only if you're sure…"

"One hundred percent. And I'm going to speak with our trainer to see if there's anything we can buy to help combat the winters too. Like heating pads or something. I don't want you to be uncomfortable."

"That sounds great." I smooth my hand over his chest. "I also asked Roberta if we can move our sessions to a video call."

"Did she agree?"

"Yeah, she did." I settle my head back on his chest, but then a thought hits me. I sit up quickly, ignoring the pinch in my hip as panic sets root in my chest. "Wait, you have a game tomorrow. Don't tell me you got yourself scratched for me?"

"I have a plane on standby to take us back to Chicago early tomorrow morning. It's going to be a rush, but I had to come and see you."

"And where are the kids?"

"With my mom."

I'm unable to do or say anything. I can't believe he dropped everything and came for me. Put his career on the line. And his health because, holy shit, this is going to impact his performance on the ice.

But the look of unconditional love shining in his eyes tells me he would do it all again without a shadow of a doubt.

He did it all for me.

"I… Will you help me pack later?"

"Yeah, I will. Let's just lie here for a bit." He tugs me closer and drops a kiss to the top of my head. "I just need to hold you for a while."

Jackson wasn't kidding when he said the plane was leaving early the next morning. The sun wasn't even up by the time the plane powered down the runway, but it meant we landed in Chicago before lunch, giving Jackson plenty of time to rest ahead of his game tonight.

I'm still in shock that he didn't think twice about the repercussions that it would have had on his career if something happened and he missed the game.

We ended up falling asleep yesterday, then lost track of time making out. By the time we got around to eating the lunch Zara had prepared, it was late afternoon. Jackson helped me pack up as much as I could. Mainly clothes and my medication, but I wasn't too worried because if I did forget anything, I could buy it in Chicago.

"The kids are going to be so excited to see you," Jackson says as we head down the I-90.

"Were they upset that I left?"

"I think they were confused at first, but then when they

walked in on me listening to the voice message, I explained that sometimes our minds can play mean tricks on us." He gives me a quick glance before focusing back on the road. He reaches out to take my hand. "Ryan had picked up that sometimes you seemed sad, so I think he had an idea."

My face falls. This is what I didn't want to happen. I didn't want to let the kids see me when my mood was low. I didn't want to wear the mask around them because I'm so damn tired of wearing it.

"I'm sorry. I tried so hard to keep it from them."

He shakes his head. "No, I don't want to shield them from things. They need to learn that not everything in life is happy and great, and I'm trying to bring them up to know that it's okay to talk about your feelings, to show your emotions, and the only way I can do that is if I do it myself. And I don't want you to hide yourself to protect them, Cas. They love you—something they told me yesterday morning —and if there's days where you feel lower than others, it's okay to show that. They'll probably smother you in cuddles and make you watch *Bluey*, but trust me, it works."

A warmth spreads through me, knowing that I'm accepted and welcome as I am. But there's one important piece of information he just dropped that comes rushing to the front of my mind.

"Wait, what?" I gasp. "They said they love me?"

His face softens as he smiles. "Yeah, they do."

I duck my chin as my eyes blur and cheeks ache from my smile.

"Fuck," I say under my breath. "I... Fuck, Jax. They have no idea how much it means to me."

He squeezes my hand.

"They know." He winks.

When we pull up outside Jackson's Lake View home, there are several cars parked outside. I glance over at him, and the confused expression on his face tells me this is unexpected.

"What's up?" I ask.

"I'm just wondering why there's some of the guys' cars here. They should be at home because morning skate would've been over and done by now."

We get out and begin unloading the car. The front door swings open, and Elliot stands there wearing the costume Jackson was wearing at Peyton's Halloween party.

"Finally! I was starting to think you'd ditched us and decided to stay in California!" he calls out with a wave. "I mean, I wouldn't blame you—they have Disneyland. Oh, I'd come help you, but I don't have my shoes on. Plus, you look like you've got it all handled."

"Don't worry, El. You stand there and watch," Jackson deadpans.

Elliot responds with a double thumbs-up.

I only have two cases and a few suit bags, so we manage between us. Once we've got all my luggage inside, I slip out of my coat and let out a relieved exhale.

"I need coffee, stat. And you need to nap for your game," I tell Jackson, stepping up behind him and placing my hands on his hips. "Maybe we can nap together once your goalie's gone back to his own house."

"Okay, this is cute and all, but sexy nap time will have to

wait because I have a surprise," Elliot interrupts. He puts his hands between us and tries to wedge us apart.

"Actually, why don't you start with why you're in my house?" Jackson asks.

"Because I had the best idea yesterday after you left, and being the genius that I am, I made it happen. So, if you would stop being cute, you'll find out what it is." He motions for us to follow him into the living room. "Come on. Don't just stand there."

I throw a worried glance to Jackson, who looks equally confused, but we follow Elliot into the living room.

I startle as a streamer pops, showering us with confetti.

"Welcome home!"

I place my hand over my chest, my heart beating rapidly against my breastbone. Holy shit, they scared the crap out of me.

Standing in the living room are Blaine, Alex, Jacob, Ethan, Zach, and Peyton.

"Kenny would be here, but he's on kidlet duty," Elliot adds, referring to the Thunder defenseman Adam Kendrick.

"And Carter is in Denver, but he said to say hey." Zach smiles.

I'm about to open my mouth when the two angels who have stolen my heart jump up from where they were hiding behind the couch.

"Surprise!" Ryan and Isabela shout together, then proceed to burst into laughter.

"Wow…" I say barely above a whisper. I'm struggling to find any words because I wasn't expecting this kind of welcome.

The kids jump off the couch and run over to hug me. I crouch down, wrapping an arm around them both.

"Did we surprise you?" Ryan asks quietly.

"You sure did." I smile. "That was the best welcome I've ever had."

Isabela's arms tighten around me, her silent way of telling me how she feels.

When I stand back upright, it's Blaine who talks first.

"We wanted to start off by saying we're sorry that we've been shit friends to you—" He grimaces. "Sorry, I forgot there's little ears around."

"It's okay," Jackson says around a huff of laughter before Blaine continues.

"I know we work together on a professional level, but I, and I'm sure I speak for everyone here, do consider you a friend, and we had a bit of a reality check yesterday when your man yelled at us."

My head snaps to Jackson. "You yelled at them?"

Jackson rubs the back of his neck, something he does when he's not feeling so sure of himself. "Yeah, I was angry and scared and kinda let my emotions take the wheel."

"It was warranted," Zach points out, then looks at me. "The times when you've been there for us, both on a personal and professional level, have meant a lot to us, and we're sorry that we haven't shown you the same respect."

I shake my head. "It's okay."

"No, it's not. Friends know where friends live. Friends check in on each other. Friends notice when friends are struggling and make sure they know they have support," Peyton adds, and then his lips tip into a smirk. "And friends tell each other when they're dating our teammate."

Heat travels up my neck at the knowledge these guys now know, but I also feel overwhelmed. It's been a long time since I had this. I can't remember the last time I had more than two people in a room who cared about me.

"I…" I lower my head, feeling emotional. "I don't know what to say."

"Tell us you're staying in Chicago," Jacob says.

I turn my head to Jackson. A soft smile spreads over his lips, those blue eyes I love so much dancing with happiness.

"Yeah, I'm staying." I take Jackson's hand, interlocking our fingers together. "I'm not going anywhere."

I'm aware of cheers and someone clapping, but my gaze stays locked on Jackson's.

"I love you," I say, just loud enough for him to hear.

"I love you too."

"Wait!" Elliot shouts, breaking the moment. "Does this mean we've gotta be on our best behavior now our agent is in town?"

"Well, I'd hope you'd be on your best behavior regardless…" I pause. "Why? What have you done?"

"Nothing!" he says a little too quickly. "Nothing bad, anyway. And it's probably nothing. It's probably so irrelevant, it's like having the 'does pineapple belong on pizza' debate."

I furrow my brows. What the hell is he going on about?

I look over at his twin, hoping maybe he'll give a clue on what's going on. Blaine's face is lit in amusement, and Alex is hiding his face behind his hand, but the pinks at the top of his cheeks and his shaking shoulders give him away.

"Is everything okay, El?" Jackson asks, wearing a matching frown.

"Yes! It's great. Oh, look! Ethan's without crutches now. Bye to the old man jokes. So, are we gonna have lunch together before we nap, or are we being kicked out?"

At the mention of him, my eyes land on Ethan. He's without his crutches, one arm wrapped around Jacob's waist, and he looks happy. No sign of pain or discomfort.

Maybe I can do it. Maybe I can speak with Ethan about it and finally put the anxious thoughts to the back of my mind and get the surgery.

While the chatter starts about where to order lunch from, I take a seat and add it to my list of things to do to be a better partner for Jackson and to be the best for Ryan and Isabela.

To overcome my fears and continue to put myself first.

Chapter Twenty-Eight

Jackson

We end up losing to Edmonton. Coach isn't pleased, but if I'm being honest, it will take a lot more than a loss in regulation to ruin my mood right now. We threw our normal routines out the window today, and maybe that's why we didn't get the win.

The guys ended up staying for lunch, and I didn't get my preferred nap time. I wasn't expecting them to be there when we got home from the airport. Yeah, I kinda went off on them yesterday, but I know they have a good heart. Sometimes it's easy in life to get wrapped up in other things that we often forget those around us. I'm not going to hold it against them, but what they did for Hayden means a lot.

And I know Hayden was really touched by it too.

Then when my mom came to pick up the kids for the night, she threw an exaggerated wink over her shoulder before she closed the door. It means Hayden and I have the night to ourselves.

I've been eager to get home since the game ended. I was

first to wrap up my post-game cooldown and the first to hit the showers. But as I finish doing the buttons on my shirt, there's one thing I need to do before I disappear for the night.

"Hey, guys," I say, getting their attention. "I just wanted to say thank you for what you did earlier. I know it meant a lot to Hayden. He hasn't had it easy since he retired, and seeing you turn up for him, knowing you're in his corner…" I look at them one by one, flashing them a grateful smile. "Thank you."

"Aw, it's okay!" Elliot bounds over in his boxer briefs and one sock. He wraps his arms around me in a tight hug before releasing me. "I'm sorry we were such ding-dongs. Will he be coming for Christmas dinner? Jacob said he's making this big cake." His eyes go comically wide. "Gonna be so good."

I chuckle. "Thanks, bud, but I think we're going to have a quiet Christmas this year. But how about New Year's?" I glance to Peyton for confirmation as he's hosting this year's New Year's Eve party.

"Yeah, just don't think you can get away with sneaking off to my bathroom again without us noticing, eh." He smirks.

I grin and flip him off. "Like you give a damn."

"Truth, dude." He shrugs. "But seriously, you're always welcome. Whether I'm hosting a party or not."

"Thanks. I appreciate it."

We chatter among ourselves and finish getting dressed, and I promise Blaine I'll speak with Hayden about creating a group chat with all of us.

By the time I'm walking through my front door, I'm greeted by the warmth from the fire and the smell of my favorite chicken pesto alfredo. Hanging my coat in the closet, I'm about to call out to Hayden when I round the corner to the living room and find him asleep on the couch. His lips are slightly parted, and the sound of his soft snores make me smile. I walk over to him quietly and perch on the edge of the couch. Lifting my hand, I trace over his cheek with my fingertip, then along his cheekbone before moving down to the corner of his mouth. The feel of his day-old stubble scratches my skin, and the prickly sensation sends a shiver down my spine.

There's no stress lines or tension in his features. He looks so peaceful. Fully relaxed.

It's wild how someone's brain can play tricks on them like his does. How can someone so incredible as Hayden, who has the biggest fucking heart, feel like they're not worthy enough?

My eyes burn, and I have to squeeze them closed to stop the tears from falling.

The love I have for this man is monumental. It exceeds the love I used to have for him. My heart is so fucking full of him it feels like it could burst from my chest. I'll show him every day how much he is loved.

And I will prove to him every day that he is worthy and that he is enough.

Hayden's eyes flicker open. He glances around, almost disorientated, before taking his glasses from where they were resting on his chest and slipping them back on.

"Sorry, I wasn't supposed to fall asleep. When did you get home?"

"Just now," I say quietly, leaning forward to take his lips in a gentle kiss. "I didn't mean to wake you."

He kisses me back, all tired and pliant. "Mmm," he murmurs without taking his mouth off mine. "I made you pasta. It's in the oven to keep warm."

"Thank you. Why don't you get into bed, and I'll join you once I've eaten?"

"I might take a shower, then I'll wait for you in bed." He sucks my bottom lip into his mouth, and I groan. He trails his hand down my chest before resting at the juncture of my thighs. My cock begins to thicken in my pants as he skims his fingers over me teasingly. "We've gotta make the most of having the night to ourselves. Not having to worry about being quiet and waking any kids up."

"I like the sound of that."

He sits up and gives my quad a squeeze.

"Good. Eat up because you're going to need your energy."

After exchanging another heated kiss, he heads upstairs while I head into the kitchen. The pasta is still warm from being kept in the oven, and I try not to eat too fast. I don't want to give myself indigestion, but I'm so eager to go upstairs and get my hands on him again. The sound of my en suite shower is like a new type of foreplay. Here's me, rinsing my dish and drinking a glass of water while the man I love is upstairs, getting himself ready so I can explore his delectable body with my mouth before burying my dick deep inside of him.

I shiver and have to give my dick a squeeze to calm myself down.

When it's time to head upstairs, I make sure to turn off

the lights and that the fire is out, then stop by the family bathroom to brush my teeth.

My room is lit by the small novelty lamp I keep in here for whenever the kids need to sleep with me. It projects a million stars onto the ceiling, creating a galaxy that is relaxing to watch.

"This is romantic," I tease, but I like it. It sets a different tone to my bedside lamp.

Hayden's propped up against my headboard, bare chest on show while the sheet covers his waist. His dark blond hair is still damp, making it look almost brunet.

But his gray eyes sparkle brightly from behind his glasses.

"I thought it was cute. I never would have put you down to be an astrophile."

"I can't say that I am, but it works when I need it."

He hums, bobbing his head in understanding.

Standing at the foot of the bed, I don't take my eyes off him as I flick open the clasp of my belt and pull it off in one smooth swoop.

His eyes turn heavy-lidded, lips parting slightly.

I undo my cuff links, then release each button one by one, slowly revealing my chest. I stop when I reach the top of my abs, earning a groan from Hayden.

Smirking, I drop my hands to the button of my pants. The imprint of my hardening cock is evident, but I don't remove them, choosing to leave them unzipped and open. Tugging my shirt out the back, I continue my ministrations, parting the two halves once all the buttons are done to show off my naked chest.

"Take it off," he demands.

Without a word, I slip the shirt off my shoulders and drop it onto the floor.

"Now, the pants." His voice comes out like gravel. "Take it all off, Jax. Let me see you."

Keeping my eyes locked on him, I push my pants down, kicking them off once they reach my ankles. I tug off my socks next, then hook my thumbs into the waistband of my boxers. My hard cock slaps against my abs when I pull them down, and the hitch in Hayden's breath has me grinning wickedly.

I climb into the bed next to him, hand splaying on his stomach as I lean over to capture his mouth in a slow but heated kiss. He tastes like toothpaste and something so distinctly him, and I moan when he slides his tongue into my mouth.

His fingers circle and flick over my nipple, and my cock is an iron bar against his warm thigh.

"Lie on your side," I murmur.

With one final kiss, he rolls over so his back is to me, bending his outer leg at the knee. I take one of the pillows from behind me and place it under his knee, and the position exposes his hole perfectly. Retrieving the lube, I cover his mouth with mine as I begin to work him open with my fingers.

I'm dripping with precome by the time I roll on the condom and shift so my chest is pressed up against his back and wrap my arms around him. He angles his head, allowing me access to his mouth. I slowly thrust inside, swallowing down his moan.

Our kisses are tender and unhurried. My thrusts are

slow and deep. He reaches back with one arm to hold the back of my head, keeping me close.

"I love you, Jax," he whispers between pleasured groans.

"Love you always, Cas."

And this is how I want to spend the rest of my nights, wrapped up in him.

"Daddy!" Isabela shouts as she runs down the hallway. She throws her bag on the floor, then collides with my legs. I reach down to scoop her up, blowing a big raspberry on her neck. She erupts into giggles, trying to push me away.

"Hey, Dad. Where's Hayden?" Ryan asks.

"He's upstairs, bud. He'll be down shortly." I put Isabela down on her feet again. "Why don't you take your bags upstairs, then I'll make us some pancakes."

Their eyes go wide. "We get pancakes?"

"Yeah, but only if you take your bags upstairs."

The promise of pancakes is always a winner. They collect their bags from the hardwood floor and run up the stairs.

Mom lingers on the other side of the kitchen island, watching me with a look in her eyes that I haven't seen in a while.

"You okay?" I ask.

"Yeah, I'm fine, sweetie. I'm just happy to see you happy again."

"Double the happy in that sentence," I chuckle.

She picks up the dish towel and swats me with it. "I

mean it. This warrants the double happy. It's been hard seeing you struggle. Okay, maybe 'struggle' is the wrong word because you're doing a fantastic job with those kids and your career, but it's been at the expense of you losing a bit of you, and that's been hard to see."

I swallow thickly. She's not wrong there. I lost myself along the way, trying to be the best version of me as dad and the best on the ice. And since Hayden's slid back into my life, I'm starting to breathe a little easier.

"I love him, Mom."

She nods knowingly. "I know. And you know what? Those two didn't stop talking about him all night. They were asking me questions I didn't know the answers to, but I learned he's six foot two and he's thirty-nine years old. He was born in Maine but grew up in Nova Scotia and played for Boston for twelve years and was known as one of the most amazing power forwards of his generation."

"Wow, you did your research," I smirk, and her eyes sparkle.

"I did, but I don't want to learn about him from Google. I want to learn about him from *him*. You better bring him at Christmas, Jackson, or I'll be loading your plate with sprouts."

"Gigi!" Ryan calls, saving me from replying when he skids into the kitchen. "Do you have the gift we got for Hayden?"

I'm unable to hide the surprise on my face, but it's Hayden who echoes my thoughts. He's being dragged into the room by Isabela.

"You got me a gift?" he asks.

"Yeah!" Ryan beams, a proud glint in his eye.

"Oh, yes." Mom opens her bag and pulls out a small plastic bag. "Here it is."

Ryan takes it carefully and hands it over to Hayden. Isabela lets go of his hand and starts jumping excitedly in front of him.

"Open it!" She giggles.

Hayden casts me an amused look, then opens the bag. He pulls out a coffee mug that has illustrations of Bluey and Bingo on it with tiny pink hearts. He examines it in his hands, turning it over, and then he looks inside. He sucks his bottom lip between his teeth, his eyebrows furrowing as he begins to blink rapidly. I walk over, wondering what could cause him to get upset, and then I see it. Written inside the rim of the cup are the words "Remember, I'm always here for you."

Pride blooms in my chest. I look at my kids, and their faces are lit up with their bright smiles. There's a chance they got it purely because it's *Bluey*, but the words couldn't have been more perfect for Hayden. We're always going to be here for him, and I'll make sure he remembers it.

"Do you like it?" Ryan asks.

Hayden nods, lips still pressed together. He lifts his head, eyes glassy behind his glasses. "I love it. I'm going to use it every day."

They cheer, then engulf him in a hug. He crouches down, wrapping an arm around both of them. He squeezes his eyes shut as a tear falls down his cheek. A lump forms in my throat.

I'm very lucky to have the life I do, and there's never a day that I take it for granted.

But this?

Seeing the man I love embrace my kids with such love and affection. To know that their happiness is just as important as mine to him. It's everything.

They are my entire world.

"I'm going to get going," Mom says, her voice a little tighter than usual.

I round the island and bring her into a hug. "Thank you."

"Anytime, sweetie." She returns my hug and pats my back. She gives herself a small shake when she lets go. "Okay, kids, give Gigi a hug, and make sure you're good for your dad and Hayden."

Ryan and Isabela give her a hug goodbye, and then she steps up to Hayden. A smile spreads across his lips.

"Welcome to the Wilde family, sweetie, and let me warn you, we're not called the Wildes for nothing." She winks and pulls him in for a hug too.

Once my mom leaves, I whip up a batch of pancakes like I promised, and then I make Hayden a coffee in his new mug. He's still smiling at it when we sit down in the living room to tell the kids about us.

"Okay, me and Hayden have something we want to tell you," I begin, sitting on the other side of the sectional so I can face them. Isabela is sitting next to Hayden, trying to tug the sleeve of his sweatshirt up his arm.

"Are you boyfriends?" Ryan asks, then smiles coyly. "I was kinda hoping you were. Hayden's really cool."

My head snaps to Hayden. He looks as shocked as I am.

"Yeah, we're boyfriends, and if it's okay with you two, I'd like it if Hayden lived with us."

"*Yes!*" Isabela throws her arms up in the air in such a

dramatic way I can't help but start laughing. I turn to Ryan, waiting for his response.

"I'd really like that, Dad." He tilts his head up to Hayden. "Will you stay? I promise not to use real pucks in the house again."

"What?" I shriek.

Hayden holds his fist out to Ryan to bump. "That sounds like a deal to me."

"Can we watch *Bluey* now?" Isabela asks. Before we can answer, she's picked up the TV remote and loads up the streaming app.

"I guess so," I chuckle.

With the kids occupied, I scoot across the cushion and press my shoulder into Hayden's.

"Hi," I whisper, dropping my gaze from his eyes to his lips.

"Hi." His smile is gentle.

"Are you ready for this? It's not always going to be fun. There's going to be days where they test your patience and make a mess and nights where they knee you in the balls without a care in the world."

He laughs softly, his eyes full of love. "Yeah, I am."

I close the distance and press a kiss to his lips.

"I'm really glad you're here, Cas."

"Me too, Jax. I'm glad I'm here too."

Epilogue

Jackson – one year later

I take a step back and admire my handiwork. The blue light provides a nice ocean feel to the tank, where three moon jellyfish bob around. The tank is a D shape, because apparently you can't keep jellyfish in an aquarium with straight edges, and has a built-in LED system. Hayden told me all about how the tank would change color, so I made sure I found one that could do the same.

"I think he's gonna love it, Dad." Ryan smiles up at me, mirroring my posture with his hands on his hips.

I glance down at my son, amazed every day at how grown-up he is.

"Yeah? You think so?"

He nods confidently. "Yeah, I do."

Hayden's been away for two days in Toronto on business and is due back this afternoon. I've been wanting to surprise him with his own jellyfish tank for a while, but with my schedule and making sure I found reputable sellers, it hasn't lined up until now. I spent weeks emailing with Roberta asking for her advice and what kind of tank and type of jellyfish she has so I could replicate it at home, knowing how much Hayden loves them.

Ryan's also been so excited to get this set up because this is the first pet we've had as a family. Not that we can cuddle up or pet a jellyfish, but the novelty is still there.

Plus, there's something else me and the kids want to ask him, so it kinda ties in nicely.

"Have you got everything ready for him?" I ask, picking up the empty packaging to take out to the trash.

"Yep, and Izzy is finishing up her drawing now." He motions for me to follow him into the family room, where Isabela sits at the dining table, her coloring markers scattered everywhere.

"Daddy, look!" she says excitedly and holds up her drawing.

I take the sheet of paper from her, and my eyes burn as I take it all in. There are four stick-figure people, two large and two small, all joined up by their stick arms like they're holding hands. Daddy is written under one, along with Isabela's and Ryan's names, and Hayden is on the other end. Underneath the four stick figures, there are big block letters that say, "The Wilde Family" and a bunch of love hearts in various sizes and colors.

"This is beautiful, peanut. Hayden's gonna love it."

She beams. She's grown so much in the last twelve months since we started her specialized programs at school and created the right environment at home. My mom still takes care of the school runs, and often, they stay overnight with my parents when I have a game, but most of the time when I'm on the road, they stay at home with Hayden. He's adjusted his travel schedule so he can be home with them more, and the difference we've both seen, and her teachers too, is significant.

Ryan has moved up a group in hockey, and Hayden makes sure he always attends his practices even if I can't. He really looks up to Hayden. Always wants his advice and often asks for his help whenever he's struggling with something, whether it be on the ice or homework.

Seeing the relationships develop between him and my kids is something I never would have expected, but it's come to mean absolutely everything to me.

"And this is mine," Ryan announces, handing his drawing over. It's a similar concept to Isabela's, without the stick men. He's drawn Isabela wearing her Bingo costume, which is her current favorite. So much so I had to buy another one recently because she's worn it so much. Then, Ryan and I are in our hockey gear, both of us holding hockey sticks, and Hayden's in a suit, but it's what he's written that causes a choked noise to escape me.

'Hayden, will you be our Papa?'

When I decided I wanted to ask Hayden to marry me, I spoke to the kids first. Their happiness is the most important thing to me, and I'd never do anything that would upset them. As expected, they were so excited about the idea of me and Hayden getting married. Isabela demanded to be a bridesmaid, then asked when we could get her dress, but it was Ryan who almost knocked me off my seat.

"Do you think we could call him Dad?" he'd asked.

I'd let him know that as long as Hayden was happy with it, they could choose what name they wanted to call him.

But the second they turned their attention back to the TV, I hid in the kitchen and cried.

Because how fucking lucky am I to have these two incredible kids.

"Is it bad?" Ryan asks, his voice hinted with worry when I haven't said anything. "I can do it again."

"No, no. Ry, this is beautiful too. He's…" I swallow the lump of emotion in my throat and look at my son with glassy eyes. "He's gonna really love this. I promise you. I love it."

Ryan lets out a relieved sigh, then turns to his sister. "We better clean up 'cause he'll be home soon."

Home.

There was a time when I never thought I'd hear those words again in association with Hayden. The home we had together back in Boston was tainted by the actions of our past selves, but we're both in a different place now. Not just geographically. We're older. Matured. We've both been through things that have shaped us in ways we wouldn't have otherwise expected. I've got kids who rely on me.

Rely on *us*.

Laura hasn't been in their life as much since I told her to get out. We did talk things through a few days later, and I told her the surprise visits had to stop. I wanted to instill stability and structure into Isabela's life, and having her mom turn up whenever she felt like it didn't fit into that plan. She's seen them twice in the last twelve months, and part of me worries that it's because of how I flipped out on her.

But then I see how happy and healthy my kids are, and I know I'm doing my best and giving them everything I can.

And now they have Hayden too. Who I have to remind almost daily not to spoil them. That he doesn't need to buy them a gift every time he leaves the house, and he doesn't need to spend money to show his love.

But that's just who he is. It's his love language, and I love him for it.

He hasn't had the surgery yet on either his knees or his hips, but I'm not forcing the issue either. I can understand his fears, even if I have to watch him struggle with pain. He ended up speaking with Ethan at Peyton's New Year's Eve party, and I think it settled some of his anxiety, but he's still working up the courage. All I can do is be there for him. Support him and love him and distract him when his mind tries to take him down a different path. He has changed his medication though, and he's no longer getting himself worked up about not being able to perform in the bedroom. He still has struggles sometimes, but he doesn't beat himself up as much anymore.

I also met Roberta, too, during the off-season. I mentioned to Hayden that I wanted to have a session together so I could learn what I could do better, and after our joint session, she asked to see me alone. She let me know that there will be hard times, and depression isn't something that's fixed with medication or disappears overnight. But she told me that if *I* ever needed her, because sometimes the people who are closest don't have an outlet for their thoughts, that she was there to support me too. Luckily, I've not needed to take her up on her offer, but I can't deny it's been hard sometimes. Watching the person you love struggle with a demon in themselves and no words you say or actions you do is enough.

But every day, I always tell him how much I love him, and I always show him with actions.

The kids' heads snap up at the sound of the door opening, and then it's chaos mode. Isabela throws herself off the chair and hightails it down the hallway, Ryan inches ahead. They crash into Hayden, wrapping him in a tight hug.

"Wow, hello," he chuckles, dropping his bag to the floor so he can hug them back. "Did you miss me?"

"Yeah!" they reply.

"Well, I missed you too." He lifts his head and looks at me. His lips quirk in a soft, loving smile. "Hi."

"Hi." I lean against the doorjamb to the living room. "Missed you."

"Missed you too." He stands up and ruffles Ryan's and Isabela's hair. "Daddy's turn."

I grin. The first time he called me daddy, he tried so hard not to laugh. We're not into that, but we still find it amusing whenever he uses it.

I open my arms, and he steps into them. He smells like the cold winter air and his spiced aftershave. I take a deep inhale, then press a kiss to his cold lips.

"I've got a surprise for you."

He nudges his glasses up his nose. "A surprise?"

"Yeah. Come see."

He takes off his coat, and then I hold my hand out. The kids follow us into the living room, giggling excitedly. His shocked gasp makes me grin widely when his eyes land on the tank.

"You got me jellyfish?" he asks, spinning around to face me.

"Yeah, we did." I give the kids a look, a silent sign to go

and get their drawings. They disappear into the kitchen, returning moments later and standing at my sides.

"We have something we'd like to ask you," I say, then reach out to take his hand. "Hayden, I was nineteen when I first met you, and a part of me knew the moment I locked eyes on you that you were the one I was supposed to be with. We made so many memories during our time in Boston, and I like to think of that as part one of our journey. But this? This is part two."

The pinch between Hayden's brows tells me he's trying not to cry.

"Fourteen years later, you found me at a time I was struggling and thought I wasn't quite enough. And your patience and your gentle love made me fall in love with you again. Only this time, I brought two extras." I nod my head to Ryan and Isabela, who are both shining toothy grins up at him.

"The gut feeling I had when I was nineteen wasn't wrong. You are the one I'm supposed to be with. You are the one I'm supposed to bring my kids up with. You are the one who I want to share lazy Sundays with and cook while listening to Frank Sinatra with."

I let go of his hand and get down on one knee. Slipping the ring from my pocket, I hold it up. "I love you, Hayden Issac Cassidy. Will you marry me?"

He sucks in a shaky breath and nods. Tears cling to his eyelashes behind his glasses, and his voice cracks when he answers. "Yes. Yes!"

The kids start clapping and squealing in excitement. I slip the platinum band onto Hayden's finger, and then he grabs hold of my hand and tugs me up. Cradling my face with both hands, he kisses me hard. My cheeks are damp with my own tears and his. I wrap my arms around his shoulders, holding him tight to me.

"Me and Isabela also have a question!" Ryan interrupts.

We separate with a chuckle, quickly wiping at our faces with our palms.

"Wow, I'm so lucky tonight." Hayden lets out a choked laugh, then takes a seat on the couch.

Isabela hands over her drawing first, and his face lights up.

"Wow, peanut, this is amazing!" he praises, running his finger over the letters at the bottom. He raises his head to look at her. "You think of me as family?"

"Yeah!" She nods, bouncing on her toes.

"Wow, I love this so much. Thank you."

"And this is mine," Ryan says, handing his drawing across.

The corners of Hayden's eyes crease with the smile that seems everlasting on his face, and I see the exact moment he sees the question at the bottom. His eyes widen, and his head snaps to me with questioning eyes.

"Is this real?" he asks, barely audible.

I nod. "It was the kids' idea, but I love it."

His eyes immediately fill with tears again, and his hands begin to shake.

"I… I don't know what to say."

"Say yes!" Ryan bursts, his arms going in the air. "If you don't like Papa, we can call you something else."

Isabela climbs onto the couch and wraps her arms around his neck. "Pleaseee!"

Hayden's laugh turns into a sob as he wraps his arm around Isabela, and Ryan takes his other side.

I crouch down in front of him, taking the drawings from him and putting them on the table. Placing my hands on his knees, I rub my thumbs in soothing circles.

I blink back tears, unable to wipe the smile from my face. He takes a deep breath, then slowly exhales. Nudging his glasses up, he wipes at his eyes again and takes a few minutes to collect himself.

"I would love to be your papa," he says to the kids, then looks at me.

Sometimes those gray eyes can appear to be stormy, like rough seas at night. But right now, they are filled with so much happiness and love they almost twinkle. Although that might be down to the Christmas tree lights.

"Papa and Mr. Wilde, two titles I never thought I'd have."

I rise on my knees and lift my hands to cradle his jaw in my palms. I press a slow kiss on his lips. There's no need to hurry right now because we have forever to go.

"Welcome to the Wilde family, Hayden. We're all glad to finally have you home."

THE END

Want a spicy bonus scene where Jackson and Hayden sneak off at a team event? Visit my website
https://www.jodioliver.com/bonus-content

Acknowledgments

Thank you for picking up Power Forward! Jackson and Hayden have lived in my head since I introduced them in Trade Deadline, and I was so excited to dive into their story. For me, Hayden's journey was incredibly important to tell as mental health is something most hockey players will struggle with at some point during their lives. Ethan experienced a level of anxiety in Off Season as he struggled to accept his near-retirement, whereas Hayden's career ended due to an injury. I personally don't believe the subsequent mental health issues that often follow a career ending injury are spoken about enough, and I hope I was able to tell Hayden's story with the respect and thoughtfulness it deserved, while also keeping within the lighter theme this series is known for.

As always, I couldn't have done this without some awesome people!

Rachel, the loml. I would be lost without you. You are the Chilli to my Bandit, and one day we won't have an ocean between us (and I won't accidentally-almost set your house on fire, I promise!).

Becca, I'm so grateful to have you in my life! For brainstorming with me when I was stuck to being my cheerleader every step of the way. I'm so excited for all the exciting stuff we have planned.

Leslie, my goddess of a PA! You are a literal superstar

for putting up with my chaoticness (and my rogue gifs when I send something by accident). I'm so thankful for you and all of your help, not just with managing my unorganized butt, but with this novel too!

Eryn, Tyler, Roberta, and Jesse - my wonderful sensitivity and beta readers! I couldn't have done it without you. Thank you so much for your patience, advice, expertise and encouragement. The love you showed for Jackson and Hayden means the world to me.

Colleen, thank you for all of your help and advice with Isabela's autism journey.

Thank you to Kari March for this incredible cover, and Wander Aguiar for another gorgeous image. Sandra at One Love Editing for your patience of a saint with edits, and for Lori and Jeanelle to fixing those pesky typos that seem to appear no matter what.

My Sin Bin crew! I teased you so hard during this! Your unwavering love and support means everything to me, and I'm so, so grateful for you.

And to you, fabulous reader. Thank you for picking up Power Forward. I hope you enjoyed Jackson and Hayden as much as I loved writing them.

About the Author

Jodi Oliver is a British author who writes MM sports romance, happily ever after guaranteed. She loves donuts, dogs, and ice hockey, and when she hasn't got her head in a book or hiding in the writing cave, you can find her at an ice hockey game.

She lives in England but dreams of living in the Canadian countryside, with some highland cows and otters.

You can find her on Instagram @JodiOliverAuthor or in her Reader Group 'Jodi Oliver's Sin Bin'

JodiOliver.com

About the Author

Jodi Oliver is a British author who writes MM sports romance, happily ever after guaranteed. She loves donuts, dogs, and ice hockey, and when she hasn't got her head in a book or hiding in the writing cave, you can find her at an ice hockey game.

She lives in England but dreams of living in the Canadian countryside, with some highland cows and otters.

You can find her on Instagram @JodiOliverAuthor or in her Reader Group 'Jodi Oliver's Sin Bin'

JodiOliver.com